MADISON WADE

Whistle for the Wind

AN OCEAN'S DAUGHTER NOVEL

First originally published by Madison Wade

ISBN 979-8-9852727-2-7 (pbk)
ISBN 979-8-9852727-0-3 (hc)
ISBN 979-8-9852727-1-0 (digital)

To the friends who read these words
when they were only dreams and misspellings.

PART 1

The Diary

CHAPTER 1
The Dream

I SAT STILL ON MY BED, thoughts boiling over in my head.
Jonathan had left me in my room, alone with my mess of a mind;
and now, I desperately wanted him to come back in, kiss me,
and force the reckless thoughts to dissolve. My mind was an
unsolvable puzzle, with missing pieces and distorted images. *He's
just a friend... or is he?* Over and over, I tried to answer the question
that had penetrated my thoughts, but there was no solution in
sight. Why couldn't Jonathan return and answer the question for
me?

He's just a friend. He's just a friend. He's just a friend. No
matter how many times I forced myself to think it, I couldn't
make the sentence true. Over the short time I had known him,
Aaron Getty had become more than just a friend. He understood
the pains that I thought no one in my life would be able to
comprehend. He helped me escape from a miserable world; one he
had lived in his entire life. He was my protector. He fought by my
side against pirates that had enslaved us both. But if it had been
up to him, I wouldn't have fought at all; instead, I would be hidden
and protected while the battle was occurring. He kissed me. *He
kissed me!* And it was magical, like the books on my shelf. Aaron
was not just a friend, no matter what I thought or said.

But Jonathan – I couldn't lose him. I couldn't imagine my
life without him. He cared for me before I knew the pirates,
before I learned how to truly be brave. He saw the immature child

that I was and still chose to pursue me. And when I said yes to him, I found a home, a comfort, an unfailing love that was deeper than the ocean we sailed. I couldn't just give him up for a man I met only a few weeks ago.

My head began to throb. I didn't want to think anymore. I fell back on the bed, resting now on the pillow. My blankets, my pillows, my ceiling, my home once again surrounded me. I stared intently at the wooden planks above my head, praying that somewhere in the splinters the answer to my questions could be found. I turned down my lamp until the flame flickered away in a puff of smoke, letting the darkness of the room close my eyes so that all I could do was listen to the ocean waves crash against the ship. With each breath I took, a wave crashed and receded, putting my mind at ease. Or, at least, they tried to. Exhaustion leftover from the week's events began to wash over me, and I could no longer resist the temptation of sleep.

Aaron. He was standing in front of me on the main deck of the *Adventurer*. A warmth like joy seemed to surround me. I ran over and wrapped my arms around him, and with that, his smile grew. As I looked into his spring-green eyes, the whole world around me seemed to change that very color. Green, like the world of the land, not the sea I sailed.

"Can't we act like we are still on the pirate ship? Can't we be with each other like we were then?" asked Aaron. The green sky around me began to spin, like clouds before a heavy storm. I suddenly felt sick to my stomach.

"Can you love me again? Can you?" he asked again. How was I supposed to answer that question? I hadn't stopped loving him – had I? I struggled to find the words, but not even a whisper left my lips. His green eyes seemed to stare into my soul, and the spinning seemed to slow. I lost my balance. Aaron placed his hand on my shoulder. I stared at his hand, but as I stared, the hand morphed into one cut open, sliced through by the same knife I used against Gargan. Shock replaced every other feeling. I faced Aaron again, but it was no longer Aaron. Gargan faced me with his malicious grin on his face. A scream of fear filled my ears. It was my own. But I couldn't remember opening my mouth. I scrambled backward.

"I didn't know that you were so scared of me, Carter," smirked Gargan. "Don't worry, everyone knows you're nothing but a squeamish, fearful little girl, and nothing you say or do is going to change that. You can't even kill a man. Not even one as horrible as me," Gargan continued as he walked closer to me. I began to shake uncontrollably, collapsing to the ground, curling close to the mainmast, as if it would protect me from him.

"It is interesting to see your true feelings about me. Are you really *that* scared? And you call yourself brave -- ha! Are you even brave enough to kill a man that only exists in your dreams? Come on, girl! Kill me!" he shouts. I only shrunk back more. He leaned over, putting his face much too close to my own, with a wicked sneer on his lips. His breath was rotten, his teeth were black. A sword appeared in my hands, already stained with the blood of a stranger.

"Can you kill me? Can you?" Gargan continued yelling in my face. I flinched and stared at the sword as if it contained the answer. "Can you?" he kept shouting. I sat there, shaking, and braced myself for the worst. But the yelling subsided, and I watched as Gargan's face morphed back into Aaron's. Something about Aaron's green eyes had changed now; they were no longer mesmerizing.

"Can you?" Aaron asked in his calm voice. The sound of his voice reassured me that I was safe, but by now, I didn't know what he was asking me anymore. My eyes were wet with tears. I moved out of his reach, then I covered my ears, fighting away his sweet voice. My eyes squeezed shut.

Then they opened. For a moment, my vision was blurred by the salty tears that were stuck behind my eyelids. My blanket had slipped off the bed and was lying on the floor. I was shivering, but the damp sheets and clothes revealed that I had been sweating. It was a dream. *Just a dream.* Reassuring myself of this truth wasn't enough to calm my fears. Scenes of the nightmare repeated in my mind. Gargan, Aaron, the blood, the questions. I leaned over and grabbed my blanket, wrapping it around my shoulders while taking deep breaths, rocking back and forth. *It's not real. It's not real.* I never fell back asleep. Eventually, sunlight crept into my room through the porthole. I could hear footsteps above me as the crew prepared for another day of sailing. Normal. Today, my life could be normal. My eyes wandered the room as if searching for any sort of motivation to move from my place on the bed. I heard a shout from above; Jonathan was giving orders about the sails. Jonathan. Aaron.

Aaron. Gargan.

Can you?

"It's not real," I whispered into the deafening silence.

CHAPTER 2

Good Morning Home

I TOOK ANOTHER LONG, DEEP BREATH and stretched my legs over the side of my bed, planting my feet on the worn planks of wood. I was home. No matter how many nightmares plagued my sleep, it could not change the fact I had beat the odds and fought my way back to the *Adventurer*. I stood up with my blanket still wrapped around my shoulders and walked over to the mirror. My hair was a disaster, but that was the least of my worries. The cuts I had received in battle had started to scab over and the bruises had turned a dark purple-black color. Neither my mind nor body had forgotten Gargan's tortures. Careful to not disturb the perfect balance of my blanket on my shoulders, I picked up my comb and began to brush through the tangles in my hair. The last time I had stood in front of the mirror, my hair had nearly reached my hips. Now the blond strands tickled my neck. It was just another physical reminder of my time with the Gargan.

In the silence, I could hear the floorboards outside my room creak. It was like I had been pulled back to the pirate ship. Seeing and feeling that I was back home wasn't enough for me to truly believe I was here. I quickly put my comb down and scanned the room for something to use as a weapon. The door opened before I had the chance to grab anything. I tensed with fear.

Jopie shuffled into the room, her eyes tired and a blanket wrapped around her shoulders and trailed behind her as she walked. I released a sigh of relief, and a smile replaced the fear on my face. I walked over to Jopie and wrapped my blanket around her as well. She smiled up at me, letting a small giggle escape from her lips.

"You look tired," she said with a grin. Her thick brown curls overflowed over my arms, and she lifted her chin to rest it against my chest. Her skin was still paler than normal and her face was still thin from the days she spent abord the pirate ship sick, but Jopie's brown eyes twinkled with the excitement of new. New home. New life. One where she lived, not served or faded into nothing. One where she had a future.

You're safe, see? I tried to convince myself. I rolled my eyes playfully, trying pitifully to match her enthusiasm.

"Good morning, Jopie," I whispered. "How was your sleep?"

"It was good, Carter," she assured me. I nodded, comforted by her response.

"You should still be with Martin," I commented. She smiled a bit bigger and rolled her eyes.

"I wanted to come and see you."

"Okay, well, let me get ready and I will take you back to Martin," I said. She nodded in agreement. I quickly finished combing through my hair and found some clothes, changing out of the ones I had soaked with my sweat in my sleep. Together, Jopie and I walked to Martin's cabin. He gave us a welcoming nod and I promised to check on Jopie soon. Then I made my way to the main deck, where I met David at the helm.

"Hello," he said, with a wide smile on his face. Oh, it was good to be home and surrounded by such friendly faces. This moment could almost convince me that the pirates were truly behind me.

"Why didn't someone wake me up? I should have been up hours ago!" I asked. In reality, I had been up, just too afraid to climb out of the bed. A voice behind me answered.

"You needed it." I turned around with a glowing smile. Jonathan stood behind me with a playful smirk on his face. I walked over to give him a hug, but I was stopped in my tracks when Aaron's green eyes came into view. My repressed feelings for him seemed to collide with the memories of my nightmare. Suddenly I couldn't breathe. Jonathan's smirk faded into a frown of concern as he placed his hands gently on my shoulders.

"Carter, are you okay?" Jonathan asked. For a moment, I couldn't respond. Then my eyes met his, I took a breath, and nodded. I knew that wouldn't be convincing enough for him.

"Yes, I'm fine," I replied, masking my fear. Aaron made his way over to Jonathan and me, flashing his irresistible smile my way, keeping Jonathan's concerns at bay for a few moments longer.

"Captain," Aaron said, standing at attention , I could see the muscles in his arms tighten. He was built for so much more than the swab position that Gargan assigned him to and the torture that pirate had force him to endure. I knew Jonathan would recognize his strength as a sailor and use him as an asset, rather than a slave. As long as he didn't spot Aaron's love for me as well, everything would be okay.

"Aaron, that isn't needed," Jonathan assured him, relieving Aaron of his stiff position. Jonathan placed his hand on Aaron's shoulder. Aaron's eyes almost seemed to widen. I knew he wasn't used to being treated well by his captain. His captain. My captain. My Jonathan. It was almost like I had forgotten how much had changed on the *Adventurer*. It still seemed shocking to me that Jonathan was the captain of the ship, though, I am sure everyone else had become quite used to the idea, comparatively.

"What position would you like me to man, sir?" Aaron asked. Jonathan thought it over for a moment.

"How about you just shadow the other crew members for a little bit, figure out how we run our ship, and help out with the activities when you can. I'll see after that," Jonathan said. A faint smile formed on my lips as I listened to the two talk. Jonathan's idea was a much better way to decide what Aaron was good at over time than to make him perform all of the positions in one day, like I had been forced to do on the pirate ship. *The pirate ship.* The mere thought of that horrid place sent me spiraling into a pit of fear again. Aaron nodded then left to work with Fallier. Then, Jonathan turned to face me.

"Are you okay?" he asked me, concern filling his eyes. Jonathan hadn't been distracted long enough to forget. I gave him a small smile.

"Yes, of course, I am sorry for worrying you," I replied,

shaking my head as if I had made a stupid mistake of some sort. The mistake being that I was still afraid of a pirate ship I had escaped from only a few days ago.

"Carter, I know you," replied Jonathan. I merely nodded in reply, keeping my smile plastered to my face. He gave a quick nod and smiled back at me. It was as real as mine. He must have realized I wasn't going to give in. "Now where's that hug you were about to give me?" I chuckled softly and hugged him, breathing in the scent of him, but there was no changing the fact that I had ruined the moment. For a split second, I blamed the frustration I felt on Aaron, but, in my heart, I knew it wasn't his fault. He had no idea of the struggle I was feeling, attempting to choose between him and Jonathan, nor did he know about the dream that had haunted my thoughts. He didn't know how wrecked I was by the memories of the pirate ship. I couldn't blame him.

I walked down toward the main mast and began to climb up to the crow's nest. I noticed Jackson, a man with black-brown hair and dark brown eyes, was at the crow's nest. From what I knew, Jackson was about nineteen years old. Other than that, I knew very little about his background. He joined the crew when we returned for Captain's funeral. I hadn't been able to meet him until yesterday, and we had not yet had a chance to share in conversation. .

"Hello First Mate," he said when I joined him at the top. I smiled at him and nodded. I thought about how odd it was to be called the first mate after all my time on the pirate ship where I was nothing more than a possession. I imagine it was odd for Jackson as well, calling a girl he hardly knew a title with such power. I wondered who they had named first mate in my absence. *Probably David.*

"I can take the crow's nest for a while, if you want," I suggested. He gave me what looked like a nervous smile. "Is everything alright, Jackson?" I inquired, tilting my head in concern. He gave me a quick nod, and shook his head, shaking away the awkwardness of the moment.

"The nest is all yours, First Mate Key," he exclaimed, placing the telescope in my hand.

"Jackson, call me Carter," I sighed when he called me

first mate yet again. It was too formal for my liking. Jackson smiled, this time with confidence in his eyes. It seemed he finally understood that I was friendly.

"Of course," he replied, "Carter." I gave him an encouraging smile in return, and Jackson began his way back down towards the main deck. I looked out into the ocean, breathing in the air. My gaze reached out over the horizon, then back down at all the men on the deck below me. These men were my family; they weren't going to attack or harm me. Here I was safe. Now I had to just start believing that again.

CHAPTER 3
Captain's Words

THE WIND BLEW THROUGH MY SHORT BLOND HAIR, the golden strands batting at my face. At first, I leaned over the edge of the crow's nest, looking out over the blue ocean. The life in the waters below was hardly visible, but I knew it was there. Memories filled my mind of the girl that lived only a few weeks ago, swimming in the waters like one of the fish, one with the sea life. Parts of that version of me still lived, somewhere inside of me, I was sure of it. I just had to look through all the wreckage the pirates had left.

"Carter, make sure you're actually looking for anything dangerous and not just staring out into the sea," David called out to me with a warning tone in his voice, pulling me from my thoughts. I brought the telescope to my eye and looked down at him. His smirk amused me, and he knew it. Slowly a smile formed on his face, and I pointed my telescope towards the ocean. For hours I sat up at the crow's nest, looking out to sea and sky, searching for any danger that might be coming our way. Once again, I let myself get lost in my thoughts, but this time, I forced myself to not think about the fear the pirates had left me with. I had thought so much about the past weeks that I had forgotten about the coming days. In only a few months, I would be turning sixteen, the age when my mother married my father. I wondered if I was going to be married soon. I swallowed hard. Marriage felt like miles away, somewhere on the other side of the horizon. I had changed so much; there was a new Carter Ellen Key, and I was doing my best to try and figure her out. I couldn't marry someone when I didn't truly know who I was anymore.

"Carter, I need to see you in my cabin, please!" I heard Jonathan yell up to me. I nodded and began my climb back down, pulling my mind out of the clouds. I landed on the main deck with ease. Jonathan closed the door to his cabin as he went inside, and, only moments later, I was running over to the door. I didn't knock, I just walked right in.

The cabin was plainer than I remembered. It almost felt empty. So quickly I had become too accustomed to Gargan's quarters. The lack of feathered hats and shining swords on the walls made me feel much more at home, while simultaneously reminding me that I had almost lost home and exchanged it for a prison. Jonathan sat at his desk staring at some papers with a quill in one hand. The other was raking through his thick blond hair. He was probably preparing to write a log entry. He wasn't the man he was when I left him, and yet, he seemed even more himself now. A captain of the place he called home.

"Jonathan?" I said softly, making my presence known, even though I was sure that he knew I was there. Jonathan looked up at me, the pain of anger and sadness was visible in his eyes. Immediately, I frowned; I hated seeing him so upset. He didn't seem to be like this a few minutes ago. *What's wrong?* He waved his hand, signaling me to come closer. I walked over to his desk slowly.

"I realize now what Captain meant about you," Jonathan mumbled half to himself. I sat down in the seat in front of Jonathan's desk. I knew he was talking about Captain James, his teacher, and my second father.

"What on earth are you talking about?" I replied. My mind was still scrambling to make sense of his words. Jonathan's eyes seemed to carry a pain I could never understand. I also carried a pain he couldn't understand.

"Carter, he told me that you would get into trouble and that I needed to keep an eye on you." At that, we both chuckled a little, breaking some of the tension in the room. It couldn't have been a truer statement. Then Jonathan continued. "Captain told me that you brought the energy to the crew, but as a captain, I would have to contain it; which, by that, I think he meant to keep you safe? He told me that one day, well before the storm. But his last words to me, right before he locked me in the hold with the crew, were these: when the time is right, I needed to remind you of a promise. I didn't know what that meant, and I still don't. I assume you do. I thought I would wait a while, maybe a month or so, just to give you some time to grieve. We all needed time. I didn't realize you would be lost to us so soon after. I-I thought you were dead, and I missed my chance to fulfill Captain's last words. I thought I had lost my chance to remind you of this promise. Captain said it was more important than anything else," Jonathan explained. His blue eyes glistened with tears that teetered at the edge of his eyes. It was more than just the promise that he lost. He lost me. A lump grew in my throat.

"Yes, I remember that promise," I whispered to myself. Memories of the night before I became a crew member flooded my mind. He had called me over before I went to bed. I thought it was an odd promise, never to leave the *Adventurer* no matter what happened. It was the day after I became a crew member, and I was angry with the 'make Carter feel important' charade. I did not realize what he meant when he said later that I was special. Why did it take his death to open my eyes?

"Could I ask what that promise is?" Jonathan asked, and yet the look of expectation on his face seemed to make his question a command. He wanted to know why it was so important. I knew that the day I disappeared from his world, Jonathan was probably so upset that he hadn't said anything to me. Regret was powerful. But it didn't give him the right to know about the promise. It seemed personal, private, and, for some reason I decided not to tell him. If it was so important, I needed to carry its weight alone. And the pirates had taught me something, trust is difficult to come by and easy to break. I should have trusted Jonathan, but the fact that I couldn't be open and honest with him about the conflicted feelings that were tugging my heart in two directions signaled otherwise.

"I'm sorry Jonathan, but I can't tell you," I answered. Jonathan's eyes saddened, his jaw clenched, and he looked at the wooden desk. Guilt pressed itself against my chest, but I knew I had made the right decision. It wasn't a difficult promise when I made it with Captain, but now I understood its true weight. And this was my weight to carry. Alone.

"Is that all he told you?" I asked Jonathan after a few moments of silence. He shook his head but didn't say a word.

"Are you going to tell me?" I asked him. Jonathan looked up at me and stood up from his desk. I couldn't tell if he was hurt, disappointed, or angry. Maybe it was a mixture of all three.

"He said that I should wait to tell you. He already had the feeling I would choose you as first mate. I suspect he knew we would have this discussion eventually. You see, Carter," his voice softened, "you happened to be the subject of conversation more than once in our meetings. I just didn't expect ...well I didn't expect to lose you." I nodded in understanding, not wanting to press him any further. Then I made my way towards the door. When I grabbed the door latch, Jonathan placed his hand on mine. My eyes met his.

"I am your love first, and above all else," he whispered. He still wasn't smiling, but the way he looked into my eyes was enough for me to know how much he truly meant it. A chill ran through me, and my stomach churned. I prepared myself for the kiss that was soon to come, but it never did. I couldn't help but be disappointed. Jonathan opened the door with my hand under his and we walked back onto the main deck, hand in hand.

The sun had turned golden while purple and pink clouds seemed to smear across the sky. The heat that had warmed the backs of all the crew members throughout the day had finally begun to subside. Jonathan gave me a polite smile, released my hand, and approached David who was at the helm. Jackson had once again taken the crow's nest. Fallier and Aaron were checking the ropes and untying knots. Aaron looked over; I must have caught his eye. He smiled but didn't wave. The smile was enough, though. His green eyes sparkled. Being here seemed to give Aaron a new glow. Then I remembered what Jonathan just said to me. A knot tightened in my stomach. What was Aaron to me? My love or my friend? No one on this ship could help me answer the question. I hoped the words I would eventually hear about Captain's last moments would lead me to the answer, but I had a feeling that they would only lead me deeper in the dark.

I made rounds on deck, ensuring all the jobs were completed or adequate before everyone made their way down to dinner. When the time came, I ate alongside Jonathan, and, while he tried to make sweet, casual conversation with me, my thoughts and feelings forbade me to fully engage. After dinner, I asked Jonathan if I could head to bed. Jonathan agreed; the look on his face revealed his concern. Still, he reminded me that I would wake up bright and early to work the next day. I nodded, leaving Jonathan, knowing the first thing I wanted to do when I entered my cabin.

I entered my room and sat down on my bed. I had never felt so lost in my own home. My eyes locked onto the bookshelf in front of me, analyzing the worn covers for a title that may magically make my troubles disappear. I stood up as my eyes settled on an untitled work – my father's journal. I had read bits and pieces, opening to random pages on days when I wished I could hear my father's voice and time had made it go quiet. But I had never read the entire thing straight through. Come to think of it, I doubted if I had ever even read the first page. Maybe I had skimmed it once or twice, but I couldn't remember. I opened the cover and began to read the words my father had left for me on the parchment. Suddenly the pages were flying through my fingertips. The lamplight illuminated every sentence. He didn't write every day, but enough for me to watch him fall in love with my mother, become a captain and a father, mourn my mother's death, and lead the *Adventurer* with the strength I could only dream of having. I watched as the days progressed until I realized I was on the final day of his journal. Of course, he didn't know it was the final day. I read these words slowly and carefully.

I will never be able to give my daughter everything. I can't teach her about loving a boy or when to get married. All I can give her is my knowledge of strength and determination. It will carry her far but not far enough. If only Arianna were still alive. Maybe my daughter would have a chance. I searched for Arianna's diary again today, but I found nothing. Every day I look for it, hoping it will pop out and I can give it to my little Carter. In my heart, I know it never will be found, lost with the woman I loved. But I continue to search for my sweet Carter. Even though she is seven, I want her to know her mother. I know that, as a captain of a trade ship, I am never guaranteed a day. So I pray that I can give Carter the journal so that she may know her mother.

Tears rolled down my cheeks as I read some of his final thoughts, which were centered mostly around me. Throughout his journal, he had mentioned the diary he had never found. For seven years he had searched, only to be taken from his home by Gargan. I hated Gargan more than ever. My father just wanted me to know my mother. I sighed and closed the journal, placing it on my nightstand. In the porthole, I could see the faintest ray of sunlight creeping over the horizon. It was time to get to work, as I had promised Jonathan I would. I hadn't even gotten a wink of sleep. An entire night I had spent awake, searching for a way to put my mind at ease. But I was left with more questions than answers yet again.

CHAPTER 4
Healing

I SHUFFLED TIREDLY UP TO THE MAIN DECK. It was still dark outside; it barely qualified as morning. Jackson was at the crow's nest and David was at the helm, both waiting to be relieved of their night duties. The moment I wondered where Jonathan was, he appeared on the deck. I shot him a smile, which he returned. Hopefully pretending to be awake would make it true. I made my way to the crow's nest, relieving Jackson. I watched as he and David both quickly went to their cabins, then, I turned to gaze at the dark expanse in front of me, a deep purple with a glow of daylight peeking over the edge.

My mind went back to the day Jonathan and I had shared the sunrise, while we were headed towards the ports. He had just made me his first mate, just declared his love for me. We had lost our captain and Jonathan had become one. It seemed like yesterday, and yet, it felt like a lifetime ago. It was a lifetime ago. I forced myself to avoid the memories of what happened between then and now. Instead, I redirected my thoughts to last night. I thought about my father's search for the journal. If my mother had died in childbirth, how had the diary been lost with her? Surely, she didn't keep the diary impossibly hidden every day of her life. My brain tried to solve this miserable riddle. I remembered that my father had been amazing at solving riddles, but it seemed he wasn't able to solve this one. If he couldn't, how could I?

"Carter!" exclaimed someone right behind me. I let out a

scream against my will. *Gargan! How is he here?* My heartbeat sped up, but I turned around to see Leonard with his hands raised.

"Sorry, I didn't mean to scare you," he apologized quickly. I forced a small smile and nodded. There was a tiny part of me that still believed I was in danger.

"No worries, Leonard," I assured him. He nodded, then informed me that he would be taking over the crow's nest and that Jonathan needed to see me; though, he referred to Jonathan as Captain. That still seemed odd to me. It would take a lot of getting used to. I nodded and thanked Leonard for letting me know and I made my way down to the main deck. Time had passed all too quickly. It wasn't until now when I noticed how bright it was outside. *How did I miss the sunrise?*

I approached Jonathan, and as he caught sight of me, he surrendered his position to Gluar, who hardly ever took the helm. I couldn't help but wonder what Jonathan needed to speak about. He took my hand and I released a breath. The warmth of his hand seemed to ease the fear in my chest, but I couldn't figure out why I was scared in the first place. We entered the captain's cabin. He offered to me the chair beside his desk and then sat down himself.

"Jonathan?" I asked, wanting to know why he had called me in here. He looked at me; his eyes looked sad, but at the same time, full of love and admiration. It was an odd combination. I wanted to know what he was thinking, scared that he would be asking me about the nightmares. *How could I even begin explaining them?* But the way he looked at me filled my stomach with butterflies. A battle could have been going on outside and he would still worry about my needs first.

"Carter, I'm worried about you," he said softly. Despite the waves against the ship and the crew working hard outside the door, the cabin fell silent. I bit my lip. There was no escaping this one. What was I supposed to say? That I was having vivid nightmares that forbid me to sleep? Or that I would get so lost in my thoughts that, when I returned to reality, I believed I was still on that dreaded pirate ship? And on top of all that, I was trying to figure out what my feelings for Aaron truly were? And now I was trying to figure out a mystery that my dad couldn't solve? It was too much. Instead, I sat silent, hoping he would break it for me.

He did.

"Before you were…lost, you were recovering from a shark attack. Then you came back to us from pirates with deep cuts and wounds all over you. And I know you wanted to get back to work and you were mostly worried about Jopie's health, but I am worried about yours." I forced myself not to release a sigh of relief. He was only worried about my physical issues. Those were so much easier to solve.

"Jonathan, Martin checked me out when I arrived, remember?" I reminded him. I could tell in his eyes that he remembered, but Jonathan shook his head. Jonathan's stubbornness was endearing. I couldn't help but smile very faintly. He noticed.

"What are you smiling at, Carter? I'm being serious. Your health is a serious matter to me," he replied, but he wasn't angry with me. He was pouting.

"You're just reminding me why I love you," I said softly. This got him smiling as well. But it faded much quicker than I had expected.

"Carter, I want you to have Martin to examine your wounds. Please, for me?" he pleaded with me. And I couldn't resist him, so I nodded. "Thank you," he replied, then he stood up. "Send Martin to me, once he's finished with his examination." I shook my head.

"Jonathan, I can report to you myself," I insisted. He raised his hand to stop my argument.

"No, I have made my decision," he replied. "I know all your tricks, Carter," he chuckled. I let out a huff of frustration. He smirked playfully at me and I tried to hide my smile. He pecked my lips and my smile revealed itself. "Now get going," he whispered. I nodded and slowly left his cabin. His smile glowed in my mind. His kiss replayed in my brain. The moment-turned-memory kept the smile on my face. I walked out of the room and immediately ran into Aaron.

"Carter!" he exclaimed. I smiled back at him, but my stomach was doing flips. How could I kiss Jonathan, tell him that I love him, and still have these *feelings* for Aaron? It wasn't fair… to anyone. The answer to that question would have to wait, again.

I had my orders from my captain, my love, and I would not be caught ignoring them.

"Aaron, I would love to talk, but I am headed to Martin's. Captain's orders," I informed him, trying to sound regretful. I desperately wanted to avoid my romantic confusion. Aaron frowned and nodded.

"Okay, well, I would love to talk with you soon," he said. How could he have lived the life he lived, filled with tortures, and still seem so innocent and pure? I couldn't break his heart, but I couldn't break Jonathan's either. My breaths grew faster. I couldn't think about it all right now. I gave him a quick nod and quickly left for Martin's. When I arrived, Martin gave me a smile. Jopie was sitting up in a bed, busy sewing some fabrics. She looked up, saw me, and smiled.

"Hey Carter," she said with a bright, beautiful smile on her face. This alerted Martin, who was busy scribbling away in a journal.

"Ah, Carter, good to see you," Martin said as he approached me. I replied with a polite nod then explained to him why I was there. He listened intently then had me sit down in a chair. Jopie watched from her bed, interested in Martin's work. He started by looking at the shark bite that had been camouflaged with other wounds I had received on the pirate ship. According to Martin, my legs were healing over fine. A miracle, really. Then I revealed the wound on my arm from when Gargan had stabbed me. I had stitched it myself. I hadn't ever examined it after it was stitched up and now I wished I had. It didn't look to be healing properly. All bright red and swollen. Martin's fingers grazed over the wound and I winced in pain. The frown on Martin's face grew. Jopie moved to the edge of her bed to get a closer look.

"Did you stitch this?" he asked me. I nodded. With a heavy sigh, he continued. "It was a good thought, but, unfortunately, I'm going to have to cut it, clean it, and re-stitch this for you." I swallowed hard, remembering the pain I experienced sewing the skin up the first time. Jopie and I traded places and Martin gave me something to stifle the pain a bit. As I lay down, he asked, "Why didn't you make me aware of this when you first arrived?"

"I was more concerned with Jopie," I replied. Apparently, Jonathan had been right after all. He always was. I almost rolled my eyes, but I conjured some self-control. Carefully, Martin began to remove the stitches in my arm. I clenched my jaw. Despite the pain reliever Martin had provided, his work still hurt. I closed my eyes, pretending that it would somehow make the pain go away.

"Jopie. Get the silk from my cabinet," he said. I blinked my eyes open to see Jopie slide off the bed and go to the cabinets, pulling a spool of silk out. He took a glass of water and carefully poured it over the wound. I groaned in pain. Jopie cut the silk for Martin and he began to restitch my stab wound. The entire process was painful, and as I closed my eyes, I saw myself sitting on the floor in the halls of the pirate ship. I had held in the screams then. The memory of Gargan stabbing me replayed in my brain over and over again. When I opened my eyes to escape the cycle, they stung with tears.

Martin picked up a rag, wet with vinegar, and used it to gently clean the surface of my skin. I released a few breaths. Jopie returned to her place on her bed. With the arm that wasn't being stitched, I wiped the tears from my eyes.

"Done," Martin announced, and I carefully sat up. "Now, to ensure that it doesn't get infected, you need to limit the use of your arm for a while. I know how difficult that will be for you, but those are my orders. I will explain all this to Captain Powell, and we will talk about what duties on deck you will be able to perform. I will return, and then you will be permitted to leave my cabin. But until then, you will stay put with Jopie." I nodded again, and Martin left the room. *Captain Powell?* The oddity of it almost made me forget about the pain. But it didn't keep me distracted for long. Thankfully, I didn't have to look far to find a friend.

Jopie and I began to talk about her time on the ship so far and what she had been learning from Martin. For a while, this was enough. But time, worry, and pain started to pull me away. As much as I wanted to be engaged in the conversation, my mind was wandering. If I couldn't work, what was I going to do? Confront Aaron? No. Tell Jonathan that I may be going insane? No. Solve the riddle my father couldn't solve?

Maybe.

CHAPTER 5
The Search Begins

Jonathan made the decision. I wasn't allowed to perform my duties for the next week, to allow for the stitches to heal. I had just returned to the *Adventurer*, and now I wasn't able to perform my duties. Despite the pain, my body itched to help the place I called home. Instead, all I could do for the next seven days was supervise – and search. With all these questions rolling around in my brain, I was ready to find some answers. I began each morning of those seven days rising before the sun. This was when I could search for the diary uninterrupted. I spent mornings in the hold, searching every nook and cranny, using my oil lamp to light my way. Once I noticed the sun rising, I returned to deck, stood alongside Jonathan, and supervised the work on board as the crew completed their jobs, while my mind did backflips trying to solve all the problems that seeped into my thoughts.

Once, on day three, while Jonathan was busy with David, discussing their course, I snuck into the captain's cabin. My father was a captain, so my mother would have access to the space. *Maybe she hid it here.* I searched the desk drawers, hoping to find her diary or something that may lead me in the right direction. The thought crossed my mind that, if it were something in here, my father would have seen it. But I had to believe there was something that he missed. It was the only hope I had left. I checked the desk for secret compartments like some characters had done in the books I had read. No luck. With a defeated sigh, I stood up only to hear the door being opened. I froze and turned to face Jonathan. He titled his head in confusion.

"Carter? Is everything alright?" he asked, closing the door behind him. For some reason, this search for the diary wasn't something I wanted to share with him. Not while it was still a hopeless mess. Not while there was still so much I didn't know. I swallowed hard. He moved closer and took my hands into his. I looked down at our hands and then looked up at him. "What's wrong?" he whispered. But the shakiness of his breath said so much more. Kind, gentle, concerned Jonathan made my heart skip a beat. It made me consider telling him the truth. But this wasn't his burden to bear.

"I-I just thought I left something in here the other day," I fibbed. I hated lying to him. Why did I feel like I needed to lie? He frowned.

"What did you lose?" He asked. *What did I lose?* I asked myself.

"Um, my father's wedding ring," I replied. He titled his head in confusion. "I was wearing it the other day, and-and I couldn't find it this morning and I thought it might have been in here." He shook his head, but his eyes remained locked on mine. I bit my lip, nervous he had seen straight through me.

"Jonathan…" I whispered. Before I could say anything more, he pressed his lips against mine. I kissed him back. This was not the peck on the lips like the other day. This was passionate, intense, and its spontaneity made it even more exciting. His hand raked through my short hair and my arms wrapped around his neck. The world around us faded into the waves. I only pulled away to take a breath and kissed him again. Time stopped. His hands moved to my hips, pulling me closer. Meanwhile, my mind was trying to figure out the reason behind this kiss -- this gift. That is, until my heart decided that I didn't need to worry about the why. I just wanted him. I leaned in again, but this time, he pulled away, dodging my lips. I blinked open my eyes, staring straight into his.

"I missed doing that while you were gone," he whispered. I grinned.

"Me too," I replied. And suddenly, I was reminded of

Aaron's kiss, back when we were on that ship. I tried to push the thought away, but it was useless. With a small smile, my hands slipped off from around his neck and I held his hands for a moment, then let go. He smiled at me.

"I should go, keep looking…" I sighed, caging myself back into my lies. He nodded.

"Let me know if I can help," he stated. I gave a kind smile and walked out of his cabin. Now I was a liar and a doubter, and with the one man that I thought I trusted.

***

Day seven came faster than I had expected. I found myself in Martin's again, with him examining my arm, ensuring that I was fit to return to my position. An entire week had passed, and I was still no closer to finding my mother's diary. What did I think? That it was going to magically appear, with the convenience that only existed in the novels I had read? He took the stitches out, which was slightly less painful than when he took the stitches out a week ago, then wrapped it in bandages. My thoughts were the only distractions from the pain, so the spiral continued. I raked over the ship in my mind, wondering what I had missed. I had searched everywhere, and still, nothing.

"Carter? Did you hear me?" Marin's voice asked, shaking me out of my thoughts.

"Hm?" I turned to face the man who had been examining my arm.

"You're clear to go back to work," he informed me, though now his words lacked confidence. I gave him a smile and thanked him for his help. He gave me a nod and I left Martin's office. As soon as I left, my thoughts once again began to bog me down. *Maybe I should have told Jonathan about all of this*, I thought to myself. But then I shook my head, responding to myself. I couldn't tell Jonathan about the search. I didn't want to put another problem on his plate. I had put him through enough trouble already.

I found myself on the main deck, though I couldn't remember walking there. Jonathan rushed up to me with hope in his eyes. I couldn't help but smile at how handsome he looked, but the secret I held prevented me from sharing in this hope he felt.

31

"So, what did Martin say?" he asked.

"It's healing well and I'm clear to get back to work as usual," I replied, giving him the smile that he wanted to see. Still being cautious of my arm, he gave me a gentle hug and kissed the top of my head. I wanted to melt in his arms right then and there. I wanted to hug him tight as I told him about the nightmares, the flashbacks, the diary. I wanted to kiss his lips and pretend that the past that was haunting me and the secrets I kept were all a bad dream. But I didn't. Instead, I returned his gentle hug, gave him a polite smile, and took a step back. His eyes looked into mine, happy but still concerned. Could he feel me drifting away, becoming a girl who keeps secrets and lies through her teeth? Could he see what I had become? Carter Ellen Key, a pirate in disguise.

CHAPTER 6
The Bookshelf

As the sun began to set on my first full day of working in a week, my body was about to collapse with exhaustion. I was surprised at how feeble my arm had become after just a mere week of not using it. After completing my final evening duties as a first mate, I left for my room. On my bed lay my father's journal, open to the last place I had scoured for any sort of clue as to the location of my mother's diary. I had failed. This entire past week had been a waste. I stomped over to my bed and slammed my father's journal shut. I stared at my bookshelf, defeated, angry. Now more than ever, I needed this diary.

I moved to stare at myself in the mirror. I looked horrible; my hair had been disheveled after a long day's work. My face had turned red with both anger and fatigue. I turned back to the bookshelves. All those stories had given me so much hope, and these past few weeks had shown me the truth. My nightmares had replaced the fantasies I once believed in. Tears had started welling up in my eyes – tears of anger and defeat, not joy and love as the stories had promised. I began throwing books from the shelf to the floor. Throwing things helped release my anger. So, I kept on. My bed, my floor, my desk, I didn't care where the books landed. The tears that had been pent up in my eyes began to roll down my cheeks. Thud after thud, my books hit the ground. I turned to face them all and sat down on the wood floor and cried.

"Mother, where are you?" I whimpered. I covered my face

with my hands, though there was no one to see me. Eventually, I looked up at the mess I had made. What a mess I had made. My tears slowed, and I took a few deep breaths. I began to pick up my books, my hands still shaky from my childish meltdown. I placed the books in no particular order back on the shelves. *The Sorrows of Young Werther, Candide, Gulliver's Travels, Robinson Crusoe.* One by one I picked the novels off of the floor. Some novels were so worn I could no longer make out the titles. As I picked one up, the binding snapped off of the cover. A gasp escaped my lips as my eyes scanned the cover for the title. *Love in Excess* by Eliza Haywood. I snorted -- that was one of the few books on my shelf I specifically avoided reading. And now, it seemed to be the very problem I was juggling. I picked up the pages, still woven together, and skimmed the first page. My eyes widened when I read the smudged words in the center of the page.

The Diary of Arianna Key. I stared at the first page in awe. My mother's diary was in my hands. The very thing my father was searching for was hidden within the books I loved so much. How could I have missed it? My father once told me that my mother loved reading more than I did, and he gave me her collection after she passed. I shoved whatever books that were still on my bed onto the floor. I sat down and carefully turned the page, not wanting to snap the fragile threads that kept the pages bound together.

For my child. If anything is to happen to me.

I couldn't look on to the next sentence. This was for me. Not Father. It was in my bookshelves. Not his. I swallowed hard. I had to keep reading.

My child, if you are reading this, something has happened to me and I am so sorry that I have not been there to watch you grow. Know that, even though I am not with you, I love you dearly. I hope that the words in these pages help you as you continue to live your life. Please, read, and don't make the same mistakes I have made. My angel, I hope to see you again one day. I pray that this finds you and your father well.

I looked from the page, staring at the half-empty shelves in front of me. A message to an unborn child. She didn't know if I was a boy or a girl. She didn't know my name yet. But she loved me anyway. And she left a piece of her with me. I held it in my hands. Carefully, I turned to the next page, where the ink was faded more than the first. It was older – the true beginning. What was written on the previous page was left for me, put there when I was known. This page was written when I wasn't even a dream. This was written for my mother, by my mother.

The first two words read *Dear Diary*. Then I closed her diary. I couldn't bring myself to read another word. I didn't know what to do. I had to talk to someone about this book. She wanted me to talk to my father, but he wasn't here. The second person I would have talked to was Captain, but James Rosten was gone as well. I didn't know who to hide my secrets with… hide my mother's secrets with. I wanted to tell Jonathan; he had known me for a long time, and he was the captain of the ship. But then he would know how much I had been hiding from him, and I would be burdening him with more stress, defeating the purpose of me hiding things from him in the first place. I thought about telling Aaron; he had many major life experiences similar to my own. But I didn't want to tell him and not tell Jonathan. It felt unfair, even wrong. I couldn't tell Jopie. While she was so kind and caring, she wouldn't be able to help me. The dolphins wouldn't understand. Then I thought of someone.

I carefully took the old cover and placed the pages back inside, to act as a shield of sorts. I looked around my room. It was a mess, but cleaning could wait. The information I held in my hands could not. Remembering that David was working tonight, I made my way up to the main deck. I saw Jackson in the nest, David at the helm, and Adam inspecting the ship. David caught sight of me and tilted his head.

"Carter is everything alright?" he asked. Adam overheard, looked to David, who nodded at him, then Adam took over the helm as David walked over to me.

"David, I need to speak with you privately," I said to him. David glanced down at the dairy and gave me a curious look. I picked David for a reason. He knew me better than anyone on the ship, except maybe Jonathan and Aaron. And if anyone could keep a secret from Jonathan for me, it was David.

"Come with me," he said, not taking his eyes off of mine, his eyes full of concern and worry. Silently, the two of us made our way to his cabin. I had only come into his room a few times; just to wake him when I was ordered to. It looked very similar to mine, but instead of being full of books, it was filled with maps and sketches of ships, mostly the ship known as the *Lord's Pearl* – his father's ship.

David's father, Lewis Carson, was captain while his mother lived on the land, working as a cook. David lived with his mother and his father visited him, giving him updates on ship life. One day the *Lord's Pearl* docked, but Lewis didn't show up at David's house. David was eight years old when that happened. Soon after Lewis's death, David and his mother became homeless, unable to make rent. When David was nine years old, my father stumbled upon the pair and listened to their story. His mother begged him to bring David along, and my father didn't refuse. David made his way from a swabbie to an advanced crew member over the years and grew closer to my father through the studies of ships and oceans. I had to believe I was choosing the right person to share my mother's secrets with.

"Now, what is it you wanted to talk about?" he asked, sitting down on his bed, offering the place next to him for me. I took a breath, bit my lip, and sat down beside him.

"I wanted to talk to you about this," I said, staring at the dairy, moving my fingertips around the edges.

"What is it?" he prompted. I stared at the worn cover and carefully uncovered the pages.

"It's my mother's dairy." The room was silent for a moment as David's eyes scanned the ragged lettering on the first page. Then he looked up at me once more.

"Your father searched for that…" he began. I finished his sentence.

"Ever since my mother died. I know, but it wasn't for him to find. It was for me."

C H A P T E R 7
David

"WHAT DO YOU MEAN?" HE ASKED, giving me a questioning look. I pointed to the passage below the heading of the diary. He carefully took the diary into his hands and read the words. Once he finished, he placed my mother's diary back into my lap. He took a breath and put his palms against his forehead.

"Are you okay?" I asked him quietly. David glanced over at me, and then he lifted his head from his hands and sighed. He looked up at the ceiling for a moment or two, and then he faced me again.

"The real question is, are you?" he asked. It was my turn to look away. I let a few moments of silence pass between us.

"David, I don't want you to tell Jonathan about this," I said softly, breaking the silence, not answering his question. He looked at me confused. I faced him; my gaze unyielding. Eventually, he nodded. I could trust him. "Can you tell me about her?" I asked.

"I never knew your mother," he began with a sigh. "You know that. But according to Robert, Arianna was a lovely and smart woman. Also, according to Robert, you look a lot like her. Your father said that when she died, he was crushed, even though he was holding you in his arms. You were born and your mother was lost. Every night he would go through their room and search for her dairy, knowing for a fact she kept up with one every night. He never found it. I can't believe she hid it for you to find - on your bookshelf. He just wanted to find it for you."

I swallowed hard, not knowing what to say for a moment. Her life for mine. Was it worth it? Did my father think I was worth his wife's death? *That's unfair of me*, I thought immediately afterward. But my mind was spinning. I had never really thought of my mother's death as my fault. I didn't know much about the whole thing, or her. She was never there. Life with a mother was just as fanciful as the novels I read. But to truly think about her, as a part of my life that had been taken away, clouded all my memories with an undefinable hurt. To think, she could have been there through all of it, but she wasn't, because of me.

Now more than ever, I wanted to know her. Maybe she really did have the answers and the guidance that she promised in the pages. I looked at David again. He was staring at me with sad eyes.

"Tell me how she died?" I asked him, my voice broken with newfound pain. He gave me a sympathetic frown.

"Carter, I know as much as you. She died shortly after she had you. There were complications after. There was no reason for me to know. I wasn't here. But I'm not the only crew member on this ship. There are men here who were on board when you were born - when your mother died." Of course, there were other crew members, but none of whom I wanted to talk with. Fallier, Gluar, Adam, Leonard were all men that, while they were happy to see me alive when I returned from the pirate ship, would rather not have a woman on board the ship. Talking to them about my *feelings* would only reinforce their ideas that a girl like me didn't belong here.

My eyes fell on the worn cover. If I wanted to know more about my mother, I had two choices: reveal my secrets, or turn another page.

CHAPTER 8
Questions

The two of us sat in the cabin silently, both of us staring at the same thing – my mother's diary, which I held in my hands. David then moved his hand and gently rested on my wrist, pulling me from my thoughts.

"Now I have a question for you," he began, "Why me?" I turned my head to meet his gaze then opened my mouth, but nothing came out. It was like someone had taken all of the words out of me. I shut my mouth and composed my thoughts. I had to make sure I worded my answer right. I didn't want to overshare.

"David, I chose you because I knew you could keep a secret from anyone. Even Jonathan. I-I didn't want him to know I was searching for the diary, and now I've found it and I want to get to know my mother," I explained. It wasn't the whole truth, not by a long shot. But it was enough that, hopefully, he would believe me. David bit his lip, seeming concerned with my explanation.

"You don't want Jonathan, the captain of our ship, to know? Why, Carter? He loves you. You - you love each other, right?" he asked. For a moment, there was another silence as I tried to compose my answer in my mind. David broke it with an awkward laugh. "Or is my social awareness as bad as they say?" he attempted to joke. I gave him a small smile and shook my head.

"No, David, I do love him. But I don't want to burden him any more than I already have. I know it was hard for him when I was…gone.”

"It was hard for all of us, Carter," David interrupted. "We had failed you, your father and James. After searching for you and never finding you, the weight of defeat hung over the ship and no one could escape it." I nodded a little not knowing what to say, then took a breath.

"Which is why I don't want to tell him. He would only be more worried about me. He is a captain of a ship. He doesn't need to be worried about me or my mother's diary. It's my issue. It's personal…" David said nothing in response for a moment. "Please don't tell him, David," I begged him.

"Does this have something to do with that other boy? Aaron? That you brought back from the pirate ship?" he questioned me. He wasn't aggressive, but his tone was clear. He wanted the truth. My eyes widened in surprise at his question. He was stabbing at me blind, but still managed to puncture my heart.

"No, it doesn't," I replied firmly, clenching my jaw ever so slightly. David nodded, but something in his eyes seemed to say he didn't believe me; and, despite confidence in my answer, I didn't know if I believed me either. But I couldn't let that show, not right now. I took a breath. "David, can I trust you not to tell him?"

"Yes, Carter. I won't tell him," David answered. "But please, tell him yourself, soon." I nodded but I wasn't going to make any promises.

"Thank you, David," I murmured as I stood up, holding the diary tight in my hands. He gave a small nod.

"I should return to my post," he sighed and moved to the door and opened it for me, hinting at my need to exit. I stepped out of David's room and out into the main hallway. David made his way up to the main deck and I turned to head to my own room; instead, I ran into Aaron, who looked to have been exiting my room. His face lit up in a smile. Why was he even *up* at this late hour?

"Carter! I am so glad I found you!" Aaron exclaimed in a whisper. As he stepped closer to me, knots formed in my stomach. Looking at Aaron brought thousands of different emotions, causing my heartbeat to quicken. The kiss on the pirate ship – that foul pirate ship. I gave him a smile, but the clashing of memory and nightmare made a true smile impossible. I think part of me wanted to let myself love him, and another part of me wanted to pretend that the pirate ship didn't exist. Judging by the look in his spring-green eyes, Aaron had already made his decision about me. *If he knew about Jonathan and me, he would hate me.* More secrets to keep.

"What is it?" I asked him, my thoughts coming back to reality. I slipped the diary under my arm in one swift motion. Aaron stopped right in front of me and took my hands gently into his own. His green eyes trapped me again. He was so happy, I wished I knew what was going on in his mind. I was sure to find out.

"I just haven't seen you in a while," he sighed. "Since we arrived here, we've both been busy. Me training to work aboard this ship and you recovering and performing your duties as the first mate. I thought at this hour we would both be free." I gave him a smile and a nod. He planted a kiss on my cheek, shocking me with his affection. He chuckled at my facial expression. "You are truly beautiful." I blushed at his words and shook my head. I unlatched the door to my room, hoping to escape this conversation. But he walked in before I did. I moved quickly, placing the diary back on the shelf before he spotted it before he turned to face me.

"Have you enjoyed learning about my home?" I asked him, trying to act casual, more normal, *something*, but my stomach was doing flips. Was I happy he was in my room? Was it bringing back all of those terrifying memories? Was it both? Aaron nodded with a smile in response to my question. Again, I tried to push the confusion out of my mind.

"Carter, thank you so much for bringing me here. For saving me from that place. To be honest, it has been an adjustment." He paused, his expression growing somber. "Actually being able to trust the men around me. Not live in fear that they will take my life at any moment," he said as he sat down on my bed. Even while saying this, Aaron was sitting stiff on my bed, alert and ready to attack. The pirates were haunting me in ways I couldn't explain, and I had only lived there for a week. His life was spent with them.

"I can only imagine how hard it must be, Aaron," I said

gently, moving to sit beside him. I placed my hand on his shoulder, rubbing the fabric of his shirt with my thumb.

"It's a good struggle to have, Carter."

"It's one that no one should have to endure," I countered. For a moment, Aaron clenched his jaw. But he relaxed a moment later.

"You shouldn't have to endure it. But here we are both readjusting," he muttered. There was a bitterness in his voice that made me flinch at his words. They stung like an insult would have, but they weren't. The tension of his tight words hung in the air, taunting us, reminding us of the pain I had been *trying* to escape.

"Aaron...it-it's okay. We're --"

"Are you joking?" he snapped. It was stunning, really, how quickly he shifted from kind to harsh. Like all of it was pent up inside. "Please tell me you're joking." All I could do was stand with my mouth agape. He laughed without a hint of joy. A lump grew in my throat as he stood up from the bed, pacing my cabin like it was a cell, locking him in with me. With each breath, the room seems to grow hotter, like rage could be warmer than the sun.

"Aaron, of course it's not okay," I started again, this time with an even voice. I sounded like my father, or Captain, when they were trying to calm me down.

"Then why would you say that!" he shouted. I answered, even though he wasn't really searching for an answer.

"Because maybe I want it to be okay. Have you ever thought that maybe I just would like to move on? Is that wrong of me?"

"No! Of course it's not wrong! I want to 'move on' as much as you do. But we can't just pretend it didn't happen," he countered, each word strained by frustration and confusion. I so badly wanted to pretend it didn't happen. I pushed my fingers through my hair, moving the blond strands off of my forehead. *This* was a situation I didn't want to endure.

"Aaron, we are arguing in circles over nothing," I said delicately. His knuckles grew whiter at each word that left my lips.

"There you go again. Calling it nothing. Saying it's okay. Praying to forget it all." Now he was trying to make my blood boil. It was working.

"It was one week of my life. It was miserable. It changed

me. It changed me in ways that I didn't necessarily want to, Aaron," I argued, standing up to meet his gaze.

"It was one week of your life, but it was my life!"

"I know that! You know that! Then why are you so upset and pitying me?" Somehow between this moment and the last my voice had grown to a shout.

"Because they ruined my life!" he yelled back, gripping my shoulders tight, his thumbs digging into my skin. I winced, clenching my jaw tight, not because it hurt, but because *he* was hurting me. The very next breath, his knitted eyebrows softened as his eyes grew wide. His grip loosened and he let his hands fall. White splotches on my skin marked where his thumbs once were. Those spots would fade, or maybe bruise, but even bruises blended in on my skin. This pain was temporary, but this moment was searing in my brain like a brand. Based on the dread and guilt filling Aaron's eyes, he knew it.

"I don't want them to ruin you too," he whispered into the space that was filled with a new kind of tension. One I had never encountered and had not the slightest clue how to understand. I couldn't wallow in this mixture of love and anger. It was too much, simply put. With everything else I was juggling in this moment, this awkward pain could not be one of them. I had to let it go. I had to just...forget it.

"Aaron, they haven't ruined me," I insisted gently, placing my hand on his arm. A lie. "And they haven't ruined you, either." Another lie. Aaron rolled his eyes, but a faint smile pricked at his lips. I released the faintest sigh of relief.

"Would you forgive me for all this?" he mumbled. I gently rubbed his arm and nodded.

"Forgiven and forgotten."

C H A P T E R   9

Whisperings

IT WAS IMPOSSIBLE TO FALL BACK ASLEEP. Thoughts of Aaron, of David, of Jonathan, and of my mother's diary scampered around in my mind. Every secret I kept, every lie I spoke throughout the day haunted my thoughts, forbidding me rest. Whenever I thought I had escaped them, I could feel the ghosts of Aaron's thumbs pressing into my skin. It took hours for fatigue to grow stronger than my fears. Even when I fell asleep, my sleep was restless. There was no hope for me, or at least it felt that way. Nightmares greeted me in darkness; every hour or so I would escape them, waking up, and starting the whole process over again. That is, until the cycle was interrupted.

"Come on first mate," he whispered in my ear. Then he planted a kiss on my cheek. I could feel it even as he pulled his lips away. Jonathan. Instead of bringing on butterflies, it only reminded me of my conversation with Aaron last night. I pushed the thought away. Today, worrying about secrets and decisions and romances was not an option I was allowing myself to have. Today I would be my old self. Carter Ellen Key before the pirate ship. I rolled over to see Jonathan's smiling face. He kissed my nose and I rolled my eyes playfully. He chuckled and warmth filled my chest at the sound. *Home, remember? This is what home feels like*, a voice in my mind seemed to say.

"Okay, okay, let me get up then," I sighed with a smile. "Before the sunrise, preferably." He chuckled and moved so I could sit up. I shooed him out of my cabin, and with a reluctant smile, he promised to meet me on the main deck. I cleaned up a bit and headed up to the main deck, just before the sunrise. Jonathan's eyes met mine as the sun broke over the horizon, like a scene in one of my novels. Except not everything seemed as perfect; his eyes seemed concerned, and the morning's playfulness had disappeared. Then I noticed David walking away from the helm, where Jonathan was now standing. I tilted my head, concerned, and rushed over to him.

"Carter, what's going on?" he asked me, taking my hands. Confused, I looked into his eyes. I glanced at David again. Surely he hadn't told Jonathan about last night. I looked back at Jonathan.

"What are you talking about Jonathan?" I asked him. He frowned like he was disappointed in me, like Captain and my father had when I was a kid. He had no right to treat me like a child, which fueled a fire in my chest. "Don't you dare give me that look," I said, clenching my jaw. Jonathan sighed at me.

"I hoped you would enlighten me," he replied.

"I don't know what David told you, but –" I started, my voice raising.

"David didn't *tell* me anything!" Jonathan snapped back. I crossed my arms over my chest. How did the moments from this morning suddenly feel so far away?

"Obviously, he said something!"

"What would he say to me, Carter?"

"That I'm keeping secrets from you!" *How are we shouting at each other now?*

"Is it true?" he questioned me. I opened my mouth to shout back at him and nothing came out. It was true. He turned away from me.

"When did we start keeping secrets from each other?" he asked when the silence was no longer bearable for either of us. Suddenly tears were glistening in my eyes.

"I don't know. It's just easier," I muttered in reply. So much for today being another normal day. Normal – could it even exist anymore? Before he could reply, I stomped away from him. I heard him call after me. My jaw tightened and I turned on my heels to face him for a moment. "Can you just let me be for just one moment?" I snapped at him. He groaned, but I couldn't deal with this. I couldn't have both Aaron and Jonathan frustrated and in love with me. It didn't seem very fair. I approached the edge of the ship and jumped, diving into the water. Maybe here I could truly forget, because sleep was not a strong enough adversary for my problems. The dolphins, my only escape, were the only ones that would listen. I whistled. After about fifteen minutes of desperate calls, Aurora, Sunset, Luna, and Dawn swam over to me, and I explained everything to them. It had only been a couple of weeks since they had brought me back home, and so much had happened that I just kept rambling on. Every hour of my return seemed to be haunted and I had stayed silent through it all. Until now.

"Carter, I'm so sorry," Dawn squeaked.

"It's nice to be back with you guys. It's been too long." They all agreed. I suggested we go for a swim. Without waiting for a response, I headed north through the waves, diving under the surface. But when I came back up for air, the dolphins were waiting behind me.

"What's wrong?"

"Shouldn't you be on deck?" Luna asked me.

"What do you mean?" I scoffed, like her question was ridiculous. It felt ridiculous. Only a few short weeks ago, I had spent time almost every day with them.

"I mean, you are the first mate. You're a leader now," Luna replied. I swallowed hard. *Why will no one just let me forget?*

"She's right," Aurora chimed in, her whistle somehow gentle. "While we love your visits, they just can't happen as often anymore." Another normal routine I was losing. I glanced back at the *Adventurer* I had swam away from. Then, I faced them again.

"No, no, no, I am not giving up my time with you," I squeaked back. That same moment, I heard my name shouted on deck. It was almost an echo I could ignore. But when I turned back, I realized the dolphins had heard the noise. I looked at them and frowned. "I promise I'll be back soon." The dolphins whistled goodbye and held the promise close to my heart as I climbed back aboard the ship. I couldn't lose the dolphins -- my friends. It just wasn't an option. Of all the normal things of life that had been taken away from me, the dolphin pod could not join that list. Back aboard the *Adventurer*, I found myself face to face with Jonathan. Again.

He grabbed my wrist and dragged me towards the captain's cabin. Despite being home, everything about this felt like the pirate ship. The strong grip, the angered eyes. My mind tricks went to work, painting a new scene for my eyes. This wasn't home. Suddenly I was back with the pirates. I could hear their shouts and smell their stench. My heart rate quickened, and I began to slow down, trying to escape the grip Jonathan had on my wrist.

"Stop," I breathed, terrified. My hands began to shake, and Jonathan turned to face me. At first, he still looked angry, which made me want to shrink back in fear. But as he looked into my eyes, the fire in his began to fade into concern. He released his grip on my wrist and stepped closer to me, wrapping his arm over my shoulders, and leading me towards the captain's cabin. He whispered "I'm sorry" over and over, but I couldn't bring myself to reply, not yet. I managed to glance up, finding overwhelming grief in his eyes. Slowly, the images of the pirate ship faded, and I began to breathe normally. I sat down in a chair near his desk in the captain's cabin. No swords or feathered hats on the wall. *See, Carter, you're safe*, I reassured myself once again. He sat down across the desk from me. For a few moments, it was silent between us. It wasn't a heavy silence, or, at least, it didn't feel that way to me.

"Carter, we need to talk," Jonathan whispered gently.

"I'm fine," I replied without hesitation.

"Stop lying to me," he said with a slight edge in his voice. There was another silence; this one was heavier than the last. After a few moments, Jonathan spoke up again. "Carter," he sighed, "I want to carry these burdens with you. I love you." At that, the mask I had carried since I had arrived back home finally fell from my face. It wasn't a loud cry or an ugly cry; it was silent, as tears slowly slipped down my cheeks. He didn't move to hold me; he knew that I didn't want his sympathy. I took a few deep breaths and wiped the tears from my eyes.

"I'm sorry, Jonathan," I said. He nodded, forgiving me. I

told him about the diary. How I searched for it because my father was searching for it. How I found it inside the cover of one of my old books. How I was too afraid to read it. Jonathan listened with wide eyes, then explained how he had searched for it since I was captured and how Captain had also searched for it. All of these amazing men looking for my mother's old diary, a woman I didn't even know, just so I could grow up with a piece of her. Now that I had it, I was too scared to read it.

I didn't tell him about the nightmares, the flashbacks, or how people said or did things that made my mind think I was still on that pirate ship. I didn't want him to think I had gone insane. I didn't tell him that I had kissed Aaron on that pirate ship and that there were feelings that seemed to draw the two of us to each other, but when I saw Aaron, I was reminded of the nightmare that was my life only a few short weeks ago. One mask may have fallen, but another quickly took its place. Some secrets needed to stay mine, and mine alone.

"You should read it, Carter. Tonight," Jonathan told me. I nodded. "Next time, please tell me. You know, instead of jumping off the ship." He gave me a weak smile. And I couldn't help but smile back. All these secrets couldn't take away his contagious smile. After another few moments, he stood up. "Take all the time you need, Carter, then join us on deck. You are the first mate; your crew needs you."

"That's what they have you for," I chuckled in reply.

***

After the sunset, I made my way down to my room. Jonathan told me to read the diary tonight but sitting on my bed with my mother's memories in my lap, I didn't know if I was strong enough. My fingertips moved up and down the cover and across the edges. I took a deep breath, finally deciding Jonathan was right. I needed to read this.

I opened the cover and carefully turned to the second page. *Mother help me.*

CHAPTER 10
Sleepless Night

THE FIRST WORDS BEGAN to explain who she was, introducing herself to the diary – to me.

Dear Diary,

My name is Arianna Katelyn Wilson. I am sixteen years old and live in North Carolina. I went out to buy this dairy today because I have a crazy, amazing, ridiculous problem. I love two men, Robert Key, a going to be the first mate of a trading ship, and Edward Jacobs, another first mate. Just my luck, right? Well, I told mother and she wasn't too happy that I had fallen for two men tied to the seas. She said it would have been better if I had fallen for a blacksmith or a businessman. But when I venture to the ports, businessmen are not the men that stand out to me. Still there is more to them that meets the eye – which Mother refuses to acknowledge. Robert and Edward are both well educated. I met Edward when he came to the port for supplies and he ran into me. He bought the bread I had made the trip for and I have dreamed of him ever since. Every few months or so, he drops by to see me and my family and always holds a dinner that he pays for himself. Then there's Robert. I met him when he was walking back to his house from school and I was coming home from the market, a long time ago, when we were only seven or eight years old. Now he works at the ports, saving his money and preparing to become a captain of his first ship. That's his dream: to lead a ship out on the seas and explore the world. It may seem childish, but I love listening to him talk about his dreams. The way he is so confident about his dreams excites me. And what do you know; now he's going to be first mate. He is heading onto his ship next week. His dreams are coming true. I am so proud of him, but I am so going to miss him.

When I told Mother all of this, she said that she couldn't help me with my romance problems. She claims that she had the perfect romance, an arranged marriage. Now she wishes she did the same for me. But it's too late for that, thankfully. Mother said I would have to get through it on my own. But love is so hard to work through alone, so I bought a dairy with the money I had saved up and I just am going to write. Maybe all my problems will solve themselves. Maybe not. Either way, I will have someone to talk it out with, or rather, write it out with.

Your new friend, Arianna

I stopped for a moment. Information about my mother floated in my mind. She lived in North Carolina. At sixteen years old, she had a problem very similar to the one I was facing. She loved two men, and I…cared deeply about two men. Except she didn't meet one of them after being sold to pirates. But she didn't see love as a bad thing, a killer of the independent self, as I did. Maybe because it wasn't a bad thing, or maybe because she was born and raised on the land that put limits on what women could do. I sighed and returned my focus to the dairy. She continued talking about Robert and Edward and her amazing memories of them.

Dear Diary,

I don't really know how I should feel. I am very proud of Robert; he gets to be a captain on his first ship instead of being a first mate. I was so excited for him, but when I went to congratulate him, he wasn't so excited. He explained that the only reason he became the captain was because the man who was supposed to be the captain died suddenly. He seemed so crushed, even though he hardly knew the man. Sad and happy at the same time is very hard to feel, I now know. He leaves tomorrow and won't be back for at least a month or two. I will definitely miss him. Is this why mother hated that I loved men that were tied to the sea? Because they would always leave me alone here on the land? Surely, she knows I can go with them. Can't I?

Your friend, Arianna

I imagined a young version of my father, a man a bit older

than Jonathan, or maybe Jonathan's age, taking charge of a ship and living a life of leadership rather than one of learning. To me, he had always been a leader, a father, but once he had been filled with dreams, like me. All too quickly his dreams became a dark reality. I remembered his diary, how he wrote of the hardships of being a new captain on a new ship. It reminded me of when I became the first mate. He was ignored and disrespected for a while by nearly every crew member aboard his ship, even by those who eventually grew fond of him. At least I had men like Jonathan and David that supported me through the harsh words. I realized I was getting too distracted and was no longer reading. There were many entries left to read and the night was only so long. My eyes fixated on the cursive lettering. Weeks went on and Edward and Robert came and left Arianna in North Carolina.

Dear Diary,

I can't write too long today. I am sorry to write that Mother died today. Father even left work early. He doesn't even do that for my birthday. Her funeral is tomorrow. I wish Robert and Edward were here. They won't get the message until it is too late. Father said that he couldn't quit his job, so I have to work at the shop by myself. Right now, I don't know how I can even manage myself, let alone the shop. I know this sounds ridiculously selfish on the day of my mother's death, but the shop is not my dream. I'm scared. And I am very, very sad. But most of all, I feel so alone. I know what Mother said about falling in love with sailors, but at least they can take me away from the loneliness I have to endure.

Yours truly, Arianna

My breath caught and my eyes grew wet with oncoming tears. I felt silly, nearly crying over a grandmother I never knew, and yet, seeing her through my mother's eyes had me convinced that I had met this woman. Arianna felt a pain that I would never feel: the loss of a mother. That thought gave me a new pain that I couldn't quite explain or define. I felt guilty and angry and cheated all at the same time. I glanced out my porthole, into the darkness. There were only a few hours left until sunrise. I had to keep reading. Entry after entry I took in more knowledge of Arianna, getting to know more of the mother I never knew. Her questions continued about which path to take and which man to marry.

Until suddenly, they stopped.

Dear Diary,

I have found myself wanting Robert more than ever. I realize now that he is the one that I truly love. It's not just his polite personality, but the way he believes in his dreams and acts on them, and cares for me even when he is far away and loves me with his whole heart. I now realize that my love for Edward, while it was strong, was a fantasy love. An infatuation. He is kind and polite, but I don't know him. And he doesn't know me. He doesn't know about my dreams and fears and everything in between. This may sound awful, but I don't miss him when he leaves. Or maybe I used to, but never have I missed anyone so much as I miss Robert now. It's as if someone tore out a piece of my heart and is teasing me with it. Every time I see Robert, I fall in love with him more each time, and every time he leaves, it hurts more than the last. This time, I'm not letting him leave without me.

Sincerely, Arianna

I stopped again, letting the words wash over me again and again, as if it were the ocean itself; the words became the waves holding me under the water, pushing me into the depths every time I tried to escape. This pain that she felt, this longing, did I have it? I knew that I longed for home when I was on the pirate ship, but anyone would. With both Jonathan and Aaron living on the *Adventurer*, how was I ever to experience this "longing"? Then again, the way she described it, I didn't ever want to experience it. Only two entries later, she saw Edward again. I gulped.

Dear Diary,

Edward was at the ports today. I informed him of my mother's tragedy. He was mournful, of course, and I felt bad for him because the hard news didn't stop there. I told him that I was leaving. I told him that Robert was going to come to the ports soon and I would live with him for the rest of my life. Something sparked in Edward. He wasn't just broken by the news, and he wasn't shattered either. It was as if something had snapped, quick and seamless. No tears, no silence. The Edward I knew, or I thought I knew, changed before my very eyes. Outraged, he yelled and stomped around the shop. I would never admit this to anyone, but he scared me. I was afraid he was going to hurt me, the way he was talking. He said that he once loved me, but, after hearing what I had to say, his 'heart was wiped clean.' His exact words. Apparently wiped clean meant everything was gone: his polite demeanor, his caring words, all of it. Not just his love for me. His love for anyone. He said he would return the favor someday. 'You broke my heart, and I will break yours,' he had said. I told Father when he finally came home after I had cleaned the mess that Edward had made in the shop and washed my face of the fear-filled tears I had shed. He didn't believe me, saying I was exaggerating and that a man of Edward's status would never act in such a manner in front of a 'delicate woman.' I hope Robert gets here soon.

Yours truly, Arianna

I paused for a second, taking in the information. After reading the entries about Edward through my mother's eyes, I would have never expected the man to take this sudden emotional turn. I swallowed hard. What if Aaron reacted the same way if I told him about my relationship with Jonathan, or if Jonathan would react that way if I told him about my feelings towards Aaron? I did not want to find out. In my gut, a knot began to twist in my stomach. This Edward man seemed to be so filled with hate and anger. It was shocking how quickly love could change into hate. They were two sides of the same coin. I swallowed hard.

I had to keep reading if I was going to finish before sunrise. I quickly read through the entries following, reading of Robert and Arianna sailing away on his ship, this ship, and marrying him. I read as she realized she was pregnant with me, how happy and scared she was. I realized I was reading the final entry all too soon. Her handwriting was ragged, sloppy. The words were difficult to read, but not just because Arianna's handwriting was poor.

Dear Diary,

I held my beautiful girl in my arms. Robert and I named her Carter Ellen. She is so small. So beautiful. But something is wrong. I can feel it. And the way Martin looks at me, I know there is something not right. It's hard to explain. I'm scared that I'm not going to see my baby grow up. What is my little one going to do? What will happen to Robert? We knew this would be a risk, but now, with death knocking, I am not ready.

Robert mentioned that Edward is aboard, which is odd. He isn't allowed in here, thankfully. He better not hurt my husband. Or my Carter Ellen.

Oh, Diary, I am so scared. I hope this isn't goodbye, but I think it may be. I'm crying thinking about leaving this world behind with my family in it. But mother once told me something about tears. I remember her every time I find myself crying. She told me that teardrops come through anger and right before bravery. They're triggered by sadness to prove you have a heart. They are a sign of courage because you know there is something better than the moment. So, when a tear drops from your eyelashes you know you've won the war.

Oh, Mother, I hope you're right. This war doesn't feel won. My sweet Carter growing up without me does not feel like winning the war.

Goodbye Diary. You've always been there for me.
Thank you, Arianna

Then I noticed something scribbled on the right margin of the final entry. With teary eyes and shaking hands, I turned the diary to read the words. They were written in the same ink, but the handwriting was completely different. My eyes widened with shock as I read the words.

Carter Ellen, I came for your mother. I will come for you, too.

CHAPTER 11

Hunted

ANY TEAR THAT I HAD THOUGHT ABOUT SHEDDING disappeared in an instant. Everything that felt sorrow in my heart was replaced with fear. Edward was coming for me. And he wanted me to know it. And the worst part was, my mother wanted to save me from him, protect me from men like him. She didn't know Edward still wanted revenge; she didn't even know why he was on board the day she died. As I looked out the window, I noticed the sky had turned from black to a deep purple-indigo color. I could catch Jonathan before we had to begin our day, and I needed to tell someone. Something like this I simply could not keep to myself. I moved to the edge of the bed and put my feet on the floor. I stood up, but soon I fell back onto the bed. My body wanted to sleep more than it wanted to share my discoveries. I stared up at the ceiling. There was a man somewhere trying to find me, coming for me, and all I could manage was lying down in a bed. I looked out the porthole. *For all I know he is coming right now*, I thought, *then again, it could be ages until he finds me. Maybe he won't ever find me*, I tried to convince myself. By this hope alone, my eyes flickered closed.

I was standing on the main deck, staring face to face with a man that resembled my imaginings of Edward. His hair was jet black with icy blue eyes. His smile was perfectly placed, like a prince in fantasy books, but with this edge that seemed to reveal he was hiding something.

"Come here, my precious girl, take this bread. It is the least I can do," Edward said, lifting a piece of bread to my hands. I smiled back and took the bread from his hands. I took a step closer. He wrapped his arms around me. "You're safe with me," he whispered. It was then when I felt the knife stab into my back. I closed my eyes in pain. When I looked up, Edward's perfect smile disappeared and had turned into Gargan's evil grin. But it was still Edward's face. It was a terrifying sight. My vision soon began to blur. I saw Edward lean closer to me as my eyes closed. Then I felt his lips press against mine. But the pain only worsened. I felt his lips leave mine, and my knees crashed to the ground, like he had been holding me up the entire time. I heard him whisper in my ear again, "My precious girl, it is a shame to kill you, but I must. You aren't crying. I guess I must be winning." I felt the knife leave my back; the pain that followed was sharp. I blinked my eyes open to see Edward throw the knife aside. My eyes closed again. I felt two hands slowly guide my body to lay on the deck. "I'm sorry child, matters must be settled. Wounds must be healed," Edward said, as I exhaled my last time.

I jerked awake. Eyes wide with fear. Breathing heavily, I looked around, confirming that it was all only just a bad dream. The blanket was disheveled, half of it off of the bed. The image of his eyes was locked in my brain, along with Gargan's black-tooth grin. I picked up my mother's diary from the nightstand and held it tight in my hands. The sunlight was gleaming through the porthole; sunrise had come and gone. Again, I had missed it. *Why hadn't Jonathan come to wake me up?* I thought to myself. I needed to get up, get to work, and tell Jonathan about my mother. I only put down the diary for a moment to get ready for the day, then picked it back up immediately and left my room.

I made my way through the halls and onto the main deck. Most of the crew was on deck and at their posts. I received a few confused or concerned looks as I made my way to Jonathan, who was at the helm. When Jonathan spotted me, he gave me a smile and waved me over to him, commanding Jackson to take his place. I reached him and he planted a kiss on my cheek. I gave him a small smile, then both of us looked down at the diary in my hands.

"Let's go to my cabin," he replied. The two of us headed

to the captain's cabin, hand in hand. In the corner of my eye, I spotted Aaron who saw the two of us, and the confusion in his eyes nearly broke my heart. I would have to talk to him about that later. What I would say, I would figure it out later. I looked back to Jonathan, who had followed my gaze to Aaron. Then he looked at me again. If he was concerned about Aaron, he didn't show it. He opened the door and led me inside. The two of us took a seat at the desk. I placed the diary on the desk and slid it over to him.

"I read the entire thing last night, Jonathan. Every word," I told him. Carefully he picked up the diary and opened the cover, looking over the words on the first page. It looked like he was analyzing my mother's handwriting. He had been searching for this during his time as captain, and now he was holding it in his hands. It was probably just as amazing for him as it was for me.

"And?" he asked. "What did you learn?" He looked up at me with a new curiosity in his eyes.

"Well, to start with, a man is coming for me," I answered, leaning back in the chair, crossing my arms. The diary fell out of his hands; the curiosity in his eyes turned into concern.

"Who? Why?" he asked. I placed a finger over his lips.

"She was in love with two men, Robert and a man named Edward. Her mother didn't approve of either of them because they were sailors, but my mom didn't care. When her mother died, she decided she wanted to spend the rest of her life with Robert. When she told Edward this, he exploded, heartbroken but worse," I explained. I stopped to breathe in and hold the tears back, just thinking about all this was overwhelming. He took my hands into his. I paused, looking at our hands, taking another breath before finishing my thought.

"Edward was on the *Adventurer* the day I was born. Mother didn't know why. And she didn't want him near me or my father," I continued. "But somehow, he found a way into the room my mother was in before she died. He left a note for me in the margin of the last entry. He said he was coming back for me. I don't want him to come. I don't want him to take me." My voice caught and Jonathan moved to wrap his arm around me, pulling me close to his chest.

"It is okay to cry. It's just me," he whispered in a soothing tone. I leaned against him, listening to his heartbeat as slow tears rolled down my cheeks. "He is not going to take you away from me," Jonathan promised. It was a kind gesture, but I knew he was trying to convince himself of this as well. Neither of us knew what the future held for Edward. Or me. My jaw tightened. If the pirates taught me anything, it was that my life could change any second. And I had to be strong enough to beat the punch.

"Look, Jonathan, I know he is coming. You can't do anything about it. The fight is between me and Edward; he doesn't even know you exist, let alone that you're in love with me. He will kill you if you try to get involved. This man is *insane*. Please, don't get yourself involved. I've already beaten a pirate captain; how hard could it be?" I stated. I knew the answer to the final question. I may have escaped the pirate ship, but the pain still haunted me. There's no real defeat. Jonathan knew that too, but neither of us dared to say it out loud. Jonathan just nodded. I could tell he wanted to say something more, but he held his tongue. I decided to give him some time to think about the words. *I can help on the main deck while he worries about all of this. I can't be worrying; it will only make my performance on deck worse. I need to get my mind off Edward,* I thought.

So, I began to stand up from my chair and head for the door. Jonathan jumped up and wrapped his arms around me. It shocked me at first, but then I wrapped my arms around him.

"You won't die. I can feel it," he whispered in my ear, and then squeezed me tighter. Then he gave me a quick kiss. I smiled, but inside I was falling apart. I shoved the tears out of my eyes. *It doesn't matter what Mother says about teardrops. I can cry all I want, and Edward will still search for his revenge! The victory may just come with tears of joy. Mother, your tears didn't help; you haven't won.*

CHAPTER 12
The Helm Helps

I slowly walked out of the captain's cabin, but I didn't dare take my eyes off of Jonathan. Until I had fully closed the door behind me, I held my gaze on him. Sadness enveloped me, but I knew that Jonathan could not get involved when the time came. *If the time came*, I reminded myself. Still, I couldn't risk his life for a problem my mother had; one that I was now forced to deal with. No matter how much I wanted to convince myself it was nothing, I couldn't. My luck when it came to avoiding men that wanted to ruin my life was virtually non-existent.

    I stepped onto the main deck, where a whole new set of worries flooded me. Thankfully, Aaron was too focused on his work to notice that I was back on deck. I had some extra time to figure out what I was going to say to calm *that* situation. Fallier had taken the helm and Jackson was at the crow's nest. The helm wasn't one of Jackson's favorite positions, I had learned, so I wasn't surprised to find that the two had switched. I stood observing the crewmen around me, then I looking out towards the ocean. Someone was out there, searching for me. And that someone wanted me to pay for my mother's actions. I shook off these thoughts and walked up to the helm. Fallier didn't even take his eyes off the seas in front of him as I approached. I was so amazed by how well Fallier stayed to his task, that I almost stepped away. But something pulled me to him. I knew that he could answer my questions, but I didn't know if he would. Fallier and I had very few conversations. He was so quiet and much older than me. He and Gluar were always together. When I was younger, I thought that he didn't like me, and as I got older, I realized how right I had been. Fallier was a strong believer in not having women on board the ship, especially after my mother's death. He believed that women were bad luck. He confided in Gluar and only Gluar. Hardly ever would I find him talking to another crew member about anything other than ship-related issues. The looks he gave me when he thought I wasn't looking had kept me at bay, until now.

"You knew my mother for three years, didn't you?" I asked him quietly. Fallier's eyebrows lowered, but he didn't face me.

"Do you need to talk about this now, Carter?" he questioned me. In his voice, there was an edge of pain, as if I had brought back terrible memories. Maybe I had. I realized I had never talked about my mother's death with hardly anyone who was alive and here when she died. Only Captain James and my father. My longing to know more only grew stronger hearing the sadness in this voice, despite how awful that sounded.

"Yes, I need to talk about this now. I need to know what my mother was like. She was important enough to have all the captains of the *Adventurer* searching for her diary. I want to know why," I replied, not in a demanding voice. I was trying to remain calm and non-confrontational. I saw Fallier glance at me then return his eyes to the sea. He sighed.

"First of all, they didn't search for her diary because of her, they all searched because they wanted you to have it." I gulped; he made it sound like a bad thing. Then Fallier continued.

"She was different from any woman I had ever met before. Your father was in love with her and she was in love with him. Their marriage never failed to surprise me. You know, she chose to leave North Carolina to live here with Robert." He shook his head with a faint smile on his lips, which made me smile. Never did this man smile in my presence. He kept talking, and I kept listening.

"She was small but strong. She was quiet and, at the same time, vocalized her opinions. What mesmerised me the most was her eyes, not the color, but the way her emotions played out through them. Behind her happiness was constant sadness and beyond her truthfulness were dark secrets. I never understood what she was hiding, and it seemed no one else noticed it; except, of course, your father. Nonetheless, I see some of those emotions developing in you. Every once in a while, I will see a spark of Arianna in you.

"Your father joked about making your mother captain, but sometimes I think he was more than joking around. When she passed," he paused for a moment, "when she passed, your father was heartbroken. Everyone was heartbroken. She carried a life force that the crew members of this ship could not ever understand until after she was gone. She was inspiring, kind, a friend to all she knew. For weeks after her passing, your father struggled to carry out his duties aboard the ship. None of us blamed him. We all carried grief, but he carried it the most. And he had you to take care of, which he struggled with at the beginning. No man plans on raising a baby girl on his own while being a captain of a ship. It's unheard of. Early on, it was Martin who took care of you... kept you healthy. That is until you were old enough to start remembering things. Then your father was able to truly raise you as his own. But now I am getting off the subject. Is that good enough?" He looked at me expecting an answer, but I was still dwelling on all he had told me. I nodded. Now, I knew everything and more. I knew what she was like aboard the ship, I knew what she was like in her words, and I knew what happened to everyone when she died. But I soon realized I still had one question unanswered.–

"Was there a man named Edward aboard around the same time my mother passed away?" I asked quietly, trying to respect Fallier's vulnerability. Fallier gave me a curious glance, and then, once again, returned his gaze to the horizon. He began to talk again.

"Yes, I do recall him being here. Edward was the captain of a battleship if I recall correctly. He said he was an old friend of Arianna's. He also had emotions masked underneath his politeness and delight. His dark secrets seemed to nearly escape his lips, but they never did come through. He only stayed for two days, and the second morning he was here, Arianna had passed. Edward sadly left the *Adventurer*, promising that he would visit you when you were older," Fallier replied then glanced at me once more, "How did you know Edward was even here in the first place?" It was a good question, and now I had to answer it.

"He was mentioned in the journal that I was reading it last night," I replied, being sure not to specify which journal. Fallier nodded, accepting my answer

"Yes, your father was fond of Edward. Edward was a successful man, captain of an American battleship, as I said before. The *Cobra*, I believe, was its name. She was a wonderful ship; the *Cobra* was fast on the waves, however, was not very well known, because her size wasn't noteworthy. At least, that was the situation years ago. Still, I can't imagine he would leave his position on that ship." Fallier explained. His eyes once more locked onto the horizon. It was as if I had disappeared and it seemed Fallier had locked away his thoughts from me. I nodded and thanked him for his time, and he only nodded in response, which didn't surprise me. I left the helm and began to pace the ship, observing the men around me who were performing their duties. But my thoughts remained on Edward.

Edward was a captain of a battleship, a battleship that was small, quick, and, for the most part, unknown, which meant it could come at any time, any moment. And no one would stop him. Because everyone loved Edward. My father was even fond of Edward. No one would defy him if he found the *Adventurer* and came aboard. After all, he would only be coming to pay me a visit.

CHAPTER 13
The Land

"Hey, what was that about? With Jonathan?" I heard him ask, breaking my thoughts. I swallowed hard, realizing I had never come up with an answer for Aaron. I turned around to face him. With no real answer, I didn't have much option other than to act oblivious.

"What do you mean?" I asked, tilting my head.

"Him holding your hand into the cabin. I feel like that was quite bold, and quite inappropriate," he replied, raising his eyebrows as if to emphasize how shocked he still was. It made me crack a faint smile, despite all the lies I was tangled in.

"Oh, and you're sneaking into my room isn't?" I chuckled, watching as his face turned red. Maybe I could squirm my way out of this one.

"Yeah, but it wasn't public," he mumbled, smiling as well. I rolled my eyes, playing into the white lie.

"This is a small ship, Aaron. Word will spread if you aren't more careful." Now the red had spread up to his ears. Instead, I turned and made my way up to the crow's nest to relieve Jackson. Hopefully Aaron would take those final words seriously, and buy me more time to sort through my mess of feelings.

I let my mind focus instead on the blue waves that blended into the blue sky before me. For a few hours, I stayed at the crow's nest, leaning against the mast to relieve the pain in my feet. I felt the sun beat down on my tanned neck and watched as the sun began to set in front of me. I paused for a moment, realizing our direction. West. It seemed odd since our last stop at the ports had also been in America. And then I saw it. A black speck that bent the line of the horizon. My heart jumped and sank simultaneously at the sight. I swallowed hard.

Land. How were we approaching land already? It had only been about a month since James Rosten's passing. Normally our routes took us across the Atlantic, to Spain or Portugal, which took longer to arrive at. A couple of months at least. But if we were arriving at a port this soon, it meant we were returning to the United States once more. I swallowed. I had known of some of the issues that had occurred in recent years, the United States refusing the trade with England. Things may have gotten worse. I, as the first mate, should have known that information. But here I was, knowing absolutely nothing, not paying attention, lost in my own issues.

I announced that land was ahead, and there were only a few cheers from the men below. It seemed to weigh on everyone's heart that something was amiss. My stomach jumped to my throat. A little over a month ago I was begging to go on the land, explore and adventure a world I knew nothing about. Now it only brought up memories of Captain James's death, Karak, and worst of all, that horrible ship. An image of Gargan's bloody hand flashed in my mind again. I shook my head, pretending that nightmarish memories could be shaken away. I hadn't realized until now that Adam had come to relieve me of my position. I gladly accepted, made my way down the mainmast, and found Jonathan, at the helm. He took notice as I approached him and commanded Aaron to take over his position. Aaron shot me a smile, which I returned, politely. The last thing I wanted was for the boys to realize I was still conflicted about my feelings I had about them.

Jonathan and I walked side by side, then entered his cabin.

"Is something wrong?" he asked as soon as he closed the door of his cabin, I ran my fingers through my blond strands of hair.

"How are we already heading to the ports?"

"Cater, we are always headed to the ports," he replied,

chuckling. "We are a trade ship after all." I sighed, slightly frustrated, and his smile dissolved.

"I mean, we are headed back to an American port. Did our routes change?" I asked him. The look in his eyes changed and he nodded.

"Yes, our routes changed. Because of the size of our ship, I didn't feel the need to risk trade across the Atlantic, especially since the option to aid the trade in the United States was available. The tension is rising between England and America, and I do not want our home to get caught in the cross-fire," he explained, then shook his head. "I am so sorry for not telling you. I got so caught up in-"

"Jonathan, it's not a problem. I understand, and I know now, so no harm was done," I assured him. I chose not to tell him that I was hurt that I didn't know when it seemed everyone else did. I chose not to tell him that deep down I was scared to go on land and that the idea of the ports in Spain and Portugal sounded so much more appealing because I knew Karak wouldn't be there to sell me to a stranger. No matter how insane my thoughts were, I couldn't shake them. But I couldn't blame him for the hurt I felt. After all, hadn't I just kept my mother's diary a secret from him for over a week? Not to mention all the other things I kept from him that he still didn't know about. My reassurance seemed to be enough to calm Jonathan down and he gave me a smile. A knot settled in my stomach, and I suddenly wished I had told him the truth, but the moment for honesty had passed.

Somehow, while lost in my thoughts, I maintained my façade and walked back out onto the main deck with Jonathan. He moved to stand behind Aaron, who was still at the helm. I glanced around at the rest of the crewmen that were working, none of whom seemed to share my hidden fear of the ports. Even Aaron seemed a bit happier knowing we were headed towards land. I knew I could not be alone in my fear. My companion just wasn't on the main deck. Quickly, I headed down towards Martin's cabin.

I expected to see Jopie in a bed, wrapped up in blankets, trying to fight the sickness she had caught on the pirate ship. But when I walked in, I saw a much different scene. Jopie was up and about, reorganizing Martin's medicine cabinet, placing herbs of all kinds on shelves, organizing them by color, or by smell, or by what they cured. I smiled, happy to see Jopie enjoying herself. In the back corner, Martin was writing furiously, with a clear smile on his face. I assumed he was writing log entries on how Jopie was recovering. Jopie turned away from her work, and her eyes widened with surprise when she saw me standing in the doorway.

"Carter! What are you doing here?" she exclaimed as she ran over to me, wrapping her arms around me in a hug. I hugged her back with a small smile on my lips.

"I needed to tell you something," I replied. Jopie's eyes glistened with excitement as she quieted down to hear the news that I was about to tell her, though I knew in just a few moments the smile would fade. I hated to be the one that told her, but I didn't want her to be kept in the dark as I had been. "We are heading towards the ports, Jopie. We're going onto the land," I explained to her. Her excitement was wiped away by fear, as I expected. But at least she wasn't alone in her fear. Neither of us were. Not like my fear was in any way comparable to hers. I tightened the hug, pulling her close to myself.

"It's okay," I whispered, "I'm scared too." Martin glanced over at me when he noticed the sudden silence. He gave a sympathetic smile to Jopie, who couldn't see it because her face was buried in my shirt. We both were afraid of the land, but at some level, my fears were irrational. Jopie's, however, were not. I could only understand a fraction of her fear. I had been sold to pirates as a slave, but I had not spent my whole life as one, nor had I been mistreated, no, tortured because of the color of my skin. Jopie and I both had a fear of the land, but hers was so much greater than mine. I couldn't even pretend to understand.

Jopie let go of me and her arms fell back to her sides. She looked up at me; I could see the tears welling up in her eyes. She lifted her hands to wipe the tears from her eyes before they were able to roll down her cheeks, but a single teardrop hung on her eyelash and I was once again reminded of my mother's last entry.

"Teardrops come through anger and right before bravery," I whispered in Jopie's ear, quoting my mother. "You are so, so brave, Jopie. It's okay to be angry, but be brave enough to live your own life, however that may look. It's okay to be scared of the land. You won't have to go if you don't want to."

"I think I am going to go on the land with you if I can," she murmured in my ear. Despite her words, I could tell by the look in her eyes that she wanted Jonathan to order her to stay on the ship. But if he said she could go, she would. Jopie was a brave girl, if she had the opportunity to prove herself brave, she would take it. It was something of me that I saw in her. Or something of her I saw in myself.

"I'll be here if you need anything," I promised her. I gave Jopie a hug, and then slowly walked out of the room. She smiled back at me, and then returned to her work organizing the shelves. I watched her for a moment, then closed the door behind me. The hallway was quiet, but I could hear voices coming from the kitchen, where I was sure everyone was eating dinner. I peeked inside. I wasn't really hungry, and I didn't want to sit among the crew members if I didn't have to. As I scanned the room, I realized that Aaron was missing. With a frown, I went to the crew's hall in search of Aaron. When I reached his room, I knocked, but I didn't wait for an answer. Only a second after my final pound on the door, I entered his room. Maybe I was being rude, but my worry for him was stronger than any concern for manners.

Unsurprisingly, Aaron's room was very plain; his bookshelves were empty, and his walls were bare. Aaron was sitting on his desk, staring at papers. Next to his desk, lying on the floorboards was the cloth bag that he had taken from the pirate ship. *The logs*, I realized. I had forgotten about the logs I had torn from Gargan's records. Slowly I walked over to Aaron. As I got closer, I was able to make out the date on the logs he was reading; they were the ones written while I was aboard the pirate ship.

"Aaron?" I said, making my presence known. Aaron jumped a bit with surprise, turned around, and stared at me in shock.

"What are you doing here?" he questioned me.

"I knocked before I came in," I replied, though it wasn't much of a defense.

"Oh," Aaron sighed, confusion crossing his face for a moment, then turned back to the ship logs. I walked up to his desk, picked up the log entry he was reading, and I quickly skimmed it over. It was an entry on Gargan pointing a gun to my head, asking me how I escaped his prison. I had reluctantly told him the answer. The shame of betraying Aaron to the enemy flooded over me again. I felt a pang of sadness, then overcome by anger. *Why had he chosen this one to read?* I looked up, meeting Aaron's gaze.

"Why this one?" I questioned him. Aaron stared at me, confused by my reaction. "Why?" This time when I asked the question, it came out as a cry. Quickly Aaron stood up, put his hands on my shoulders, and pulled me close to him, wrapping his arms around me. I knew he was trying to comfort me, but I still tensed up, still sensitive after the interaction we had shared just a few days ago. He didn't seem to notice, so I forced myself to relax.

"He didn't do anything to me. He already knew it was me," Aaron whispered in my ear, forcing me to calm down and listen. I looked up at him, confused. What was he saying? Gargan knew? And yet Gargan had threatened to kill me, even though he already knew who helped me. It sickened me to know that Gargan's threat on my life, or Aaron's, could not have been changed with my answer. All he wanted was to see my reaction. He truly was evil. I wondered if I had given him what he wanted, squirming under the threat of his gun. Fear swam in my gut as the memories once again flooded my mind. I was drowning in them.

"So, what did you come in here for?" Aaron asked, stepping out of the hug, and pulling me out of that terrifying sea of nightmares. I looked up at him and took a breath.

"We are reaching the ports tomorrow," I mumbled. Aaron gave me a small smile, placing his hands on my shoulders.

"It will be good to see land," Aaron exclaimed. I only nodded. Land meant something different for the two of us. And it didn't seem like he had noticed that yet.

"We need to get back to the main deck. Dinner will be finished soon," I stated. Aaron agreed and we both made our way to the door, walking side by side. He glanced my way as we reached the door, and I looked up at him, slightly confused.

"What?" I asked him, with a small smile beginning to form on my lips. The look on his face made me curious, like he was hiding something. But before I could figure it out, he took my face into his hands and planted a passionate kiss on my lips. My brain lost track of what was up and down and right and wrong; he was my gravity, holding me in place and making me float all at once. And I kissed him back. I forgot what I was saying, what I was thinking. The nightmares and fears I had carried with me all day long had disintegrated into nothing. His lips moved against mine with yearning. But then the pieces of my mind fell back into place. I pulled away and took a breath, resting my forehead on his. He was smiling. What expression did I wear? Joy? Fear?

"We need to get back to the main deck," he murmured; I could feel the breath of his words against my face.

"*I* already said that," I reminded him with a whisper. The smile on his lips only grew.

"I know you did, but clearly, you didn't mean it," he replied. To this, I stood straight, no longer resting my forehead on his.

"What makes you say that?" I questioned him, my smile fading, his smile gleaming.

"Because you are still standing here with me."

CHAPTER 14
Edward Again

I LEFT THE ROOM ALL TOO QUICKLY. He kissed me. I mean, he
kissed me. He held my face in his hands. He had pulled me so
close. I swallowed hard and silently thanked the Lord that he
hadn't followed me out. Had I kissed him back? I couldn't have.
If Jonathan ever found out, he would never forgive me. My feet
were glued to the wooden boards I was standing on. I turned
back to the door, then looked down the hallway that led the way
back to the main deck. Aaron swung the door open and we were
facing each other. It was the moment my feet remembered how to
move. I quickly made my way back to the main deck. He called
after me, concern laced his words, but I ignored him all the same.
Unfortunately, he wouldn't let it go. Just before I reached the
main deck, he took hold of my hand, his grip a pinch too tight. I
jumped in surprise, turning to meet his gaze once more.

"What's wrong? Are you alright?" he asked, his eyes
desperate as they met mine. I gave him a fake smile and nodded.
He frowned. I couldn't blame him. I wouldn't believe me either
if I were him. Still, I had to find a way out of this situation. I
couldn't talk to him about this, about these feelings; not now, not
ever.

"Aaron, I really need to get to work. There is much to do
to prepare for the ports and I am the first mate. I need to be on
deck. Please, can we just talk about this later?" I pleaded with him,
though I had no intention of talking about 'this' later. Later wasn't

good enough for Aaron, it seemed. His grip on my hand tightened, squishing my knuckles together -- his green eyes locked on mine.

"Don't lie to me Cater. I grew up around liars. I know them much better than you," he said, his voice uncomfortably calm. I twisted my hand out of his grip and hugged it close to my chest.

"We will talk about it later," I insisted once more. He clenched his jaw and I watched as his eyes scanned over me, up and down -- as if he was searching me for the truth. And I didn't dare make a move. Finally I saw his shoulders drop and he released a breath. I mirrored him.

"I'm sorry Carter. I-I don't know what came over me."

"It's okay," I replied, willing a faint smile to my lips. "I get it." *Just keep piling on the lies.* This one seemed to satisfy Aaron.

"We'll talk about it later. Go lead your crew." With a small smile to convince him - or myself - that I was okay, I turned on my heels and made my way onto the deck.

Though the sun had sunk into the horizon, the sky was still a light shade of purple, not quite black yet. Only the moon and a few stars shone at this hour. All around me, the crew was preparing the *Adventurer* to arrive at her destination in the morning. Adam and Leonard were heading towards the hold to double-check our inventory. David was at the compass with Jonathan by his side at the helm. Gluar was within the masts, tying knots and untying others. Fallier was up in the crow's nest and Jackson was swabbing the decks. No one was sitting still; everyone had a job to do. I made my way through the crew members, up to the helm at Jonathan's side. -

"I assume you informed Jopie and Aaron about our arrival to the ports?" he inquired, "I didn't see you at dinner." I nodded in reply. David took this as his cue to relieve his position to me and I took over navigation. Then, I explained to Jonathan how Jopie was nervous about going on land. I didn't have to elaborate much; Jonathan understood her situation and how we needed to help protect her. Quickly, he ruled that Jopie would be hidden in the hold, as I had been my entire life, that is, before Captain James' death. In his eyes, he revealed some confusion. I still needed to explain why I had missed dinner.

"When I went to talk to Aaron, he was reading through

some ship logs from our time on the pirate ship. We talked about them for a bit after I informed him of the ports," I explained briefly. The worry that clouded Jonathan's eyes disappeared and was replaced with a different emotion: jealousy. I hadn't thought Jonathan was capable of such emotion. *He's jealous? Of what? Aaron spending time with me?* I bit my lip nervously. *If he knew what really happened…* But as quickly as the sign of jealousy came, it was gone.

"I understand," he nodded. Thankfully, he did not push for any more details, but an awkward silence fell over us. After a few moments, I started up a new conversation.

"Did you tell David about Edward?" I asked him.

"No, he would only want to help you and since you want no help on this matter," he eyed me as he said this, "I decided not to tell him." The look in his soft blue eyes was a jab at me. He was still frustrated that I was resisting his help, and now knowing I had spent some time with Aaron about shared issues probably did not help. I didn't want to hurt him, but I was piling on the pain.

"Edward is a captain of a battleship," I continued, remembering my conversation with Fallier. More bad news for Jonathan.

"That's not good," Jonathan mumbled. I did not like this energy that had manifested between us. Still, I continued our conversation.

"I know! He could just blow a cannon through our ship and sink us all!" I whispered, careful to keep my voice down so the other crew members would hear me. They didn't need to know that a revenge-filled captain was coming for me.

"Carter, that's not it. He is the captain of a battleship, while I am a captain of a trade ship. If he wants, or if he needs to, he can take authority of this ship, especially now with all the tension between England and the United States," Jonathan explained. I swallowed hard; I hadn't even thought about that.

"Wouldn't he need a reason?" I asked, fear and desperation now seeping into my words. Jonathan took his eyes off of the horizon for a moment to look at me. He was just as scared as I was. Then he looked back to the sea.

"He doesn't need a reason with all this tension, Carter. Not when war is on the horizon," Jonathan replied. War? It seemed a little extreme. Of course, I knew that for a while now, trade with France and England was restricted. But war?

Jonathan and I dropped the subject of Edward, and the war. Instead, we discussed the ports ahead. While he described it, I continually reminded myself to stay by his side. I refused to get lost again. After our conversation, I relieved myself of the position and returned it to David, and I took the crow's nest, leaving Fallier to inspect the ship once again. I stayed at the crow's nest until it came time for the nightly duties to begin, which seemed to be only moments later. Jonathan told me that I would have the second part of the night shift and recommended that I get some sleep. I agreed with Jonathan wholeheartedly. Sleep seemed to be a hard thing to come by recently.

I didn't need to be asked twice to go and get some rest. I quickly made my way to my quarters and basically collapsed on my bed. I curled up in a ball and pulled the blanket over me with a faint smile on my lips, forgetting about my fears and worries, if only for a moment. Exhaustion overtook my body, and I fell asleep before another thought could keep me awake.

***

The moon was high in the sky now, and the stars glistened around it. The silver glow of the full moon flooded the main deck. I sat up on the crow's nest while Jonathan was at the helm. The night watch had begun. I looked into the telescope and saw the land more closely, though in the dark it was difficult to make out anything. I turned to my left and saw a ship.

"Ship on the port side!" I yelled down to Jonathan. He looked over the port side and saw the ship sailing. "It's coming straight for us!" I yelled. I was sailing at full speed, and it quickly gained on us. Suddenly the ship was in full view. It was at least twice as large as our own. I got a glimpse of the name. It was enough to make me scream in fear. The *Cobra* was on her way towards us, towards me. Jonathan must have seen it too because he seemed to stiffen in shock. Before I knew it, the ship was right next to us.

"Lower your anchor!" yelled a voice on the other ship. In fear, Jonathan and I lowered our anchor. Once it hit the bottom, a plank coming from the *Cobra* was shoved across, connecting the two ships. Three men walked across in a straight line. Jonathan quickly ran in front of me, but I moved out from his protection. It was me they wanted, not Jonathan, not Aaron, not David, not any of the crew members, not even the ship itself.

"Carter Ellen Key," said the man in the back, saying each part of my name as each man stepped onto the ship. The man's hair was a glossy black with a streak of gray. He seemed to be around forty years old. When he talked, his words flowed out of his mouth like water in a river. His eyes, just as I had imagined, were as cold as ice.

Jonathan took my hands into his and squeezed it so tight that it almost hurt. I didn't dare release my hand from his painful grasp; it would be much more painful if I let go. Out of the corner of my eye, I saw Aaron running up to the main deck. No doubt he had heard my scream and had woken up. I gave him a glare that told him to slow down and act natural. So, slowly Aaron approached the two of us, and he reached for my hand. A sense of safety flooded over me. But then I noticed Edward looking from Jonathan, then to Aaron, and then to me. That's when I pulled away from both of their hands and stepped forward. Edward smiled down at me. For the first time, I realized how tall and muscular the man was. My mind told me to step back, begging for safety, but I resisted the urge.

"It's good to see you again, Carter. The last time I saw you, you were only a few days old," he exclaimed, smiling. He was just like Fallier described. I could tell there was darkness in his kind words. Edward looked around again.

"I don't seem to remember these two," nodding his head at Jonathan and Aaron, "Where's your father?" he asked me. His question pierced me like a splinter. Thankfully, Jonathan and Aaron answered for me.

"He's no longer with us," they answered simultaneously. I met his gaze firmly. He actually seemed to mourn, but underneath his grieving eyes, I saw a spark of joy. A flare of anger burst inside of me, but I kept it hidden.

"What about that James fellow? Wasn't he the first mate?" Edward asked after a few moments of silence. This time, I made sure to answer before Jonathan and Aaron did.

"He passed away a few weeks ago," I replied, being sure to keep calm, burying my anger deep inside of me. This time, I saw the surprise in his eyes.

"Oh, my, tough trials seem to haunt this ship," he said, half to himself. If I didn't know better, I would think him caring. Then he bent down, aligning his eyes with mine, like I was a child. "Who's the captain?"

"I am," said Jonathan without the slightest hesitation. Edward turned his head to face Jonathan. Then he stood up and walked up to Jonathan.

"Then I suppose he is your first mate," Edward concluded, pointing at Aaron. But Aaron shook his head.

"She is," Aaron said, nodding his head towards me. Edward seemed stunned, but quickly he regained his composure and walked back up to me. He grabbed my wrist. I tried to escape his grasp, but it was too tight. Then he looked up at Jonathan.

"I will need to take your first mate onto my ship. Does that sound fine with you?" Edward said quickly. It was like Jonathan was frozen -- all he could do was stand in shock. Edward didn't wait for a reply. He turned around and made his way towards the plank of wood.

"Carter!" Jonathan yelled. I reached out for his hand, but another man grabbed it.

"Carter!" he yelled again. It echoed – his voice in my ears.

I shot straight up in bed. Jonathan was hovering over me but stepped back as I jumped awake. I looked around, then stared at Jonathan. I was safe. Taking deep breaths, I managed to calm myself down.

"You're up," he whispered. A fog of worry seemed to cover his face. Thankfully, he decided not to ask any questions.

"Who's with me for night duties?" I asked him, trying to get past my nightmare. Jonathan smiled. Small and faint, but there all the same. His smile seemed so rare these days, then again, so was mine.

"Me, of course!" he chuckled. I returned his smile, but it wasn't real. Jonathan didn't need to coax me out of bed anymore. Nightmares had shooed me out from under the blankets. He took a step back and I got out of bed, glanced out the porthole, which only revealed a scene of black, and prayed a silent prayer that nightmares didn't come true.

C H A P T E R   1 5
The Decision

I TOOK THE CROW'S NEST once we arrived on the main deck, relieving Aaron of his position. Neither of us exchanged a word. I didn't know if it was the fatigue or the discomfort that kept the two of us from talking to each other. Not knowing which Aaron I would get was starting to worry me. I told him I would forget about it, but that was proving to be an impossible task. I swallowed hard; I didn't need to be thinking of that right now. I had a job to do. At the crow's nest, I held the telescope to my eye, looking out in the black, trying to make out the land from the sea. Though I could not see it, I knew we were edging closer to the ports. As I sat up there, a knot of fear began to form in my stomach. I looked away from the land and to the port side of the ship; it was the place where the *Cobra* appeared in my dream. I was being ridiculous. My mind tried to tell me that my fear was uncalled for, but my heart told me otherwise. I had to know if Edward was looming over my shoulder. My gaze raked over the black. Nothing was on the port side of the ship. My childish fear had taken hold of me and now I felt stupid. I wouldn't let it happen again.

"Everything looking okay ahead?" I heard Jonathan call from below me.

"Yes, everything is safe," I replied loud enough for Jonathan to hear. For a moment, I wondered what he was thinking. Did he know about the kiss between Aaron and me? *How could he know,*

Carter? I immediately asked myself. *You're being irrational.* After another deep breath, I let the sound of the waves put my soul at rest. No more thoughts of Jonathan, or Aaron, or Edward, or pirates.

For hours I sat at the crow's nest, leaving my mind numb and eyes wide. As dawn broke, the land came into full view. I could make out a few buildings but the details beyond that were still imperceptible unless I used the telescope. With the sunrise came the crew, ready to take over the positions from Jonathan and me. As I made my way down to the main deck, Jonathan summoned me over to him. Jonathan relieved his position to Fallier, who set his gaze on the land, and then Jonathan signaled me to follow him into his quarters. Jonathan sat down at his desk, shuffling through some papers. I watched for a moment or two before speaking up.

"Sir?" I asked him. Jonathan looked at me, at first shocked, and then a playful smile grew on his face.

"Since when have you ever called me 'sir'?" he asked me. I smiled and shrugged my shoulders.

"I thought I'd try respecting your title," I said with a playful smirk.

"And?" he said, tilting his head with a soft chuckle.

"I don't like it," I replied. Jonathan smiled and looked down at his desk, shaking his head. I watched as his smile faded away. Then he looked up at me.

"I want you to know that you are in every thought and every prayer that I have. You are the most important person in my life. I don't know why all this has happened to you. It's not fair. Now, I wonder if one day you will disappear and I won't ever be able to see you again," he began. I listened to every word intently, each syllable soaking into my skin and making its way into my heart. His words were coated with a sadness that punctured my heart. I suddenly felt guilty for pushing him away when he kept trying to get through to me.

"There's something you should know. Something that Captain told me before he died," he took a deep breath and I raised my eyebrow. "Captain said that nothing he could do or say could contain you, but you listened and obeyed. He said that he did so many things wrong, but you helped make it right. He loved you with all his heart. I realized I felt the same way about you, but even moreso. The way you smiled, the way you were so independent, the way you could disobey and argue when you thought something was wrong, and most of all, the way you never stopped believing in your dream when it seemed like it would never come true, all of these things made me love you.

"When I kissed you that night, I loved you, and I hoped you loved me back. And when Captain spoke those last words, I realized, I loved you and you didn't have to love me back. Everything you did made an impact on me, and the only way I could pay it back was by making your dream come true. But I didn't watch you like Captain had commanded, and you got lost. This time, I want your dream to come true, without anything or anyone taking you away." He finished and I could feel the guilt and the desperation he carried. He just wanted me to be happy. He just wanted me to live my dream, even when I felt sad and low. I stared at him in awe. He truly was a remarkable man. Why was I resisting him? Why couldn't I love Jonathan the way he loved me, with such purity and honesty? *Aaron*, I answered myself. I looked up once I felt the burning of Jonathan staring at me. I could never deserve that love that he poured out to me.

"You love Aaron, don't you?" he asked me softly. He wasn't accusatory, but his voice was broken with defeat. I opened my mouth to reply, but he raised his hand. "No, Carter, it's okay," he murmured. But it wasn't okay. I didn't want to lose Jonathan, I couldn't. Yes, we fought. Our lives weren't perfect. But life without him simply wouldn't be life.

"Jonathan. Wait." I grabbed his hand and refused to let him slip away. He turned to face me. I pulled him close and pressed my lips against his. He was the one. He had to be. His hands rested on my hips, pulling me closer as he kissed me back. Close wasn't close enough. One of his hands moved gently up my back and rested on the back of my neck. As he kissed me, all my memories of Aaron and the pirates disappeared. He reminded me of the joy that lived deep inside me, that had been lost under the wreckage of the last few weeks. He reminded me of the woman I wanted to be. He was my rock. Dependable. I couldn't lose him; I refused to let him go. I couldn't, not even for Aaron. He pulled away and rested his forehead on mine. I smiled and my eyes fluttered open and I looked at him. His eyes were still closed, and I listened to the sound of his breathing.

"Aaron is a friend, Jonathan. You are so much more," I whispered. Never had the words felt more confident. No word, no kiss could change my mind. Jonathan loved me, even when he believed I didn't love him. I didn't deserve him. His eyes fluttered open and his lips formed a smile as his eyes met mine. He nodded. He planted another gentle kiss on my lips that brought another pure smile to my face.

"I trust you," he whispered in reply and my smile grew. He chuckled softly and he moved to hold my hands in his. I stared at our hands. Together. They were right where they belonged.

"Let's head to the ports," Jonathan sighed with a smile on his lips. I nodded happily. He was acting calm, but the joy in his eyes was incomparable to ever before. Hand in hand, he opened the door of his cabin and we walked out onto the main deck. The fresh air hit my face and the sound of the ports filled my ears. We were nearly there. I scanned the deck when my eyes met his. Green like the grass that was closer than ever before. I watched as Aaron's eyes landed on my hand; my fingers intertwined with Jonathan's. A lump formed in my throat and I slipped my hand out of Jonathan's. Jonathan glanced over at me then followed my gaze.

"I need to talk to him for a minute, to explain some things," I whispered. Jonathan nodded and attempted an encouraging smile. I wondered, for a moment, what he was thinking. There was no time to dwell on my curiosity though. With a deep breath, I made my way over to Aaron, who turned away from me as he noticed what I was trying to do.

"Aaron. Aaron, wait, please," I said as I got closer to him and he started walking away. I grabbed his wrist and held it tight. He didn't fight my grip, but he didn't turn to face me either.

"Aaron, can we talk?" I asked him quietly. Despite the ports nearby and the hustling crew around us, the world seemed silent and still as he turned to face me.

"Sure, let's talk," he muttered, his jaw tight. How could he be so angry and upset and still so handsome? The two of us walked to my room with the tension growing between us. I opened the door and he walked in and took a seat on my bed. I stood in front of him, silent for a few moments.

"You wanted to talk? Let's talk," he said, eventually, when the silence was too much for either of us to take.

"Aaron, please don't act like that," I begged. "I do care about you."

"Oh yeah? And that's why you didn't tell me that you're in love with the captain of this ship when I was falling head over heels for you," he snapped back. I bit my lip and looked down. He had every right to be angry, but it still hurt. It hurt to know that this is what I did to him.

"I love you, Aaron," I replied. He rolled his eyes.

"Love? No, Carter, you aren't allowed to say you love me. That's just cruel."

"You're one of my best friends!" He flinched and looked away. I swallowed hard. He looked back at me with a tight smile. Somehow it was more painful than the moments where he had lost control.

"You don't understand, do you, Carter?" The edge in his voice slowly seemed to disappear into sadness. I chose to keep quiet. "You don't even know what love is, even when it's right under your nose." He stood up and walked out of my room, leaving me alone with my thoughts. Only moments ago, I was the girl I wanted to be, happy and joyful and free. Now I was locked in a cage I built myself.

CHAPTER 16
The Ports

For a moment, I stared at the door. I took a deep breath. I should have known this would happen. Why did I believe Aaron would be okay with me not choosing him? A few minutes ago, he didn't even know there was a choice. I needed to be okay with his reaction to my decision. I had Jonathan, the man I had loved my entire life. I left my room, holding onto that thought. I made my way to the main deck and spotted David and Jonathan at the helm. As I made my way over to them, I watched as we docked at the ports.

"Everyone to your stations!" I yelled. The crowd dispersed, each man heading to his position. About half of the crew was on the port side, ready to tie up the ship. Aaron and Jackson were both ready to drop anchor. I ran over to the two of them. Aaron immediately relieved himself of the duty and I bit my lip. Jackson, though, didn't seem to notice the discomfort.

"Thanks for helping me out here, Miss Key!" Jackson exclaimed. I sighed in playful annoyance.

"How many times do I have to tell you not to call me that?" Jackson looked over his shoulder and smiled at me. Then he faced forward at the sea again.

"You only told me not to call you First Mate Key," he yelled to me. I rolled my eyes and breathed a sigh of annoyance. Jackson heard me and he began to laugh. I laughed with him, trying to forget the misery I had been wallowing in.

"Well, from now on, just call me Carter!" I exclaimed.

"Drop the anchor!" I heard Jonathan command from behind me. Jackson and I worked on one main anchor while Adam and Gluar worked on another. The two groups dropped anchor then manned the capstan, pulling the *Adventurer* to shore. It was difficult work for the four of us, but with the excitement of approaching land in my veins and desperation to escape the hurt I was feeling, the difficulty seemed to fade.

"Tie her up!" Jonathan commanded. I watched as the crew members skillfully jumped onto the dock and tied the Adventurer to the posts. With both the ropes and anchors in place, the *Adventurer* halted. I moved to stand beside Jonathan once more. My disappointment and frustrations faded away. Excitement replaced the sadness and fear; I felt my joyful-self shining through once more. I was the girl that only Jonathan could bring to the surface. Jonathan chuckled behind me as the smile on my face grew.

"Carter," Jonathan said, catching my attention. I looked over my shoulder to face him. He wasn't looking back at me. He was scanning the main deck as the crew was helping dock the ship, but there was a whimsical smile on his face, so I knew that he noticed me turning to face him.

"Are you ready?" he asked me, his smile growing wider, his hand slipping into mine again. I let the butterflies of excitement fill my stomach. I smiled back, hoping he could see, then I faced the land again.

"Of course!" I answered, bouncing on my toes with anticipation. He laughed a little, but it faded quickly. It didn't worry me. Not like earlier. He was still a captain, and he had a job to do.

"All hands on deck!" he shouted, his voice ringing through the air. Anyone not already on deck, such as Martin and Jopie, were on deck in a matter of seconds. All eyes were on Jonathan and me, the leaders of the crew. Jonathan didn't need to explain what was going on. The ports were here, no longer in the near distance. He explained our job at the ports: to drop off supplies and pick up the items they had been traded for, on behalf of our employers. Jonathan also said we would be receiving some new cannons as well, due to the rising tensions in the Atlantic. I couldn't help but swallow at the mention of the war on the horizon. Knowing we would be prepared to defend ourselves eased my conscience a little bit.

"How are the sails, Gluar?" Jonathan asked.

"Nothing to report, captain," Gluar replied. Jonathan nodded and then asked Martin how long it would take to buy some new medicines for Jopie. As the two discussed this, I smiled at Jopie and she smiled back. I would eventually be able to tell her that she wasn't going to have to go on the land. Behind her smile, Jopie was a nervous wreck. Her fear built up with each minute that passed. By now, she must have been scared for her life.

"Aaron," Jonathan announced. My eyes followed Jonathan's until they reached Aaron. His green eyes gleamed in the sun, sparkling like gemstones – and just as hard. Aaron glanced at me and I quickly looked down at my feet. Aaron returned his gaze to Jonathan. I hoped that we didn't have to act this way forever. It would be impossible to lose a friend like him.

"Yes, sir," Aaron replied, raising his chin. He was strong and proud, ready for any position that Jonathan gave him.

"You will stay on the ship with Fallier and make sure everything runs smoothly. Also, make sure Jopie is safe in the hold before we leave," Jonathan explained.

"And give her an oil lamp," I cut in. Aaron raised an eyebrow towards me. His gaze made me feel uncomfortable. Though, as I turned around, I noticed everyone's head turned to face me. I realized I had never spoken up in one of these meetings before. On top of that, my command was slightly random and surprised most of the crew. But it was true, Jopie would need an oil lamp. And now, based upon the many confused faces staring up at me, I was expected to explain why.

"It's dark in the hold; she will be under there for hours. At least don't make her dread it," I sighed remembering my own time spent down in the hold. As soon as I finished, I looked over at Jonathan and David. Jonathan smiled proudly at me and David nodded in agreement. Then I looked at Aaron. He gave a shallow nod and kept a straight face. For some reason, I seemed to expect something more, but his nod would do for now. At least he was acknowledging my presence. I turned towards Jopie. She mouthed the words 'thank you'. I gave her a happy nod, hoping she understood that it meant 'you're welcome'.

"Let's go!" Jonathan exclaimed. As soon as he said the word, I ran over to the plank that led from the ship down to the ports, and I ran down onto the land. The wood of the docks was rough and threatened to splinter the bottoms of my feet. I saw the main street of the town. As I took another running step forward, I heard Jonathan behind me.

"First Mate!" he yelled, his face speaking his thoughts. His face was stern as he looked down at me. Still, there was a glimmer of a smile in his eyes. I stopped in my tracks, realizing my mistake. I wasn't just a cabin girl anymore. I was second in command; I needed to at least try to act like it. I brought my feet together and stood straight, waiting for the rest of the crew to catch up. Behind Jonathan's stern captain face, I saw David and Jackson smiling wide, probably trying to hold back the laughs that were catching at their throats. I grinned along with them. Moments later, the crew was only a few feet from me. They stopped in shock. Jonathan ran up to me, but not before someone grabbed my shoulder. *Not again!* I thought to myself. I whipped around, prepared for a fight.

"Arianna!" said a woman's voice. My eyes widened with shock as I looked at the woman. Jonathan stopped in his tracks. My tightened fists lowered as her eyes looked over me. She seemed just as confused as I was. She was probably in her late thirties or early forties. She had brown hair that reached just past her shoulders. The woman had beautiful hazel eyes and tall, lean stature. I could guess who she was.

She was my mother's best friend, Rachel. She was my mother's neighbor for four years. Even though Rachel was three years older than my mother, the two of them got along quite well. But two weeks after Arianna's mother died, Rachel and her husband moved away from my mom. This didn't keep them from staying in touch. My mother sent her letters until she married my father and joined the *Adventurer*. It seemed impossible that she was actually here.

"Oh, you aren't Arianna," Rachel sighed, clearly disappointed. "I'm so sorry, I thought you were someone I once knew." She thought she had found her best friend, but instead, she had found me. Slowly Rachel began to walk away. I heard Jonathan and the rest of the crew approach me, but I lifted my hand, signaling them to stay where they were.

"Rachel, wait," I called after her. Rachel lifted her head and turned back to face me.

"How do you know me?" she questioned me. I knew I had to be careful about how I answered. Only Jonathan and David knew about my mother's diary and only Jonathan knew the secrets that lay inside. I didn't want the rest of the crew to find out about it.

"Arianna was my mother," I replied. Slowly, she approached me once again. Her gaze continued to go up and down as if she were searching for something that I had.

"You look much like her," she muttered, half to herself, "some things, like your eye color and your wavy hair, remind me of someone else. What is your name, darling?" she asked me kindly.

"My name is Carter," I answered with a small smile. "And the other person you are reminded of is my father, Robert Key," I continued. Her eyes lit up as I said my father's name.

"Good gracious Arianna Katelyn!" she exclaimed, making me jump back in surprise. Then she started babbling all about the relationship between my mother and my father, all of which I already knew and more. I smiled. It was rare to meet someone who knew my mother so well. But inside I knew that I would be the one having to break the news that both of my parents were dead. Still, I knew it would be good to learn more about my mother, and maybe Edward, through Rachel. Wanting to be polite, I tried to remember what Rachel's last name was.

"Mrs. Price," I said, interrupting her. Rachel looked down at me.

"Yes Carter, what is it dear?" she asked me. I looked at the crew behind me. Some, like David and Jonathan, were smiling at me. Others, like Gluar and Jackson, were very confused. None of them needed to hear the questions I needed to ask Rachel and all of them needed to get started on the supply transfer.

"How about you and I go somewhere private to talk while the rest of the crew gets their work done?" I suggested. Rachel smiled and nodded in agreement. Then I turned back to face Jonathan.

"I'm going to talk with Mrs. Price for a little bit, then I will be back to help finish up the loading. Is that okay, captain?" I asked Jonathan. He smiled as I referred to him as 'captain', which I didn't do often enough, then he nodded. I turned and walked with Rachel.

"Where are we going?" I asked curiously. I looked around mesmerized by the shops and bright summer colors, but always glancing back to make sure Rachel was still by my side. I didn't want to get lost again.

"I thought we would go to my house; how does that sound?" she asked me. I nodded twice quickly as excitement filled my chest. I was interested to see how her family turned out and to meet Lewis Price.

"Besides," Rachel continued, "there's someone you ought to meet!"

CHAPTER 17
Rachel's Story

RACHEL GUIDED ME THROUGH THE STREETS of the town until we reached her home. It looked much like Mrs. Rosten's house, except it was a bit larger. I didn't know what I was expecting, but I knew I was excited to see a united family, something almost unheard of on the *Adventurer* or any ship for that matter. She guided me away from the first floor and I followed her up the stairs and into her living space where there was a bed, a small couch, a kitchen, and a man, who I assumed was Lewis, and their two children. All three of them stared at me, and Rachel didn't seem to notice.

"Can I offer you anything? Tea?" she asked me. I shook my head. Her family looked from Rachel to me, back to Rachel again. I swallowed hard, feeling like an interruption. Finally Rachel seemed to notice.

"Lewis, Anna, Connor, this is Carter," she explained to the three of them. This explanation didn't seem to satisfy them, even though Anna nodded as if it meant something to her. "Lewis, she is Arianna's daughter," she explained to her husband.

"Ahh, okay. Nice to meet you, Carter," he said with a smile, approaching me with his hand extended. I gave him a firm handshake. Anna and Connor still seemed confused, but Rachel wasn't in any hurry to explain. Instead she brought over a tray of tea and had us all sit down on the couch. Anna looked about my age, fifteen or so, with blonde hair, like her father's, tied up in a bun. Connor had to be Jonathan's age, at least, maybe even a few years older. He had a scruffy beard that matched the color of his brown hair, and hazel eyes, like Rachel.

"Arianna was one of my friends growing up," she explained to both of her children. They nodded and gave me an awkward smile. Lewis and Rachel forced conversation on the three of us until the awkwardness disappeared. Eventually, the five of us were carrying a casual conversation with ease, but I still hadn't told Rachel that my mother and father were dead. How was I to do that now? I took a deep breath.

"Mrs. Price, may I speak with you and your husband in private?" I asked her. She looked at me, slightly confused by my request, but then nodded. Rachel sent Anna and Connor down to the shop on the first floor. As the door closed, she turned to face me once more.

"Now what is it you need to talk about?" Rachel asked me. She readjusted herself, facing me more directly. With her hands, she pressed down her dress and looked up at me with a pleasant expression.

"Well, Mrs. Price, my parents, Arianna and Robert, well they, they both have passed away," I stuttered through the sentence. I waited for her face to contort in sadness or shock, or for her to start weeping. Clearly, she must have believed Arianna was alive if she thought I was Arianna. But Rachel only breathed in deeply and looked down at the floor. Without meeting my gaze, she took my hands into hers. I just stared at our hands until she spoke again.

"I had wondered about that. Who is taking care of you now?" she asked me. She was gentle, kind. I couldn't help but wonder if this is what it might feel like to have a mother.

"Well, Captain James Rosten was looking after me for a little while, but then he died a little over a month ago. I live on the ship, ma'am, and the crew is my family. They take good care of me, in fact, I am the first mate of the ship now. It's my home," I explained. Her eyebrows raised as I told her my position on board.

"My... Child, that's very impressive," she commented with a smile. I nodded a thank you.

"I wanted to speak with you about my mother, who she was, and her relationship with Edward," I said. Rachel nodded, her eyes revealing a glint of curiosity. She began by explaining most of what I already knew, such as her parents' work, her talks with Robert, and the time she and Rachel spent together. But I didn't want to tell her to stop. It was interesting to hear what she thought about my mother's life. Then she began the story of Edward. I was already listening, but my interest heightened.

"Edward was a kind-hearted man," she began. I smiled, but underneath I knew the truth. The man I knew from my mother's diary was not so kind-hearted as Rachel believed. "He would normally only come to the ports once a month, sometimes even less than that. The two met each other one day when Arianna was out in the marketplace buying food. He approached her, touching her hand, calling her beautiful – very forward. Borderline scandalous. I told her she should have slapped him away, but Arianna insisted he was kind. Edward bought the bread and the rest of the food and helped her bring it to her house. I thought it was ridiculous for Arianna to bring a stranger to her house. Every time he came to the ports after that, Arianna and her family would have a nice dinner, inviting him of course, since he bought most, if not all, of the food. Her parents seemed fond of him, but I wasn't very close to her parents.

"All the while, I saw Arianna slowly falling in love with Robert. Arianna complained that her mom was very upset that she had fallen for two sailors, but she couldn't do anything about it. She never really told Edward much about Robert, nor did she tell Robert much of Edward. It was creating a dangerous situation. Arianna needed something to pull her out of the clouds. I tried to, often, saying that she could only love one of them. She always replied saying she didn't know or soon she would figure it out. Soon Robert had left for his new ship. Arianna was left alone to dwell on her thoughts.

"Then her mother died. Arianna was heartbroken. I don't think she slept for a single moment that night, or the rest of the week. She was left alone, with no one to look after her, except for her father, who worked all day and most of the night. I was all she had, and I was about to leave with my husband. She came over to my house one day, crying. She was so alone and tired. She was running a shop by herself and didn't know what to do, nor did she care to learn. I asked her to tell me one person that she would want with her right then. She answered with the name Robert. Suddenly her eyes widened, and she stopped crying. I thought she had made her decision, but I left before she saw Edward again," Rachel finished. It was silent for a few moments. Then I began to stand up, but Rachel gripped my hand tighter. I sat down again.

"How exactly did she die?" Rachel asked me. I frowned and swallowed hard, guilt filling my chest.

"It was my fault," I whispered. It was nearly impossible to say out loud. She tilted her head, concerned. "There were complications when I was born, and she didn't make it," I explained briefly. With a sad smile, Rachel shook her head.

"Dear Carter, it's not your fault," she replied, her hand gently caressed my cheek and she lifted my chin to face her kind smile. I felt a tear roll down my cheek, but I couldn't remember when I started crying. She wiped the tear from my cheek with her thumb. "She dreamed of having a daughter like you, Carter," she whispered. I gently pulled away and wiped my eyes. I couldn't imagine my mother dreaming of me -- a few short weeks ago, I couldn't imagine my mother at all. Not truly.

"Thank you for telling me," said Rachel after a few moments. I nodded, and after a minute of pure silence, I asked her if she could guide me back to the ports. She nodded with a comforting smile on her face and the two of us walked out of the house saying goodbye to her family as we walked out. Rachel guided me back down the streets of the market place until I reached a familiar sight. The ports, filled with all of their excitement, drew me away from the sadness that Rachel and I had carried. The tears in my eyes dried up under the heat of the sun. I was on the land, safe and loved. Then I spotted my beautiful home. Jonathan waved me over to the ship.

"Thank you, Mrs. Price. I loved meeting you," I turned to give her a goodbye. Rachel came closer and gave me a quick hug.

"Stay safe," she whispered in my ear. I nodded. She took a step back and nodded at me almost like she was giving me permission to return to my home. I accepted and ran towards my ship. Jonathan and David greeted me as I approached.

"So how did that go?" Jonathan asked me.

"It went well," I replied with a smile, looking over my shoulder at Rachel walking away, back into the mess of the marketplace. Jonathan nodded and smiled, and we continued to load the ship. After twenty minutes or so, we finished loading the supplies. It was time to make our way back into the blue. Back into the place I knew I belonged. Despite its dangers, its chaos, its uncertainty, I was safe on these waves, surrounded by these men. My family.

CHAPTER 18
Secrets Revealed

THE CREW WORKED AROUND ME as I approached the helm, where Jonathan stood. Despite the loud hustle and bustle of the crew, the sound of the waves filled my ears, calming me down, allowing my thoughts to settle. Everything I feared about Edward, everything I learned from Rachel seemed to blend into the seafoam – not lost, but faded somehow. In these few moments, I was just Carter, a first mate on a ship she called home. Jonathan spotted me and shot me a smile. I smiled back at him.

"Yes, Captain?" I asked as I approached the helm, where he was waiting for me. Jonathan chuckled and rolled his eyes.

"Do you really have to call me that? It sounds weird coming from you." I held in a laugh.

"Oh, Jonathan!" I replied with a wide smile, "You are my captain and I will call you what I will." I laughed. Jonathan rolled his eyes again and wrapped an arm around me, pulling me closer to him. I bit my lip in a giddy smile. It was different, better, to be in his arms, unafraid.

"I picked you up some more clothes, and I already put them in your room. No dresses, I promise," he explained. I nodded in response and smiled up at him. Then he gave me a curious look. I tilted my head.

"What, Jonathan?" I asked.

"So, what did she say?" he asked me. I took a deep breath and stepped out from under his arm. He gave me a concerned face. The two of us relieved the position to another crew member and we entered the captain's cabin. He took a seat behind his desk and I pulled up a chair and sat across from him. I began to explain Rachel and I's conversation to Jonathan. Every once in a while, Jonathan would lean back in his chair or nod in understanding, but he refused to say a word. When I finished, Jonathan leaned forward and took my hand from across the desk.

"Well, let's hope that the Edward that Rachel knew, the kind, caring man, is the one that we meet," he sighed. I nodded in agreement, but a knot formed in my stomach, and I swallowed hard. I knew that Edward had changed since the last time Rachel had seen him. The Edward that Rachel knew didn't exist anymore. He was coming after me, it was just a matter of time. Jonathan's hands slipped out of mine as he stood up. I glanced at Jonathan and watched him walk out, giving me a soothing smile. I tried to forget about my recent thoughts, forcing them back into the seafoam. I left the captain's cabin and made my way down to my room to rest my mind. I opened the door and my jaw dropped at the sight.

"Aaron! What are you doing in here?" I asked him, astonished. I looked in Aaron's hands, where my mother's diary was open, when it should have been on my nightstand – closed. I stared at him in shock. "Aaron, what is going on here?" I questioned him. He didn't answer my questions. Aaron put the diary, open, back on the nightstand. His intense stare seemed to attack me. His beautiful green eyes were now filled with a terrifying mixture of anger, grief, and pain. I tried to step towards him. He stepped back. I swallowed hard. I hated seeing him like this.

"Why didn't you tell me?" he asked me, almost yelling. I stumbled back at his aggressive tone. I scrambled to shut the door before someone heard, then I looked from him to the diary, back to him.

"You *read* it?" I asked him in complete shock. But once again, Aaron didn't answer my question.

"Carter, an insane man is coming after you! Why would you keep this information from me?" he questioned me again. He moved towards me and grabbed my shoulders, desperate. Instantly

I grew tense, afraid of his anger escalating. But, I didn't move his hands away. Jonathan was my love, but Aaron understood parts of me that no one could. Aaron had become one of my best friends, and nothing could change that. As much as I didn't want to tell him, Aaron deserved the truth.

"Aaron, I didn't tell you because no one is going to help me. Not David, not Jonathan, and not you. If he comes, I will face him alone," I replied calmly. Aaron's hands slid off of my shoulders, his fingertips brushing against my arms, sending chill bumps across my skin. He gave me a defiant, questioning look.

"But I can help you, I will help you!" Aaron exclaimed, frustration coating his words. His fists tightened at his side. Carefully, I reached for his hands; his intensity scaring me. He noticed what I was doing and moved out of my reach. He was still hurt by my decision. I couldn't blame him.

"No, you won't," I replied firmly. Now my fists were tight. Aaron looked down at the floor; seeing him defeated softened me a little, and my fists loosened. I moved and sat on my bed with a heavy sigh. He sat down next to me after a moment, which surprised me. For a moment, the tension between us disappeared. I looked over at him and he met my gaze.

"Why is it so hard for you to let me do things on my own?" I asked him gently. Again, there was silence.

"I'm just so scared you will get hurt," he sighed, breaking the void. I was going to reply, but then his gaze shifted from pleading to sweet sorrow. "It's hard enough to accept that you ignored the spark between us that I could so easily see. I am trying to accept that we are friends even though I know that we are much more than that. Aren't friends supposed to help each other in times of trouble?" he questioned me. Aaron made a good point, but I couldn't force his thoughts of our relationship out of my mind. I knew there had been a spark between us, and Aaron knew it too. But is that what I did, ignore it? Smother it? Or did I confront it differently than Aaron?

"Aren't they?" he asked me again, with more persistence than anguish in his voice this time. My thoughts of us faded away.

"Of course, they help each other, but the best way to help me now is to not intervene. I can't risk your life for a problem with my mother's relationship," I explained to him. "You can't keep me from getting hurt, Aaron, but I can keep you out of harm's way." Aaron rolled his eyes and turned away from me. I gently turned his head back towards me with my fingertips. His eyes widened with surprise.

"Look, I don't know what made you think you could read my mother's diary, but I can honestly say that I have never been so angry and happy at the same time. A burden has been taken off my chest, but it was a burden I never wanted you to know about. It's a burden I needed to carry *on my own*. Now you are trying to carry some of the load. I won't let you do that. That is why it was a secret in the first place. Edward is my problem. My mother is my problem," I explained to him. Aaron began to talk, but I lifted my hand to stop him from speaking.

"Let's say I did let you help me. What could you possibly do?" I asked him.

"I wouldn't let Edward take you onto his ship," he blurted out just as I finished the question.

"But Edward is the captain of a United States battleship. He has the authority to take me whether you want him to or not," I countered. Aaron nodded, considering his new options.

"Then I would come with you. To protect you," Aaron responded.

"Aaron, Edward could kill you if you came with me. That would put me through emotional torture and I'm sure Edward would find a way to use that against me. You would end up hurting, not helping," I explained to him. Aaron sighed, growing more frustrated with every passing moment. I had won this argument, but the look of defeat in his eyes did not make me feel victorious.

"Just remember that I will always be here. And I am more than just a friend," he muttered. As the last word left his mouth, he stood up from my bed and made his way towards the door. *More than a friend?* I seemed to ask myself, sitting still. *Am I allowed to even think of him like that when I just told Jonathan it wasn't like that?* I was so angry with myself. I was so angry with him. He wasn't wrong in saying he was more than a friend; we had connections that no one else could share, but he was using them to prove love. It wasn't fair. It wasn't true. He was making me think twice. He was saying things he knew would convince me to love him again. *Would I love him again?* I asked myself. As soon as the question came to mind, I answered it. *No.*

I thought of Jonathan. His golden hair, his eyes like the sea, his soul so pure. I thought of my first kiss, the one we shared. I remembered the kiss he gave me when I finally made my decision. Pure happiness. Pure love. Not guilt in sight. Not sadness in thought. The memories alone made butterflies form in my stomach. I made a decision and I knew it was the right one. I knew it. I had to have made the right decision. As Aaron left my room, I refused to meet his gaze. I kept my eyes on my folded hands, not only because I was so in love with Jonathan, but also because I was scared his beautiful green eyes would sway my thoughts.

CHAPTER 19
Friends

For a few moments, I sat on my bed listening to the near-silence of my empty room. I had to get Aaron out of my head. I paced the room for a little bit, but my eyes were glued to my mother's diary, the diary Aaron had read without my permission. It wasn't working. He was still consuming my thoughts. I decided to get outside. I walked through the halls and up to the main deck, but it did nothing. I was completely lost in thought. I was thinking about what Aaron had told me, about my first kiss, and Edward all at the same time. My mind was so scattered, I barely existed outside of it. And I ran straight into Jackson.

"Whoa, sorry!" he quickly apologized. I was pulled from my tangle of thoughts and faced Jackson, shaking my head.

"No Jackson, no need to apologize. It was my bad," I assured him. I noticed a book had fallen on the floor. Jackson looked at me with an awkward smile.

"Miss Key, I apologize, I should have been paying attention to where I was walking," he replies. I couldn't help but roll my eyes.

"Well, you can't be too sorry. You are still calling me Miss Key after I specifically asked you not to," I chuckled. He laughed awkwardly.

"Yes ma'am, you do have a point there," he admitted with a soft chuckle.

"No more of that," I told him. He nodded with a smile.

"And I apologize for running into you, Jackson. I was so lost in thought; I wasn't paying attention to the world around me." I bent down to pick up the book that I assumed he dropped when I ran into him.

"And I was reading, I should have been looking out where I was going," he countered. We both smiled at each other, accepting the apologies, and I handed him the book.

"Robinson Crusoe, huh?" I asked him. Jackson nodded.

"It's a fantastic work," he replied. I nodded in agreement.

"It's one of my favorites," I told him. His smile grew.

"Maybe we can discuss it sometime?" he suggested.

"I would love that." Somehow I knew that there would be no time for such conversation. Not soon anyways. Now that I had made my decision to let Aaron go, and whatever those feelings I had for him, tension was stronger than a title wave. Not to mention all of the other emotional weights I was carrying. Talking about a book so that an acquaintance could grow into a friend was a nice thought, but that was all it could be.

He nodded, put the book under his arm, and headed towards the crew's quarters. I continued to roam the main deck, this time aware of my surroundings. I checked on the other crew members, ensuring that they were well and that all the jobs were being completed. No-one was disappointed. I accompanied Jonathan for a bit, but I tried to avoid any conversation concerning Edward, the diary, and especially Aaron. I did not tell him about the encounter that Aaron and I had earlier. I didn't tell him that Aaron might be more than a friend and how tempting those green eyes were. *Oh no, not again.* My thoughts had spiraled back to Aaron even while I was talking about sailing with Jonathan. I was an awful person. After Jonathan and I finished our conversation, I told him I would return to the main deck soon. I didn't tell him where I was going. From a porthole below the main deck, I dove into the ocean.

The water splashed over my head, cooling my skin that had been baking in the sun for far too long. I swam up for a breath and dove back underneath the waves. The *Adventurer* was my home, but this was my world. And in this world, Aaron's words couldn't flood my mind. My mind was too busy being flooded with the smell of saltwater and happy memories. I quickly whistled for the dolphins to come to join me. The sounds echoed and I waited for a reply. Soon I heard the lovely sound of tails splashing in the distance and a smile broke across my face. Aurora, Dawn, Sunset, and Luna approached me happily.

"Where have you been Carter?" Sunset clicked, "It seems that we haven't seen you in forever!" The other dolphins nodded in agreement. I felt bad. I was so caught up in all these different worries that I hadn't made time to see my friends.

"Sorry, I've been so busy lately," I apologized quickly, though I knew they would want more than that.

"With what?" Luna questioned me.

"I discovered my mother's diary and learned about this man named Edward who my mom almost married and I am pretty sure he is out to kill me," I tried to explain as best as I could. Of course, they asked questions, but at least I didn't have to talk about Aaron, or think about him for that matter. I explained what I had learned from my mother's diary in choppy, distorted whistles and clicks. Even the word 'mother' wasn't one I used very often.

"That is crazy!" Aurora squeaked. I nodded in agreement

"Why do you always have to be in danger?" Dawn whistled. I decided not to address that question. I didn't have the answer.

"How were the ports?" Sunset asked me. As we swam under and over the waves, I whistled and squeaked as best as I could, trying to explain the land, since the last time I visited, I was sold to pirates. I briefly mentioned Rachel but focused more on what it looked like. The dolphins seemed intrigued for a while, but eventually, they began to squeak and whistle about their times since I had last seen them. I tried to listen as well as I could. Sometimes they were too fast, but I understood most of it. Their stories often consisted of hunting and swimming and exploring. Quite an easy life in my opinion. I wished mine carried the same level of simplicity, peace, or joy. As we swam and as they talked, my mind began to drift once again.

Aaron's claim was stuck in my brain. But there was no place for someone "more than friends" while I was with Jonathan. It would be unfair to him. I already told him that Aaron and I were finished. And that was true. We could still be friends if he would just give up on pursuing me. He said he wanted to help me, but this wasn't helping. If he wanted to help, he would let me go.

"Carter?" Sunset squeaked. *I've been caught.* I turned and gave her a small smile, trying to pretend that I hadn't been lost in an argument that existed only in my mind.

"Yes?" I replied.

"What's wrong?" she asked me. Reluctantly, I proceeded to tell them about my situation with both Jonathan and Aaron. I explained how I had chosen Jonathan, but Aaron was still trying to convince me to choose him, whether he was doing it on purpose or not, I couldn't say. I didn't tell them that his words may have been working. Maybe.

"I'm so sorry about Aaron," Aurora empathized. I nodded kindly her way, but her words didn't help. They only reminded me how pitiful this whole situation must have seemed.

"I just wish he could let me go," I replied. That was why I had chosen Jonathan. Both men would offer to help, spend time with me, fight for me. Both, I knew, would love me with all their hearts. But Jonathan wanted to see me happy so much so that he was willing to see me with Aaron if it meant I would be happy. Aaron couldn't do that. And while it may have been admirable that he was still fighting for my heart, I needed freedom. Despite the misplaced emotions and haunting memories, I was still the independent girl my father and Captain raised me to be. I was still strong and brave. I could still fight my own battles. And Aaron refused to let me do so.

That is what I had made my decision. The peace of this realization overwhelmed me.

"Carter?" Luna said, pulling me from my stream of thoughts. "Is everything alright?" she asked me.

"Yes," I replied, smiling at her. I turned to the rest of the pod. "Yes, I'm good. Thank you for listening. And talking to me. It helped me a lot." The dolphins nodded and we began the swim back towards the ship.

C H A P T E R   2 0

Jopie's Job

WITH THESE THOUGHTS STILL ENGRAVED in my mind, we made our way back towards my home. I looked at the friends around me. I listened to their conversation, determined not to miss a word. I could see the *Adventurer*. As we approached, I realized I wasn't quite ready to board home again. Aurora suggested playing a game, like old times. Everyone stopped talking and began to think about a game that they wanted to play. The mere thought of a game sent a shiver of childish excitement up my back. It had been so long.

"How about tag?" I suggested. The dolphins nodded in agreement. The smile on my face glowed so brightly I could almost see it. As we decided on who was going to be it, I heard a familiar voice commanding me from above. My heart sank a little.

"Carter! Back onto the ship!" Jonathan yelled down to me. With a sigh, I nodded and said good-bye to my friends. Though I was disappointed to leave my friends, I agreed with Jonathan, as much as it pained me. I was second in command on the ship, as the dolphins had reminded me at our last visit. I needed to be on the ship and working, not playing around in the water. Jonathan sent down a rope and I climbed up with ease. It almost seemed to be an easier climb than normal, or rather, what had become my normal. I had forgotten how much Gargan had changed me. For so long now, this incessant pain seemed normal. I needed to keep reminding myself it wasn't.

I landed on the main deck of the ship gracefully, only a bit of the shock hitting my knees. I flipped my wet hair out of my face, sending droplets of saltwater at Jonathan's face. He chuckled a bit.

"Glad to see you back aboard the ship, first mate," he commented. I nodded with a soft smile in reply.

"How can I help onboard, captain?" I asked him. I had called him 'captain' more often, lately. I liked calling him the captain; I wasn't afraid to call the man I loved a captain. It reminded me of how proud I was of him. I couldn't keep the smile from reaching my lips. It seemed like my thoughts had truly been calmed by the sea.

"First, you and I need to go see someone," he replied. I swallowed hard. Just like that, the calm was gone. Fear overwhelmed me all too quickly. The shift must have been noticeable because Jonathan placed his hand on my shoulder, trying to comfort me. "Don't worry, it's fine," he convinced me. I nodded, still hesitant. Surprises used to fill me with excitement, but now, after the pirates, they had been filling me with fear, leaving me suspicious of what was to come. It wasn't fair to Jonathan, or the rest of the crew, that I acted this way. But I couldn't control it.

Jonathan guided me off the main deck and down the hallway that led to Martin's room. My heart began to race. *Martin's? Jopie! Is something wrong with Jopie?* Even as I reminded myself of Jonathan's reassuring words, the knot of fear in my stomach wouldn't go away. Jonathan placed his hand on the latch and slowly opened the door. When I looked inside the room, Jopie was standing on her tip-toes, hovering over Martin. I let out a sigh of relief. Then Jopie turned to face Jonathan and me as she heard the door open.

"Carter!" she exclaimed and ran over to me and gave me a big hug. I hugged her back, keeping her close. I hadn't realized until now how truly terrified I was that she was sick or hurt. She was my responsibility. *I should have been spending more time with her, caring for her. Then I wouldn't have been so scared about this visit.* Jopie's smile made all my worries disappear. She stepped away and stood alert then gave a small nod to Jonathan, respecting his rank. Jonathan smiled her way, and she was at ease a moment later.

"So, what brought us here today?" I asked Jonathan and Jopie. Jopie's grin grew as she looked at Jonathan to answer my question.

"Well, Jopie is ready to take on a real role on this ship, as a mate," Jonathan told me. My eyes widened and I happily hugged Jopie once more.

"I was hoping you would help me decide what position I should take," Jopie continued.

"I would be happy to help, Jopie," I replied. She nodded excitedly, then looked over at Martin. He gave her a small smile and she moved to hug Martin.

"Now, Jopie, don't forget to come and visit me, okay?" he whispered to her. That's when I realized the bond that had formed between the two of them. It reminded me of Captain, and how he called me darling when I was at the helm, guiding the ship through the sea. How I missed hearing his voice. Tears balanced on the edge of my eyes. I wiped them before they escaped.

"Of course I wouldn't, Martin! What makes you think I would?" Jopie exclaimed, clearly excited to become a mate, but also, maybe, too excited. She spoke as if she were hiding the truth-- she was nervous. Martin squatted down to be level with Jopie and squeezed her hands.

"Good luck, Jopie girl," he murmured in her ear. Jopie nodded. For a moment I thought I saw tears welling up in her eyes, but when she blinked, they had disappeared. Martin patted her shoulder and stood upright. Jopie let go of his hand and walked back over to my side. Jopie hugged my side and I placed my arm around her shoulder. Jonathan looked over at me and nodded. I looked down at Jopie and she smiled. With that, the three of us turned and left Martin.

"Thank you again, Martin," I said as we walked out the door. Jonathan closed it then said that Jopie and I could head on our way. Then Jonathan left towards the main deck.

"So, Jopie, what are you thinking?" I asked her. She sighed and looked up at me.

"I don't know, really. But I don't think I want to work on the main deck. I am not really built for *those* types of jobs. I think I would want to be..." but her voice trailed off. She seemed unsure of herself, which surprised me. For as long as I had known Jopie, she had always been confident in herself. Maybe the pirate ship changed her, just as it had changed me. It was unfair of me to assume otherwise.

"What do you want to be?" I asked her, trying to force the words out of her.

"I really would like to cook," she finished. I smiled, though I wasn't surprised.

"Well, let's go see Barton!" I exclaimed. With that, we skipped over to the kitchen. When we entered, Barton was beginning to make dinner. Jopie stared at the space in shock and amazement. I had forgotten that her meals were being delivered to her while she was with Martin. She had never seen the kitchen. Though small, Barton's kitchen was as clean as can be and well organized; so very opposite of the one Jopie had been working in a few short weeks ago. Now Jopie was healthy and happy.

We walked over to Barton, and I explained that Jopie wanted to become his mate. He gladly accepted Jopie as his mate, just as expected. She walked over to him, and Barton showed her around the kitchen. He explained what they were making for dinner that night, while I stood at the door, observing from a distance, making sure Jopie was ready to commit to this. She had grown stronger since I had last seen her. No longer was she thin, weak, and sickly. She had changed. She had, seemingly, moved on so well. How was I still plagued with nightmares of a man that ruled my life for only a few short weeks? It all seemed like forever ago, and yet, when I closed my eyes, it was only yesterday.

Jopie gave me a nod and smile. I knew what that meant. I gave her a wave.

CHAPTER 21
Dinner is Served

Jopie and Barton were already hard at work as I closed
the door behind me. As I walked, thoughts swirled around in my
mind, threatening to morph into true worries. Worries about
Jopie, this ship, the pirates. Aaron. Jonathan. Edward. I shook
them off as I reached the main deck. The midday sun beat down
on my blond hair. Almost at once, Jonathan called me over to him.
I sped up my steps, each one taking me further from my troubles –
at least that is what I hoped.

"Carter, where is Jopie?" he asked me as I approached. His
question surprised me. I tilted my head.

"What do you mean where is she?" I furrowed my eyebrows.

"I assumed that she would end up wanting to be your
mate," he replied. For a moment, I considered the idea. While I
would have loved teaching Jopie all I knew about the ship and the
different roles and being on deck with her every day, the thought
had never truly crossed my mind until now. Not once since Jopie
came aboard did I ever think she would want to learn my position.
When we first met, I never doubted that Jopie was strong, but she
wasn't built for the way of life I followed. I knew she would spend
most of her days with Barton or Martin. I remembered when she
had become a cook on the pirate ship; despite everything that had
happened to us, she was happy about her place.

"No, she is Barton's. Wonderful choice for her, don't you
think?" I asked him. He nodded slowly, almost like he was

disappointed that Jopie would not be present on the main deck. I found his reaction curious. "Is everything alright?" I asked him. He looked up from his gaze at his feet and smiled at me. It was a fake smile. Hardly ever did Jonathan fake a smile.

"I am perfectly fine," he replied. Though I wanted to know the truth, I decided not to push it. If he didn't want to tell me, he wasn't going to tell me. Not yet at least. I couldn't push him to tell me things if I didn't want him pushing me to tell him about my feelings, my fears, and my nightmares.

"Where can I be of use?" I asked him. Jonathan commanded me to the crow's nest, as usual. I began my climb up as Aaron began his climb down. Halfway between the deck and the nest, I glanced over at Aaron. He must have felt my gaze because less than a second later, he looked over at me, and our eyes met. The two of us were frozen for a moment, but then we quickly turned away from each other. The rest of the climb I was reminded of the deep-seeded guilt that I had been trying to forget. Aaron loved me and I had broken his heart. Aaron had loved me, and I *used* to love him. *And I could love him again.* At least, that's what he wanted me to think. Then I reminded myself of why I chose Jonathan, of my realizations with the dolphins. Slowly, my mind felt more at ease. When I reached the top, I quickly placed the telescope to my eye and looked out to sea. I prayed for the blue waves to wash away my uncertainties, but they only grew. Eventually, I couldn't help but look down at the deck below me.

Aaron and Jonathan were talking to each other, smiles on both of their faces. Jonathan had known that I loved Aaron, and Aaron knew I had chosen Jonathan. I had tried so hard to keep the two from knowing about the other. And I failed. *How can Aaron be smiling and talking to Jonathan when he can't with me?* Maybe Aaron didn't see Jonathan as a threat, maybe he only blamed me. Or maybe he thought he was already winning me over again. I looked away from the two men and back towards the horizon, the blue sea, with the afternoon sun reflecting off the waves.

***

The announcement came that dinner was ready. My stomach rumbled at the thought of food. I smiled at myself, amused, knowing I had been hungrier before. I began my climb back down towards the main deck to receive directions from Jonathan. I didn't know if he wanted me to stay here while most everyone ate, or if he would order someone else to take charge of the deck during diner time. Most of the crew had already received their orders from Jonathan. The deck was nearly empty when I approached him.

"Captain?" I started. Jonathan released a light-hearted chuckle.

"I don't think I'll ever get used to you calling me that," he said, his cheeks heating up for a moment, then they faded to normal. "David and Gluar have volunteered to wait for their dinner. So, you and I can make our way down. It is probably very important that you go, seeing as Jopie helped make it," Jonathan replied. I nodded, a smile growing on my face. I slipped my hand into his, and the two of us left for dinner, leaving David and Gluar behind on deck. We walked down, and I kept my gaze lowered, staring at the floor. My eyes shifted, my gaze landing on his hand. I wanted to grab it and pull him closer to me. My mind went back to weeks ago, just before the storm, when he gave me my first kiss. At the time, I hadn't wanted to love him; I didn't know I loved him. Now I knew; now I wanted to kiss him. The two of us stopped when we reached the door to the kitchen. I expected Jonathan to open the door first. As the two of us grew up, he insisted it was polite that he opened the door for me, even though I persisted that I could open the door myself. I looked up at him, curiosity covering my face. He looked at me dead in the eye. No longer was he happy or smiling. Now he was serious. Strong.

"What's wrong?" I inquired. In response, Jonathan reached for both of my hands. I took a step closer to him.

"I must ask you the same question," he stated, matter-of-factly. I bit my lip. I didn't know what to say.

"What?" I asked him, slightly confused. Jonathan immediately let go of my hands, and they quickly returned to my side.

"Something's wrong. I know that you are worried about the Edward thing. And I know you and Aaron are in a tough spot, but there is something you aren't telling me. The way you tensed up when I had news about Jopie. And some nights I hear you crying in your sleep," he continued. I knew my eyes widened, but I tried to control my facial expression. I did not want to talk with him about my...issues. Not now.

"I don't understand what you are talking about, Jonathan," I said, trying to make my lie seem believable. I knew I could; the pirates had taught me how. "Why on earth would I keep anything from you?" I questioned him, taking his hands, and gently rubbing his knuckles with my thumbs. Jonathan pulled his hands away from mine again.

"I don't know. That's why I asked you. But if you say so... I guess I will forget about everything," he replied in a tone that told me that he knew for a fact that something was up and that we were going to discuss it later. Jonathan was determined to get to these answers eventually, but the exact time he would get them was up to me. And I was going to avoid telling him for as long as possible. This was my burden, not his.

Jonathan opened the door and the two of us walked in. We sat down next to each other. Across from Jonathan was Jackson and across me was Aaron. I smiled at him kindly, but Aaron did not return the gesture. Jonathan looked between the two of us, then took a bite of his food. Aaron, on the other hand, looked down at his plate and shifted his food around his plate. Guilt pressed up against my chest, and I forced myself to breathe. Everything in my heart wanted to reach out and take his hand, and assure him that everything would be okay.

A lie. It was truly ironic. The longer I spent away from that pirate ship, the more I started to become a pirate. *Not anymore.* I couldn't help Aaron through this. Not now. Not yet. He needed time alone, and I needed to give that to him.

Still, the small talk of the table was growing more unbearable. As hard as I tried to force off the guilt and put on the facade that everything was okay, I always found myself silent in the end. Jonathan reached to move his hand on top of mine, but I moved it just out of his reach. In the corner of my eye, I spotted the confusion filling his eyes. I didn't want to explain how holding his hand in front of Aaron would only escalate the situation. Surely Jonathan would be able to figure that out.

It didn't matter. Aaron had noticed the reach. Now his eyes were locked on me. Unwavering.

I glanced down at my plate and the half-eaten scraps no longer looked appealing. The idea of hiding away in my room and avoiding Aaron's pain -- much more appealing. I stood up from the table and thanked Jopie for the meal, then apologized to the crew for retiring early. No one questioned it. Why would they? I was the first mate and still recovering from my time on the pirate ship. They all wished me good night, all except for Aaron. He didn't even glance my way. His silence was far more painful than the guilt. I should have expected as much. As I made my way to my room, the pain and guilt clung to me like the odor of fish that hung in the air.

Finally alone in my room, I slipped under the covers and rested my head on the pillow behind me. Staring at the ceiling, I took deep breaths. It wasn't Jonathan's fault. It wasn't Aaron's either. It was mine, for not telling them. I hadn't been completely honest with either of them since Gargan. And not just about my feelings. The fear, the terror, the nightmares. But I couldn't tell them. This was my burden, and I needed to learn how to carry it. With another breath, I closed my eyes and drifted to sleep.

I was in a large room with a chandelier of candles hanging above me. I was in a silk gown that made me look like a mermaid. I never wore dresses. For some reason, though, I didn't question it. On the other side of the room, Aaron stood, smiling at me. There was pure joy in his eyes, but there was pure fear in my heart.

"Where are we, Aaron?" I asked him. The two of us made our way closer to each other. When we were close enough, Aaron reached for my hands, and for some reason, I didn't pull away. He placed his hand on my back. Instinctively, I placed my hand around his shoulder. Our other two hands, we held out gracefully and we began to dance.

"A ballroom," Aaron answered, giving me a cunning smile. I smiled, lightly biting down on my bottom lip. Soft music filled the air and our feet began to move with the sweet sound. I could feel the powerful happiness flowing from Aaron to me, but somewhere inside of me, there was an unexplainable fear. I wanted to pull away, but I couldn't. I realized that a hot sticky liquid covered my hand. I looked down – blood. Aaron's hand had a knife in it. I looked up to warn him, but when my eyes met his, I realized his green eyes had been replaced with a stranger's. No, not a stranger's – Gargan's. The dance began to slow down, and Aaron leaned in. I tried to avoid him. I closed my eyes, not in perfect happiness, but fear. I sat up straight in bed and yelled one word.

"Aaron!"

I felt the word echo all around me.

CHAPTER 22
Midnight

I FELT A BEAD OF SWEAT ROLL DOWN MY CHEEK, or was it a tear?
I looked around me. The blankets were thrown all around and
my pillow was on the floor. The few books that were lying on my
nightstand had fallen onto the floor and the oil lamp had been
shoved to the edge of the table.

Then I heard running from out in the hallway. Fear filled
my chest. I looked around the room. I wasn't on the pirate ship. I
was safe, but I couldn't seem to convince myself of that. Curled up
in a ball, I rocked back and forth. I couldn't clear my mind. There
was a knock on the door. I never said come in, but the person
on the other side came in anyway. Aaron stepped into my room.
I jumped a little, my hand covering my mouth quickly to keep
myself from screaming. He frowned and looked down. I breathed
in slowly and convinced myself that I was safe. I tugged the
blankets closer to me. I felt bad about upsetting him, but terror
was still controlling my mind, shaking in my bones. Recognizing
the insane fear that I was in; Aaron slowly moved a bit closer to
me. The noise of his feet masked the sound of another person
coming. Jonathan ran into my room; he stood behind Aaron, who
was now kneeling beside my bed.

"What's wrong?" Aaron asked after a few moments. I took
another deep breath and came out of my small, curled-up position.
When I opened my mouth, no sound came out. There were no
words to describe the unnatural fear I was feeling. I didn't want

to tell them, and I didn't want to worry them. What would they think if I told them I was having nightmares about the pirates still? Then Jonathan bent down and placed his hand on my leg. Aaron took note of this gesture of affection; the emotion in his eyes changed for a moment, hardened, but he didn't say anything. He didn't even glance down at Jonathan's hand. He just kept his eyes fixed on me. I had to say something. They were both so worried.

"It was just a dream," I insisted. I expected to see their shoulders relax, but they remained tense and focused on me.

"Carter, you have been having some very, umm, how should I say this? Very interesting dreams lately," Jonathan replied. Aaron nodded in agreement. The two men that loved me were now ganging up against me. As if my situation couldn't get any worse.

"Recently, Adam has been sleeping in my room because you keep waking him up, either by crying or screaming. Your dreams are pretty intense," Aaron explained. I felt awful that I was disrupting Adam and Aaron and who knows how many others. But I couldn't help it that my dreams were so realistic...so painful.

"Carter, I have tried not to ask, but I need to know, for the good of this ship and the good of this crew," Jonathan decided, closing any margin for escaping this situation. I sighed, giving in to his ruling. He wasn't going to let me leave this room unless I gave him the truth. And I didn't want to lie to him anymore, even if it meant I had to share my weakness.

"Just the other night, you scared me half to death just when you woke up! What was going through your head?" Jonathan broke the silence, growing more frustrated and worried.

"I...I have been struggling with a lot of things," I began, my voice shaking. "Ever since I got back from the pirate ship, things have never been the same. I have nightmares of Gargan and that ship. And now with all the worries about Edward —"

"Carter," Jonathan interrupted me, glancing at Aaron, who turned to face him.

"He knows, Jonathan," I assured him. He looked confused, raising an eyebrow at me. Since I had spent so much of my efforts trying to keep Edward a secret, Jonathan was probably wondering why I had chosen to tell Aaron about Edward, especially now that we weren't really on talking terms.

"With all the worries about Edward, I am under more stress than I already was," I swallowed hard. "The nightmares, the fear. Sometimes I think I'm on that pirate ship. It's horrible and I don't know why it keeps happening. I'm sorry." For a moment, the two boys were quiet. Only the flicker of the flame in Jonathan's lamp and the waves outside filled the void.

"Why did you scream for me?" Aaron asked me quietly, breaking the silence. By the look in Jonathan's eyes, he wanted to know the answer to that question too but for different reasons. I swallowed hard. The truth would be hard for Aaron to hear, salt in the wound. I tightened my fists and kept my eyes on my lap. I looked up and met Aaron's eyes.

"You were there, but you morphed into Gargan, kind of," I mumbled in reply. Aaron swallowed hard. Jonathan looked down awkwardly. It was silent for a beat too long. "Don't look too much into it," I said when I could no longer sit in the tension that was filling the air that was suffocating me slowly. The two men nodded. Jonathan stood up and took a deep breath.

"Get some sleep," Jonathan told me, his voice soft. He gave me a weak smile, hesitated at the door, then left my room leaving the door open. Aaron met my gaze for a moment. I forced a weak smile.

"I'm sorry," I whispered. He shook his head.

"Don't apologize." He stood up and gave a weak smile. Aaron kissed my forehead and left without saying a word; he knew that the kiss was enough. If only he knew he was only making my stress worse. Or maybe he did know. *No, Aaron isn't that cruel.* Once the door was shut, I threw my head onto the pillow and forced myself to fall asleep. I would need it if I were going to work well tomorrow.

I woke up in a room, not my own. It was bare like the pirate rooms, but it wasn't the pirate ship. Someone walked in through the door. His icy eyes almost calmed me, but I refused to let them. His form wasn't clear though, just his eyes. I knew I was dreaming. Despite not knowing what he looked like, my mind told me that it was Edward in front of me. He continued coming closer to me. I saw bloodstains on his hands. He crept closer, but I refused to take a step back. Or maybe I couldn't step back.

"Stronger than I expected," he commented with a smirk.

"Why do you sound so surprised?" I questioned him. He gave me a sly smile. My hands tightened into fists.

"You have such low standards," he laughed. As the words left his lips, Jonathan and Aaron came through the door, their eyes were locked on me, but their eyes matched Edward's ice eyes, cold, heartless. I fell backward in shock. The bed had disappeared from the room and I crashed on the floor. I reminded myself I was in a dream, but no matter what I thought I knew, the dream kept going. All three men moved towards me. Aaron lifted his fist over my head.

"Don't, don't, don't please, Aaron! Stop!" I started crying.

"Why?" he asked me through clenched teeth. Those cold eyes weighed down on me. His fist came down.

My eyes shot open. I covered my mouth in case I screamed again. My eyes were wet with tears. I blinked a few times, my eyes raking across my room on the *Adventurer*. Edward wasn't in my room, neither was Aaron, but Jonathan was.

CHAPTER 23
Expectations

MY EYES MET HIS. Jonathan's face was stern, but I noticed a glint of surprise in his eyes. He didn't seem to act on it. He stood up from his seat beside my bed. I looked away from him and through the glass of the porthole. The sun was shining bright, nearly blinding. At least I had made it through the rest of the night. I needed to be on the main deck. I turned to get out of my bed, but Jonathan stopped me.

"It happened again, didn't it?" he said. I could see his jaw tighten. He didn't bend down to my level, he didn't grab my hand, and he didn't try to reassure me that everything was alright. The surprise had disappeared from his eyes. Only frustration remained. I grew more irritated with him. He had the audacity to be frustrated with me when it was him who invaded my space.

"What do you mean 'what happened'?" I asked him as if I didn't know what he was talking about. Jonathan placed his hand on my shoulder, keeping me from standing, as he pulled a chair over and sat down. I kept my gaze locked on him.

"Who was in your dream this time that you forced yourself to not scream?" Jonathan questioned me. *Why is he acting like this?* But I ignored his question. I had my own.

"How long were you in here?" I snapped. Honestly, I didn't want to know the answer. I was just angry that Jonathan was acting like this.

"Since I heard a scream early this morning," he replied. I

rolled my eyes and groaned, putting my hands on my forehead. Jonathan suddenly grabbed my wrist and pulled my hand away from my head. I couldn't help but jump back at his rash movement. I pulled my arm from his grip and held it close to myself. His stern gaze wavered a little, now sad, or disappointed in himself. But it didn't last long. "Do you have any other questions?" he asked.

"Related to this or just in general, because I have many," I retorted. I wanted him to know I was angry. He was treating me like a child. If he remotely understood what I had gone through, he would have never treated me this way.

"Related to this subject please," he replied, far too calm for my liking. I rolled my eyes.

"Why? Why all this? Why wait for me to wake up? To make me feel uncomfortable? Or weak? Or broken?" I asked him, my voice rising into a shout. Jonathan sighed, looking away, like suddenly he was realizing how ridiculous he was acting. My arms remained crossed. He sat down on my bed next to me. He placed his hand on my thigh. I was still angry at him, but I didn't move his hand.

"Because I need to know what is going on through your head, for me as the person that loves you, the person that you love. Not your captain, but your friend," he answered, almost in a whisper. I swallowed hard. We were both silent, then Jonathan spoke again.

"Please, answer my question now," he murmured. I relented. It wasn't worth staying mad at him forever.

"You, Aaron, and Edward. And me of course," I replied quietly. A tear rolled down my cheek, which came out of nowhere. I wiped it away quickly, hoping that Jonathan didn't notice. If he did, he made sure he didn't show it.

"What exactly happened? Last night, you didn't talk specifics about your dream. I know that what you told us last night was important, but I need to know what's happening in these nightmares, so that maybe I can put your mind at ease. I want the truth this time," Jonathan stared me in the eye.

"Okay," I replied and took a deep breath. "I was dreaming of Edward attacking me, you and Aaron were on his side, trying to kill me. Aaron knocked me out." Jonathan nodded with a small frown.

"And the other one?" Jonathan asked me after a while. As the question came out of his mouth, I bit my lip. I refused to tell him that one. It was embarrassing. Shameful.

"Jonathan, you really don't want to know. I promise," I assured him, but Jonathan shook his head.

"No, I want to know," Jonathan countered.

"I promise, you don't," I argued.

"I *want* you to tell me," he commanded, standing up to face me. I wanted to stand up, but my legs suddenly felt weak. My head fell in my hands, and I wanted to cry. I forced the tears down deep in my heart.

"I don't want to tell you," I whispered, half to myself. "You'll hate me for it." I felt like I was five again, when I didn't want to tell my father about something mischievous that I had done – even though he already knew exactly what crime I committed. I felt sad and guilty. I didn't want to disappoint him, but it was inevitable. I peeked up to see Jonathan's reaction. His eyes were wide, shocked and, more importantly, hurt. Jonathan placed his hand on my shoulder and sat down beside me.

"Carter Ellen Key, I don't care what words come out of your mouth. I don't care if you killed me in your dream and enjoyed it. I could care less if it were about falling in love with Edward. It was just a dream. I want you to open yourself up to me, and these dreams are the first step," Jonathan assured me. I looked at him, my eyes glistening with tears.

"It was a ballroom. Aaron was on the other side of the room. We danced, but the whole time, my stomach felt twisted, as if something were wrong. Then his hand started bleeding, like Gargan's hand when I stabbed it during the mutiny. When I looked up, his eyes changed into Gargan's. Then, Aaron leaned in to kiss me, but it didn't spark amazing passion or butterflies that I felt bubble inside of me. Jonathan, I felt fear. Not just nightmare fear: it was the fear I would have if Gargan or Edward walked into this room this very instant. It was real." I answered.

"Oh," he mumbled, lost for words.

"I told you. I knew that you wouldn't want to know," I

muttered, looking away from him. When the silence was too much for me, I stood up.

"We have a job to do, Jonathan. Let's not let my stupid nightmares get in the way," I said sternly. Jonathan nodded, clearly something was on his mind, but I didn't feel like asking him. I walked out of my room, brushing his shoulder as I left. Jonathan turned to face me.

"Carter," he said, catching my attention. I turned around to face him.

"What?" I asked, trying to stay composed. While I wasn't frustrated as much with Jonathan, I wanted this conversation to be over.

"If you have a dream like that about me, can you tell me what you feel?" he asked innocently. My shoulders relaxed. I nodded in response and moved to hug him. For a minute or two, we just held each other. I listened to him breathing and closed my eyes, letting myself feel some sense of rest. This was home, this was safe. A moment ago, I was so angry with him, and now, like two waves that had crashed into each other, we had morphed into one, stronger and more magnificent than the two on their own. Then he pulled away, and we walked out the door together. It was odd how quickly my emotions had changed. From anger to love and trust in just a few minutes. Was this love? Moving in and out of a current, lost in waves, hoping to find an oasis on the other side of the storm?

As the two of us walked onto the main deck, David approached us. He nodded a good morning to me, and I nodded back. Then he stood before Jonathan and gave him a smile, awaiting orders from his captain and friend.

"Report, David," Jonathan demanded after David greeted us.

"Sir, a ship has been spotted off of starboard," David replied quickly. My eyes widened in surprise. I tried to keep my emotions down. There was no reason to be nervous. Ships passed us often on our routes. This was *normal*. Still, Jonathan reached for my hand. I let him take it.

"Let's see it!" Jonathan replied with fake enthusiasm. I nodded, forcing a smile and agreeing with Jonathan. David guided the two of us out to the helm. He handed Jonathan a telescope and pointed the direction out for him.

"Well, it's not a pirate ship," David mentioned with relief in his voice. I squinted my eyes, trying to see the ship more clearly. Jonathan looked down at his feet and gave me the telescope. I stared at the ship. The flags were decorated with red and white stripes and stars in the blue shaded corner. I read the words on the side of the ship. It read *The Cobra.*

CHAPTER 24
The Arrival

"Do you know that ship, sir?" David asked Jonathan.

"I know of it," Jonathan replied, nodding his head. Then he glanced at me, his eyes full of anger and worry.

"What ship is it?" someone asked from behind me. I turned and faced Fallier, not wanting to answer him. Trying to act calm, I stared at him.

"The one we spoke about the other day," I replied, unable to say the name of the ship I had placed my eyes on. Fallier's jaw dropped in disbelief. I raised my eyebrows. I had never really seen Fallier shocked. I guess the timing surprised us both. I tried to imagine what would have happened if *The Cobra* made its appearance before I had read, or even found, my mother's diary. We wouldn't have known to be on our guard. I guess it was a good thing Edward had shown up now.

"As I live and breathe! He *is* coming back!" Fallier exclaimed, a little too loud. All of the crew turned and faced Fallier and me.

"Who?" asked Jackson.

"One of Arianna's old friends, Edward," he replied happily. Gluar and Fallier exchanged joyful glances. Adam and Leonard gave each other sideways smiles. Jackson looked completely confused, having no idea who Arianna even was. I avoided all of their stares. Aaron, Jonathan, and I all exchanged nervous glances. I didn't care if anyone noticed now. It was as if my life had reached its final battle, and I already knew the outcome. Jonathan and I held our gaze for a moment. We were both thinking the same thing: how could we keep each other safe?

All the crew watched as Edward's ship came closer to ours. I felt many gazes fall on me, but I ignored them. I had a strange feeling when I looked around at the crew. Never had I felt like I was about to say goodbye. I never thought, until now, that I would ever have to. The faces around me, most of them unaware of the danger that lurked on that ship, weighed heavy on my heart. So, I decided to focus on the ship. I was preparing myself for the worst. For all I knew, he wanted to kill me. And I was prepared to walk on that ship to fix my mother's past at the cost of my future. At least, I hoped that I was.

Before I knew it, The Cobra was right next to our ship. Out of instinct, I turned around quickly to face Jonathan. I grabbed his hands. I felt a fear rush through my body, but I shoved it away. Confidence was key if I even had a chance to come out of this situation alive. Or even, possibly, escape it altogether. Jonathan kissed my forehead. I wished his kiss had the power to put my mind at ease, as it had done so many times in the past. Not this time.

"Head to your room. I won't tell him where you are unless he asks for you. Okay?" I nodded in confidence. I wished that Jonathan would never tell him where I was hiding. But I knew that we needed to appear normal, not only for the crew's sake but also for my own. Maybe Edward wouldn't be as bad as we thought. Maybe, if we treated him well, he would find goodness in his heart and break the promise that he left in the diary. I turned around and walked down to my room. Right before I made it to the hall, I felt someone's hand on my shoulder. I tensed up for a moment. There was no way that Edward had already boarded the ship. Still, as I slowly turned around, I prepared myself for a fight.

But it was Aaron, his green eyes glazed with fear and sadness. I relaxed the moment I saw his face.

"Aaron, I-" I began but he cut me off. He placed his hand over my mouth and pulled me further down the hallway. Then he pulled his hand away.

"Carter, I don't want to let you do this, but you are way too persistent once you come to a decision. I am trying to convince myself to let you do this, but I can't bring myself to it. A knot forms in my chest when I think about your death. If he kills you like you think he may, I feel like I can only say goodbye one way," he finished. Aaron placed his hand on my neck and pulled my head closer to his. Before I could stop him, his lips brushed against mine, and surprising us both, I didn't pull back. My whole world was spinning. Right and wrong were lost in the hurricane. All I knew was this could be the last time I may ever see him, and I wasn't going to waste it on my own confusion. He pulled away, and I could feel his gaze fixating on me, as if he were trying to decide what to do next. He leaned in again. But this time, I lowered my chin, my lips just out of reach of his, and I rested my forehead on his. Whatever we were, it wasn't just friends. *We're a mess, that's what we are.*

His hand slipped on my neck and moved halfway down my back. Then it returned to his side.

"I'm sorry," he whispered, looking at the ground. *I'm not,* I wanted to say, but I knew it would only make things more difficult. I placed my hand on his chin and lifted his head.

"Aaron, I'm sorry, I don't know what we are, or what the future holds… but you were right we're more than just friends," I said, worried I would regret the words later. Aaron gave me a weak smile. Then I turned and left for my room. I felt Aaron's gaze on me until I closed the door behind me.

As soon as the door shut, I ran onto my bed and released the tears that had been balancing on the edge of my eyes. I let out every emotion; love, fear, sadness, confusion until the only thing that was left was pure confidence. It was better this way – crying now so that Edward couldn't coax the tears from me later. With nothing left in me, I walked over to the mirror and smiled. I could be hard and fearless now. I would sit pretty for Edward. I weaved my hair into a small blond braid and stared at myself in the mirror.

I heard many footsteps above, and shouts of welcoming. I imagined Jonathan introducing himself to the man who loved - then loathed - my mother, the man who came for me. I wondered what they were discussing. Maybe Edward wondered where my father was. After all the last time he visited I had just been born, nearly sixteen years ago. Were they making small talk? Was he asking about me? I looked back in the mirror. I didn't care. He could no longer fill my thoughts with fear. I wouldn't allow it.

And then I heard footsteps down the hall. This time, I knew exactly who was headed my way. I swallowed hard. What should I be doing when they walked in? I heard a knock on the door. I took a deep breath and looked at the girl in the mirror. She could face Edward. I could face Edward. I plastered a smile on my face and opened the door.

"Carter, what a pleasant surprise."

CHAPTER 25
Conversation

I TILTED MY HEAD, pretending to be surprised and confused. Jonathan hadn't come with him, which surprised me. But I couldn't let that scare me. I examined him. His hair was a dark gray; I could tell it had once been black, as my mother had described. His eyes were the color light blue, reminding me of melting ice. They seemed filled with compassion, but I knew that could not be so. He hated my mother; he would hate me.

"Sir, I don't believe I know you," I said. He smiled sympathetically but his eyes shifted for a moment. He had spotted my mother's diary on the side table. I should have hidden it before he arrived.

"Carter, you know me," he continued bluntly. I was surprised at how confident he was and at how much he knew. "How much of that diary have you read?" he questioned. And yet, when his voice was so demanding and aggressive, it was kind at the same time, like my father's voice. *How could that be possible?*

"I have only read the first few pages, sir," I replied calmly, sticking to my lie. It would only raise his suspicion if I changed my story now. Then, Edward suddenly jumped forward; he stood right in front of me. For the first time, I realized how tall he was, almost two heads taller than me. I was reminded of how small I was. I wished Jonathan were here. Why hadn't he come? Maybe Edward wouldn't have been so bold if Jonathan was by my side.

"Carter, I know that you know who I am," he said harshly,

his words raspy. I was surprised at his sudden aggressiveness and how well he could see through my deception. I had been trained by pirates on how to lie, but he was captain of a ship that defeated pirates. He could see through my amateur work. I swallowed hard. My mind scrambled to find a way to strengthen the lie. I had to keep what I knew about him a secret. But I had missed my moment, and waited too long to answer him. Without Jonathan, I couldn't see the purpose in lying to Edward any longer.

"Edward, I do know who you are. My mother truly loved you. You must know that." Edward's shoulders relaxed and he smiled once again. He took a step back, and I immediately felt safer.

"Thank you for those words, but you know as well as I that they aren't true. You are the result of her rejection," he muttered as he sat down on my bed. I watched, confused by his sudden change in demeanor. He patted the place next to him, and cautiously, I sat down beside him. He put his hand on my knee and his thumb rubbed gently. I bit my lip; no matter how kind he seemed, being so close to him made my skin crawl.

"I assume you know what's coming." I tensed up at this comment. He looked at me, his eyes sad. His hand moved to move my braid over my shoulder. I swallowed hard. "You are a wonderful girl and you deserve more than the life that you have. But I am also a wonderful man, and I do not deserve the life I have suffered through. My suffering, however, is at the fault of your mother." He paused, looking down at his feet. "She left me alone, with nothing to look forward to. When she left with Robert, she took away my future. She took away my hope. Now I know that it isn't your fault, but I know an easy way we can both make this right," he finished, squeezing my knee. I carefully shifted so that I was out of his reach. I wanted it to be over. I was losing my patience. I had said my goodbyes, my farewells, and I had finally convinced myself of the horrible fate awaiting me. There was nothing else I could do.

"Just do it then. Get it over with already!" I said between clenched teeth. Edward turned towards me, completely surprised.

"Get what over with?" he questioned me. I whipped around to face him.

"If you must kill me, then do it already," I exclaimed defiantly. He leaned back in shock.

"Carter, I am not going to kill you. Two beautiful, dead women was not what I was planning on. No, I just need you to be crushed the way I was," he replied smoothly. I was completely confused. He came to kill me, but he wouldn't, but he wanted to crush me all the same. *What does that mean?* I forced the thoughts out of my mind, knowing they would only confuse me more. Trying to figure out Edward's plan would not make things any easier. He stood up and smiled down at me like he hadn't just told me he was going to ruin my life.

"Let's go up to the main deck, shall we?" he suggested. I nodded and stood up, even though I didn't want to go. I wanted to be left alone in my room, deciphering the puzzle Edward had handed me. He opened the door, and I slowly stepped through. I followed him to the main deck with a smile still stuck on my lips. I didn't want the crew to suspect anything. The last thing I wanted was put my home – my family – in harm's way.

I expected to wince at the sunlight, but when I arrived on the main deck, the sails of Edward's ship blocked out the golden rays. His ship was so close and so big – at least twice the size of the *Adventurer*. And Fallier had called it small? I returned my gaze to my home. Jonathan was at the helm, and he looked surprised. Aaron was climbing the ropes, but his eyes were locked on me. I shot a glare at both of them, and Jonathan and Aaron both returned to normal.

"Captain Powell, might I ask permission from you and your first mate to bring Carter aboard my ship," Edward asked kindly. Jonathan raised an eyebrow.

"Why, might I ask?" Jonathan questioned. Edward tilted his head at Jonathan.

"We have things we must discuss," he replied. Jonathan nodded. Then he nodded at me.

"First mate," Jonathan demanded. Did he expect me to come over to him, right in front of Edward? He looked at me with compassion. I reminded myself that he knew what he was doing. But I refused to move. I didn't want to put him in jeopardy. "First mate," he said this time with more force. I breathed in heavily and took a single step forward. Edward's eyes widened in surprise, or maybe a warning, but he didn't stop me. Jonathan nodded, with a reassuring smile on his face. I wanted to run to him, but I forced my feet to slow. I followed Jonathan into his quarters. As soon as the door closed, I ran to him. He hugged me so tight that the emotions I thought I had rid myself of earlier were nearly revived. His warmth calmed me. Even when we let go of each other, Jonathan continued to hold my hands.

"He is giving us a choice," Jonathan whispered. I shook my head.

"He isn't going to kill me, Jonathan. And we both know this isn't really a choice – it is a courtesy," I murmured. Jonathan took a step back, his hands slipping out of mine.

"But he is going to do something. I can't just let you go with this mad man! I love you, Carter!" Jonathan exclaimed. And suddenly his lips were pressed tightly against mine. He was so forceful, I stepped back until I hit his desk, but our lips never left each other. I hugged him close. I wanted so badly to stay with him, forget the world on the other side of his door. His hands moved through my hair and I never felt safer. As his lips left mine, I whispered, "I have to go." Jonathan smiled and replied, "No you don't." We were suddenly kissing again, my arms wrapped around him, his fingers tracing my spine. We had never been so close. And I never wanted us to be apart again. His lips pressed against mine in a storm of passion. The truest love I had ever experienced.

But he pulled away. Once he stepped back, I hugged him, and I realized that a decision was made. I had won, I was leaving. Somehow, this didn't feel like a victory. He looked down at me and smiled, smoothing out my hair. Then he kissed the top of my head then moved to open his cabin door. Jonathan nodded and the two of us stepped out of the captain's cabin. Though I didn't hold his hand, I felt his shoulder up against mine. His closeness soothed me, and I was happy we had agreed on something. We loved each other more than we loved ourselves. And we were going to do what was best for each other, even when it was hard.

C H A P T E R   2 6

Losing Him

"Captain, have you and your first mate come to a decision?" Edward questioned almost immediately after we stepped out onto the main deck. The moment Jonathan and I had shared disappeared into the wind, carried far out of reach. Jonathan nodded, but I spoke.

"I will come with you on your ship, Edward. I know how important this is to you," I replied. I hoped that I sounded strong, like a first mate should. Edward nodded, giving me a polite smile. I walked over to him. He took my hand lightly and he guided me across the plank of wood that connected the two ships. It was long and narrow. I watched my feet closely, being sure not to make a misstep.

"Carter!" someone yelled my name from behind me when I was about halfway across. Both Edward and I turned around to see who was yelling my name. I met Aaron's green eyes immediately. I tried to signal him to keep his mouth shut.

"Carter be careful," Aaron began. I interrupted him quickly. Edward gave me a concerned look.

"Aaron, I will be fine," I tried to convince him. Not only did I want Aaron to know I wasn't going to die, but also, I didn't want Edward to get any ideas about hurting him.

"These people are strangers, unknown to us. How can you trust them this easily?" he questioned me. *Why can't he just let me work things out on my own?* I thought to myself, growing frustrated.

I swallowed hard. Trying to convince Aaron I was okay and keep Edward from asking questions was proving to be impossible. I prayed for God to forgive me for the lie I was about to tell.

"Edward, he knew my mother – if I don't go with him, I may lose my chance at really knowing who she was. I-I trust him," I replied, returning my gaze to Aaron. I squeezed Edward's hand and smiled up at him, then I turned back to Aaron. Aaron's mouth was agape. I felt like crying. Even Jonathan's eyes had widened. Edward looked down at me approvingly. I didn't want or need his approval. My words were enough to keep harm at bay, and that was all I cared about. After a moment, Edward and I continued on our walk towards his ship. It was massive, but even it couldn't distract me from my thoughts. I had broken Aaron's heart, pushed him away from me. I had gone to a place where he could no longer reach. If only he had known how much it hurt me too. *Could he ever forgive me? Would he even have a chance to? Or have I broken anything that we once had between us? Now am I truly alone?*

PART 2

The Cobra

CHAPTER 27
Welcoming Party

THE REST OF THE WALK, my eyes were looking down at the plank of wood underneath my feet. It wasn't because I was concentrating on my balance – I was lost in my thoughts, trying to figure out how to maneuver myself out of this situation I had put myself in. And I was still trying to figure out what exactly the situation I had put myself in was. I wanted to mend this rift without getting hurt. My chest was heavy, and my heart ached. I slipped my hand out of Edward's. He raised an eyebrow at me, but nothing more. I did *not* trust him. My words were only a lie to get Aaron off my back.

I lifted my head and faced the ship in front of me. I gnawed on the bottom of my lip, not in fear, but anger. Holding in these shouts of frustration nearly had my lip bleeding. My pace sped up and suddenly Edward had to keep up with me. Whatever lay ahead of me, I wanted to get it over with. When I finally reached the other end of the plank, I turned to face my ship, waving their way with a smile of confidence on my face. Aaron nodded back, David, Jackson, and the rest of the crew waved back, and Jonathan saluted me. *How I wish he could kiss me instead.* I turned back around and stepped onto Edward's ship.

The crew of *The Cobra* stared at me, some in awe, and some with pleasant smiles. I wondered what he had told them about me. Did they know what Edward was planning? Edward stomped down behind me. I refused to move, not without guidance or permission; I was on an enemy ship that held more powerful authority than my own. If I truly wanted to mend what had been broken between Edward and my mother, force was not the answer. Edward led me out of the *Adventurer*'s view. Then, a crew member approached me with a black sash and covered my eyes with it. I jumped a bit, confused by the blindfold, and I tried to squirm out of his reach before he tied it. But Edward squeezed my knuckles uncomfortably, warning me otherwise. *Well, maybe force is the only option.* Still, I wasn't convinced it was a good time to fight back. I was blind, using my other senses to figure out what was going on around me. I heard the creaking floorboards when the man stepped away from me. I felt someone's breath on my ears. My first reaction was to jump away, but I managed to hold my ground.

"You do everything I say, and I won't kill you. You give me what I want, and I will spare those you love most," Edward whispered in my ear, his lips brushing against my ear. I wanted to smack him away, but the last sentence struck me to the core. *How could he hurt the crew if we are here and they are aboard the* Adventurer? I didn't want to find out, and I didn't want my crew to pay for any of my mother's or my wrongdoings.

Breaking my thoughts was a sudden shove from behind me. I scrambled to find my footing, losing my balance without my sight to help me know where to step. Someone grabbed my shoulders and thrust me upright. I regained my balance, but I couldn't figure out which way to look.

"Captain, this is not the time," explained a crew member directly in front of me. I assumed he was the one who stopped me from hitting the ground.

"Watch your mouth, Henry, it can get you in some major trouble," Edward snapped back. I tensed, waiting for him to shove me on the ground, but he never did. Just as I relaxed, two hands grabbed my shoulders and spun me around. Then I heard Edward's voice coming from somewhere around me, from my left, then right, then behind me. I was getting dizzier by the second, but I needed to focus on what he was saying.

"…not allowed to know the location of any rooms on this ship, so you will be blindfolded and spun around every time you are moved from one place to another. You will cooperate," Edward finished forcefully. Suddenly, the person stopped spinning me, but

I still felt like I was moving. My feet shuffled around as I tried to find my footing. I thought I was going to fall over, but the same hands that spun me grabbed my shoulders and steadied me. I heard a whisper, and immediately I was being shoved down a series of hallways. Slowly, I regained some sense of direction, but the darkness still fooled me. I was shoved in a direction and I heard a door shut. For a moment, I stood there frozen, listening to any noise around me. After a moment or two, I reached for the cloth that was over my eyes.

"Are you Carter?" a voice somewhere in front of me asked. My hands shot down to my side and I began to listen again. I heard footsteps coming towards me and I immediately braced myself. I wanted to step back, but I didn't know what, or who, I would step back into.

"It's okay, don't be scared," said a man's voice. I felt him in front of me and sensed his presence as he walked around me. He circled me and then stopped in front of me. Suddenly, his hand was on my forehead as he moved a strand of hair behind my ear. I wanted to slap his hand away from my face, but I refused to move.

"Are you Carter Ellen?" He asked me again. Fear kept my lips pressed together. All I wanted right now was to leave this ship and be surrounded by the crew of the *Adventurer*. Or at least have this stupid blindfold taken off. I was infuriated with the way Edward had tossed me to the side after all the claims he had made. And I was frustrated with the constant darkness surrounding me, which allowed strangers to approach me and restricted me from fighting back. I clenched my jaw and felt a tear roll down my cheek. I hated myself for revealing such weakness.

"Don't cry," urged the man, once the tear had rolled down my cheek, out from under the blindfold. I felt his thumb wipe away the water left on my skin from the single tear. In a spurt of rage, my hand shot up and grabbed his wrist tight. How dare he touch me like he knew me, like he cared! Not when I couldn't even see his face. I was not letting go. I felt his struggle for a moment, but the stranger soon stopped fighting me.

"Tell me what is going to happen to me," I demanded through gritted teeth.

"I don't know," he replied calmly, but his voice wavered with fear.

"Take off this blindfold," I commanded with the voice of authority that came with becoming a first mate.

"I can't. He won't let me. Not yet," the man said, his voice now shaking. Except it didn't seem he was scared of me. I swallowed hard. I knew that 'he' meant Edward. I wasn't the only one here controlled by Edward, which was both comforting and terrifying. I released my grip, and my hand immediately returned to my side. Instead of taking the blindfold off, I kept still. Whoever this man was, I wouldn't risk punishing him by taking off the cloth. Neither of us deserved Edward's wrath. There was silence for a while. I wondered if the man had moved while I was lost in my thoughts, or if he was still standing in front of me.

"So, is your name Carter?" the man asked again.

He was still in front of me. I jumped when I was reminded of how close he was. Considering his question, I realized there was no use in resisting him any longer. I nodded in response, not daring to say another word. I felt him take my hand and guide me someplace. Whoever this man was, he was gentler than Edward.

"Please sit," he urged. I felt around me to find exactly what place to sit. It was a bed from what I felt. The man placed his hands on top of mine and guided my hands to the place I should sit. I sat down, feeling him brush against my legs as he sat down. I felt his shoulder hovering mine after he sat down. I swallowed hard. This man, this stranger, was too close for my liking. I scooted away, and the man said nothing of it.

"You aren't exactly how I expected you to be," the man began. His words ran through my mind again. I wanted to ask him what he meant, but I held my tongue. With this blindfold, and Edward's warning echoing in my mind, I didn't know what to do. It was so different than being sold to the pirates. They may have been evil and cruel, but I knew what to expect. Here, I had no idea what Edward planned for me. Here my crew was being threatened, which I didn't take lightly. After a few moments of silence, the man must have realized I wasn't going to respond, and he continued talking.

"I guess I thought you would be more like your parents. I met them once. They were very kind, nice, and welcoming. You strike me more as a stubborn person than a welcoming one," he continued. *He met my parents?* Plural, meaning he had met my mother too. But then my curiosity waned just enough for me to process all the statements he made after briefly mentioning my parents. I wanted to explain to him that if someone had just been taken onto an unknown ship, threatened their life and the lives of their family, blindfolded, thrown onto the ground, and stuck in a room with a stranger, then they might be a little stubborn and standoffish. Still, I kept my mouth shut and let the stranger continue talking.

"Maybe I can see it, the relationship I mean. Your father always seemed to be a brave one; I can see that in you. Your mother I met from a distance. She had just given birth to you. She was weak, tired." He paused for a moment. "Which one are you more like?" he asked me, though it sounded like a rhetorical question. I refused to move, but the answer ran through my head. The words Gargan had spat at me, saying that I was like my father rang through my ears, and then Rachel's words telling me how much I reminded her of my mother.

Suddenly, I felt the man's hand on the black cloth. I jolted in surprise. His hands left the blindfold immediately.

"I'm sorry I frightened you, Carter," he apologized. I only nodded. I looked to face where I thought he was.

"Let's try again," he whispered in my ear. I didn't say anything or move a muscle as he pinched the top of the blindfold. I didn't remind him that he hadn't received permission from Edward to do this, though, in the back of my mind, I knew it would be me, and not him, that would take the fall for this if Edward found out. He slowly slid it off my eyes.

The sun's rays from a porthole in the room pierced my eyes. I shut my eyelids until I thought my eyes would be adjusted. My eyes slowly blinked open as I looked down at the bed.

"Wow," the man breathed. This one word rang in my ears. I looked up to face the man who had just taken my blindfold off. I swallowed hard. He looked to be four or five years older than me and a few inches taller than me. But most importantly, I knew exactly why he had met my parents. Somehow, in some way, he was related to Edward.

C H A P T E R 2 8
Discovery

My jaw almost dropped, but I bit my lip instead. His eyes were the color of a light blue sky and his hair was as dark as the night on a new moon. His smile was kind as he reached for my hand. I watched his hand move closer to mine. When he was centimeters away from my hand, he stopped. I looked up at him to find him shaking his head. I remained silent.

"I'm sorry," he said, meeting my gaze. I tilted my head to the side, but other than that, I didn't react. "I should have told you my name. I was so persistent knowing who you are, I forgot to tell you who I am. My name is Samuel Carson Jacobs." He stared at me, waiting for an answer. I didn't give him one.

"I know you can talk. It doesn't do you any good to stay silent," he explained. I disagreed with Samuel. *Does he not know?* I wondered.

"Your mother was good friends with my father, Edward, the captain of this ship," he continued. He was Edward's son. *Good friends.* I nearly snorted. "My father wanted me to meet you. Have you ever heard of me?" Samuel asked me. I shook my head 'no' and Samuel looked down at his knees. His words swirled around in my mind. Never once had I heard of Samuel. Even Fallier, when telling me about Edward, hadn't mentioned him.

I heard footsteps outside the door. I could tell that Samuel heard it too. I turned and faced him, but I remained silent. The son of my enemy was my only hope. Samuel picked up the dark cloth and mouthed the word 'sorry'. He shoved the blindfold over my eyes and the black surrounded me again. I heard him get off the bed and he guided me until I was lying down on the bed we had been sitting on. I didn't know what was going on, but I trusted that Samuel was doing the right thing. I heard the door open.

"How is she?" asked the man who came in. Edward. His voice was forceful, angered, and loving at the same time. It was a difficult concept to grasp. I wondered if Samuel was scared of him, or of what was going on.

"She's doing fine, Father," Samuel replied.

"Is she asleep?" Edward questioned Samuel.

"No sir, I just guided her to the bed to rest, but she hasn't fallen asleep," Samuel answered.

"What has she told you?" Edward asked, as if I *was* asleep. I heard Samuel sigh.

"Nothing. She only spoke once, asking what was going to happen to her. I didn't know the answer, and that's what I told her," Samuel explained. It was silent for a moment. Then I heard footsteps coming closer to me. A strong grip grabbed my wrist. Suddenly, I was pulled off the bed and I smacked the ground.

"Father!" Samuel exclaimed, surprised, and confused.

"Listen, Samuel, this girl, this *child*, needs to be taught a lesson," Edward stated through gritted teeth. Edward gripped my hair tight and pulled me off the ground. I bit the inside of my cheeks to hold in my screech of pain.

"Father, look, you're hurting her!" he yelled. "Let go of her!" Edward immediately let go of my hair and I crashed onto the floor. I felt someone's hand on my shoulder and a hand ran through my hair.

"Carter, are you okay?" he asked me. I ducked away from his hands. I didn't need Samuel's help.

"Carter please, tell me that you are okay," Samuel begged. I stayed silent. What was I supposed to say? "Please, please, Carter, speak to me. Tell me that you are okay." I sat there, completely silent. "Father, what is wrong with you!" he shouted. I winced a bit at his loud voice so close to my ear.

"You are on the right start," I heard Edward mutter.

"To what?" Samuel questioned. He placed his hand on top of mine. I slipped my hand out from underneath his.

"Marriage. Samuel, Carter, you two shall be married."

CHAPTER 29

Goodbye

I TENSED IN FEAR. I was *not* going to marry Samuel. I hardly knew him. But according to what Edward had just said, I was. My heart pounded inside my chest. Fear, rage, confusion had all morphed into one, unidentifiable mess.

The blindfold was ripped off my face. Light from the setting sun stung my eyes. I finally saw the face of Edward Jacobs. He was so close, so happy, so vile that I almost shuddered at the sight, but I managed to stand my ground. The black cloth was in his hands. Samuel's confused gaze moved from me to Edward and back to me again. Samuel's hand was placed on my shoulder. I stood up to face Edward, shrugging off Samuel's hand without so much as a thought. In the corner of my eye, I noticed him stand up behind me.

"Do you have something to say, Carter?" Edward questioned me. I remained silent. I could tell by the smirk on his face that he thought he had won me over. I had so many things to say, but I wouldn't utter a word until the time was right: when I knew my crew was safe and I had a plan to escape Edward. Something in his face changed, as if Edward could read my thoughts.

"Come with me," he stated angrily. He grabbed my wrist and pulled me closer to him. He shoved the blindfold back over my eyes and forced me through the door. His hand guided me through the many passageways of the ship. After a minute or two of walking, he pulled me back, forcing me to stop. He pulled the blindfold off of my eyes and stood in front of me.

"You do exactly as I say, and no one dies. You are going to permit us to leave with you on this ship. Then you are going to happily wave goodbye to your ship and act like you have fallen in love with this ship," Edward demanded. "Finally, you are going to ask two members of your crew to come aboard to say goodbye. If you say anything wrong, I will shoot them in the head. Do you understand?" Edward finished. I only nodded, but questions swirled around in my mind, all of the answers lost in a current just out of reach. Then Edward pushed me onto the main deck, breaking me away from my thoughts. I saw my ship, the *Adventurer*, before me. But I felt locked away from my home; it was torture just looking at it. I could see the beautiful faces of my family, my crew. Nearly all of them had no idea what was happening just beside them. Jonathan looked at the *Cobra* and spotted me. He ran over to the edge of the ship and yelled out to me.

"Carter! Is everything alright?" he called out across the water, relief sounding in his words. It wasn't over yet. Edward placed his hand on my shoulder, reminding me of his warning. As if I needed a reminder. It loomed over me like the gray of storm clouds.

"Yes, everything's fine. Jonathan," I stopped myself, thinking over my words. *Can I do this? Can I leave him? Knowing Edward intends to marry me off to his son, a complete stranger?* Edward's hand tightened around my shoulder. "Captain, I request permission to stay aboard *The Cobra* for a few days. Captain Jacobs has asked permission to leave this part of the sea and return me in a timely manner. A week, perhaps," I felt Edward eying me, but I had some conditions as well. *The Cobra* wasn't my home, and I had made a promise to my captain never to leave my *Adventurer*. I had put that promise in jeopardy once. I wouldn't do it again. Still, Edward tightened his warning grip. The pain threatened to leave a bruise. I thought about the last thing Edward had told me to do.

"I request that you and …" I trailed off, thinking of who I wanted to share this last guaranteed moment with. So many names were running through my head at one time. I didn't want anyone to go unwanted, but only one other person could come, and I knew who it had to be.

"You and Aaron come aboard to discuss a few final things," I finished. Aaron looked me straight in the eye. I hoped – I prayed he saw this as an apology. Both began to make their walk across the plank of wood that connected one ship to the other. Aaron looked at me with longing and anger, while Jonathan looked at me with confusion and fear. But, amid everything, I could see their love for me. How I wished I could run over to both of them and hug them and pull them close to me. I needed to feel their warmth surround me and never let them go. I wanted to remind them that I loved them. That this wasn't my choice, no matter how it seemed.

"What is it?" Jonathan asked. I opened my mouth to speak, but Edward stepped in front of me.

"Carter and I have important information we need to discuss, and the discussion will take time. Much longer than the hour or two that you can provide. These discussions could be life-changing in some ways." Edward paused and looked down at me and smiled, reminding me of his plans. *How can he look so kind in front of them and be such a viper with me?* Jonathan and Aaron both noticed but said nothing. "We both have our schedules to stick to and there is no time for delay. I proposed that we need to let Carter join me for part of my journey as we discuss things. Does that sound fair?" Edward explained. Jonathan nodded, but Aaron didn't reply.

"When will she be able to return?" Aaron asked, not looking up to face Edward.

"Within the week," Edward replied, abiding by my words. Aaron only nodded. Then Edward clapped his hands together and left the three of us to our final goodbyes, neither Jonathan nor Aaron knowing how final it would be.

"Can we do this one at a time?" I suggested. The two agreed and Jonathan volunteered to leave first. It was just Aaron and I alone in the room. Only silence survived the tension that stood between the two of us.

"Aaron, I want you to know that what I said earlier wasn't true. I was hoping that you still cared about me, hoping I didn't break our friendship. I was hoping I could still trust you," I began. Aaron looked up at me with sadness in his eyes.

"Carter, you can trust me with anything, you know that," Aaron said. "Remember that time when Gargan had you and you couldn't escape. I will do it again if you need me to," Aaron went on. I nodded, but both of us knew that this time would be different. We didn't have Aaron's knowledge of the ship or my father's handiwork to help us this time. We both stood up and walked towards the door. Aaron kissed me on the cheek, before walking out the door.

Jonathan entered and it was only a matter of seconds until we were in each other's arms. I could breathe, inhaling his scent and exhaling my fear. Jonathan placed a gentle kiss on top of my head. I took another breath. I wanted more than this. I tilted my head up to face him and stood on my toes. He didn't need much more convincing. His lips started soft against mine, but each moment, each breath brought us close, and he pressed harder. I nearly collapsed in his arms. His hand went through my hair, I wrapped my arms around his neck. But then, Jonathan abruptly stopped, pulling his lips away from mine. He took a step back then moved behind me. He moved my hair away from a single point on my head. I hadn't realized a knot had formed on my head from one of my falls.

"What happened?" Jonathan whispered in my ear. I only shook my head in reply. Jonathan nodded, understanding that I couldn't tell him. He came around to face me again and grabbed my hands.

"I don't want to lose you again," he told me. I frowned. This was torture for him too. First the pirates, now this. I pictured the sight of Jonathan guiding the ship, commanding a new first mate to do other things. My heart sank.

"You won't Jonathan, not if you remember to come back for me," I replied. It may have been a lie at the moment, but I promised myself to make it a truth. Both of our gazes moved from our hands to each other. Jonathan nodded, and then kissed me again softly.

"I love you," he murmured in between kisses. Then he stepped back and began walking towards the door. I waved goodbye and he was gone. I was alone. Again.

CHAPTER 30

Doldrums

EDWARD IMMEDIATELY ENTERED THE ROOM from a door behind me that I had not even noticed. He wrapped his arm around my shoulder and pulled me close to him, making my skin crawl. I resisted him instantly. But Edward pulled me tighter to him. I thought about punching him in the gut. But I didn't know if Jonathan and Aaron were still aboard. With a wave of his hand, he could punish them for my actions. I kept my tightened fists by my side.

"That went very well. I learned everything I needed to know, and none of your friends died, which means everything went according to plan," Edward stated. My jaw tightened in anger. He eavesdropped on my conversations. My moments alone weren't truly alone. *Why am I even surprised?*

"Carter, it seems that you and your mother share a problem, from what I overheard. But I have a hunch that you already broke the news to that Aaron boy. He is broken-hearted, sad, depressed, and angry. He keeps trying because maybe you will open your eyes to the truth. And somewhere deep inside you, it's working. He is stealing your heart in pieces because the last time he tried to steal it all at once and he failed. Slowly but surely, he thinks he will re-win your heart. And you know something; I think his plan just might work. Of course, that would be if you hadn't forced him to leave you here." Those final words of his stung more than any other because they were the truth. My arm almost whipped around to punch his face, but I – miraculously – kept myself still. I reminded myself he was probably trying to get a reaction from me and gain an excuse to hurt me or my crew. I wouldn't – I couldn't – give him one.

But the stillness forced me to dwell on his words. Was it possible that Aaron could win me back when there was already such a strong bond between Jonathan and me? I was no longer being forced to choose, since I had already chosen Jonathan, but were they being forced to fight? Was I forcing them to fight?

"Carter, you are going to speak if I tell you. If I, or anyone else for that matter, command you to speak, you must do so. Do you understand?" he said, grabbing my jaw and pulling my face close to his, jerking me away from the mess in my mind. I nodded as my response. He let go and grabbed my arm. Then I turned towards Edward in a face of defiance, surprising him.

"I will never marry your son," I stated plainly. Edward was taken back, unprepared for my sudden break in silence.

"I will do everything in my power to change that statement. I won't force it, but you will change your words. I will…coax it out of you," Edward said with a smirk, stepping behind me. I feared what he would do, but I stood my ground.

Suddenly, darkness covered my eyes. I realized that the blindfold was once again being tied. I was dependent on Edward. I loathed this unwanted trust. Every time the blindfold was over my eyes, I had to give in to someone, whether it was an acquaintance, an enemy, or a stranger.

Edward shoved me forward and led me down a series of hallways. I stumbled many times, but Edward didn't care. Forward was all that was in his mind, or rather, whatever direction we were moving. He stopped to open a door then shoved me into the room. The door slammed after a moment. I never heard footsteps to indicate that he left. Suddenly someone's hands were on my shoulders. I jumped, unable to contain myself this time. The hands retracted and I was left wondering who it was, but not for very long.

"Carter! Are you okay?" he asked me. Samuel placed his hand on the blindfold, but I slapped them away. Edward was still outside, I knew it. But Samuel didn't.

"What?" he questioned me. I pointed behind me, where I assumed the door was. I hoped I wasn't making a fool of myself and pointing at a desk or the bed.

"What? Something's outside?" he asked me softly, assuring me that I had pointed to the door. I nodded, but I hated the tone he was using – like I was some child that needed coddling. I heard the slow footsteps of Samuel as he approached the door, then the squeak of the door opening.

"Father, what on earth?" Samuel exclaimed. I could picture Edward rolling his eyes and shoving Samuel out of the way to enter the room. *Why would he drop me off in this room just to invade it?* A hand grabbed mine; it was definitely Edward, based upon the force he put into it. Samuel was much gentler.

"Tell me, girl, what is it I want from you that you refuse to give?" he asked, his spit spewing on my face. I flinched a bit, showing him in my own way how dissatisfied I was. I was reluctant to answer, but Edward's warning dangled above me like a guillotine. Suddenly I understood why he was there.

"You want me to marry your son. But I swear that I won't," I replied, clenching my jaw. There was silence for a moment or two. I wished for the fifteenth time today that I wasn't wearing this stupid blindfold.

"How did you get her to talk?" Samuel questioned his father, breaking the silence. I felt a gust of air as Edward turned around to face his son. He was still so close to me. It was a good thing I hadn't moved.

"You can't ask her; you have to force her. Statements, not questions," Edward explained. *What is he trying to prove?* I lowered my head, facing the floor. The silence was awkward, made even more so by the blindfold. If I could see, I would be able to gauge the room, or at least take a step back. Right now, I could be an obstruction in their conversation, and I wouldn't even know. In the darkness, I was trapped, waiting for the next move, which came sooner than I expected.

Two fingers gently pressed against my chin, moving my head up to face someone. My blindfold was carefully taken off my eyes, and I knew that instant it was Samuel. He looked straight at me, his eyes glazed with an odd mixture of fear and compassion.

He opened his mouth to take in a breath and speak, but his head dropped in failure before he even said a word. I breathed a single sigh of relief. Edward looked disapprovingly at his son. Samuel walked over to face him. I felt awful seeing him treated this way. How could a father be so cruel to his son?

"I can't do this father. I can't force her to speak against her will," he stated with confidence. I could see the rage boiling in Edward by the look in his eyes.

"She has no will!" he yelled. I raised my eyebrows. "She lost it the moment she stepped onto this ship!" I refused to believe any word he said. His words intoxicated my mind with lies. The only way I could prove he was wrong was to stand up to him now. *But what if that is what he wants me to do?* I questioned myself. It didn't matter; I needed him to know I wasn't some glass figurine to place on his shelf. I was a woman, a first mate, a leader.

"I have a will!" I announced, the sound reaching above Edward's ranting. Both Samuel and Edward turned to face me. Samuel's jaw dropped in dismay and Edward's eyes widened and his eyebrows raised. They were staring at me waiting for more words to leave my lips. For once, I would give them what they wanted.

"I have a will; I'm going to fight and speak up for myself. I have opinions. I can't believe that you would think otherwise. You of all people Edward, you should know better. You knew my mother and my father. How on earth do you think I could grow up to become a woman with no will?" I argued. After that, I returned to silently glare at the man who was determined to ruin my life.

"I ask you again, Carter Ellen Key, before I leave you in peace, will agree to marry my son Samuel Jacobs? Or do you choose to suffer?" Edward questioned me once more. It sounded so cliché, but so terrifying. I glanced over at Samuel with an apologetic look.

"I will not marry your son, Edward. I will not," I stated. "Is that what you call coaxing, Edward? Because if so, you will need to get better at it. This has been nothing compared to the tortures I've endured." Edward shook his head, upset, and disappointed in me. Samuel's eyes widened with shock. People don't stand up to captains, or fathers, like Edward. But he didn't scare me. He turned and walked out the door. I turned and faced Samuel, then looked down at the floor. Slowly, Samuel walked over to me and placed his hands on my shoulders. I pulled away and looked up at him.

"I don't judge you for that decision. I see no reason for you to say yes," Samuel began. "We have treated you poorly here, and he is expecting you to give in to everything he says. I don't know why he thinks he can do this to you." Samuel started rubbing a bruise on my forehead, but I moved his hand away. No matter how kind he was to me, I didn't want him touching me or caring for me. That wasn't *his* job. Samuel guided me to the connecting room and showed me the bed. I nodded a thank you and he left the room, shutting the door behind him. As soon as I heard the door completely close, I fell back on the bed and stared at the ceiling. I prayed that I would live to see my ship again, and my crew, the men that I loved, the place and the people I called home.

An answer to prayer never felt more impossible. This is what it felt like to whistle for the wind. It was a phrase I had grown up hearing. Never had I used it before. Crewmen would say they were whistling for the wind when they wanted something to happen that never had a chance. The winds listening to the call and filling the sails on command, for example.

The winds were not coming for me. I was stuck in a doldrum.

CHAPTER 3 1

In the Darkness

AT LEAST THIS PRISON WAS MORE COMFORTABLE than the last. Here there were blankets to keep me warm all night. But a prison is still a prison. The sun was gone, and the purple darkness on the other side of the porthole made my eyelids heavy. I looked through the glass again, realizing my home was gone, far off in the distance. What if I wasn't strong enough? Or worse, what if Edward went back on his word and never returned me to the *Adventurer*? I held my quivering lip between my teeth.

I forced the thoughts out of my head. I would return to my home within the week, only a few months before I would turn sixteen. The time had gone by so fast. Sixteen, the age my mother got married. I hoped that I would *not* be getting married soon, at least not within the week. Not to Samuel. I wanted to marry for love – just as my mother had chosen. As the thoughts rolled around my head, my eyes closed, and I fell asleep.

The darkness surrounded me, but I heard a voice echoing in my mind. It was muddled, soft, and difficult to make out. Slowly, it became louder. The voice was Edward, whispering in my ear. I realized then that I was blindfolded.

"You must choose who you will marry by pointing at them. Let fate take control, Carter," he whispered. I gulped and prayed that I pointed at the right person. I hoped that Jonathan was in front of me. I lifted my finger. I heard the evil chuckle of Edward in my ear. I breathed a sigh of frustration and anger. I clenched my fists in rage. I knew from the laugh in my ear, I had picked the wrong person. Edward whispered in my ear the person I had chosen.

"No!" I screamed into the darkness. It was a scream of defiance and anger, not sadness and fear. But it didn't change the fact that I was falling, and my head smacked the ground soon after. The window was still dark, and only a small glow from the moon lit up my room. I heard someone run to the door; I knew that it was Samuel.

"Carter, are you okay?" he asked through the door. I breathed in and out heavily a few times, not replying. I heard the door slowly open after a moment. Samuel had an oil lamp in his hand, illuminating the room. My eyes quickly adjusted, and I realized how close he was to me. I quickly stood up. Even though he was kind, he didn't seem to understand the concept of privacy.

"What happened?" he asked me. I shook my head and forced a weak smile.

"Nothing, it was just a dream," I laughed at myself, trying to make myself more innocent. Samuel only nodded, and he walked over towards my bed. He fixed the blankets and readjusted the pillows. I nodded a thank you to him and began to walk over to the bed.

"Are you sure you are okay?" he asked me again. I nodded, and Samuel nodded in response. "If you need anything, just knock," he reminded me. I nodded again, wanting him to leave more than ever. Finally, he walked out of my room and shut the door behind him. I listened as he walked away from the door. I waited.

Once I knew he was gone, I walked over to the mirror in the room. I looked at myself in anger. Even though it was only a dream, I had let the darkness fool me. I had let Jonathan down. The name that was whispered in my ear was not his. It was Samuel's. I punched the mirror in anger, and I watched as the glass splintered over my reflection. The crack in the mirror went across my chest. I laughed, though the coincidence was anything but humorous. I wanted to go home. I wanted to get away from Edward so badly. I wanted to get out of this darkness, this death that was inevitable. But I couldn't. Not until I won this fight against the man who threatened my family.

I heard Samuel once again approach the door. He must have heard me crack the mirror, but honestly, I didn't care if he came in again. I'd happily slam my fist into his jaw. Maybe that's not what he deserved, but that's what he would get from me. I watched as the door slowly cracked open, but suddenly it stopped. I wondered what was going through his head on the other side. The door closed.

I listened as he walked back away from the door. I wanted to know what had entered his mind to urge him away from the door, from entering my room again. No matter, I was happy with him not bothering me. He was just another burden on my shoulders; just another reason for me to leave, to be angry, to defy Edward.

I went back to bed. I had to get my head in the right place. For too long I had believed that the physical and mental scars that Karak and Gargan left had me trapped in an eternal torture. But here, they reminded me of a strength within me that had been buried by fear and confusion for far too long. I had searched for answers from my father, then my mother. I had leaned on the men on my home instead of standing on my own. That wasn't an option here. I wasn't a first mate here, or someone's love. I was just Carter. And if I ever wanted to be any of those things again, I would have to fight my way home.

CHAPTER 32
Trapped

I woke up with the rising sun; my newfound determination still pulsing through me. I glanced out the porthole, and I saw the first glimpse of the sun. The dawn had just broken. *I bet that Samuel isn't even up.* I slipped out of bed and walked over to the cracked mirror and looked in the drawer. I hoped for something I could use to escape or even just prove myself a worthy opponent to Edward, but there was nothing.

I walked over to the door and took a deep breath. I silently pushed open the door and tip-toed into Samuel's room. I hated that our two rooms were connected. The illusion of privacy wasn't even well-kept. On his desk was the item I was looking for: a knife. I quickly grabbed it and slipped out of another door, one that didn't connect to mine. Once I had closed the door, I breathed a sigh of relief. For the first time, I saw the hallway I had been shoved down who knows how many times. I wondered which direction was the main deck. I listened to the noise around me. I went down the quieter hallway. From what I had learned on the pirate ship, the louder the hall, the more dangerous it was. I walked aimlessly through the ship, and I held the knife tight in my hand. Turning the corner, I caught a glimpse of Edward. I hid behind the wall. *What are the chances that Edward would not be on the main deck when I got up?* A good captain should be on deck. I breathed in, re-gripped the knife, and once again turned the corner. I stood my ground confidently. This was the Carter that faced pirates, and she wasn't afraid of an old man like him.

Edward turned around. His eyebrows raised and his eyes widened with confusion, then they narrowed with anger. A smile made its way onto my lips, only for a moment, just long enough to show him I had gotten the reaction I had wanted. From what I knew about Edward, anger was merely a mask to hide his fear.

"What on earth are you doing out here?" Edward questioned me with gritted teeth.

I flashed a smirk at him and replied, "I woke up, Edward, and decided to explore a little. Is that really a problem?" He couldn't shake me. I had endured so much worse than him. He glanced down at my hand and saw the knife, but I didn't care. It's not like the knife was the surprise – I was. He took a few steps closer to me.

"You scared of me, Carter? Don't lie to me girl. Lies will only get you into more trouble than you're already in. And, child, you are neck-deep in trouble," he questioned me as he walked closer to me. For a moment, I considered his words. If this was neck-deep in trouble, it wasn't too terrible.

"No, I used to be, but I am not anymore," I stated bluntly. Edward stiffened for a moment and then continued on his walk closer to me. I hadn't given him the answer he wanted, and I refused to step back. When he was inches away from me and I hadn't moved yet, Edward raised his eyebrows. I looked up to stare into his eyes. The icy blue color attempted to strike fear into my heart, but I shoved the fear away. Fear was not an ally.

Edward raised his hand. He was preparing to slap my face. What he didn't know was that I had gone through much worse. His hand flew across my face, leaving my cheek pounding and in pain. But I refused to let my hand jump to my face. I faced him instead, and let my knife slash across his cheek. It was time to defend myself. He dabbed the blood with his fingertips as it dripped towards his neck.

"Do you really think that hurt me, Edward? I am a first mate of a ship, and I got there as every other crew member would. Now you tell me, do you think that hurt?" I snapped at him; I let my anger loose, each word drawing me closer to a yell. Edward's eyes widened with surprise at my spontaneous uproar. I raised the knife, preparing to stab his shoulder. But he was ready, his strength surprising me as he shoved me down to the ground. My head was one of the first things that slammed on the planks of wood, bouncing twice before it finally rested on the floorboards. I closed my eyes in pain, struggling against the darkness that was surrounding my vision.

"Carter, you are still merely a girl. Nothing you say or do can change that," Edward stated. I opened my eyes for a second just to see Edward smiling down at me. I tried to grip tighter on the knife, but I was slowly fading away. He stepped on my wrist and I cried out in pain, releasing my grip on the knife. My eyes closed again; I couldn't fight the darkness.

"Father!" was the last word I heard.

***

I woke up in a dark room surrounded by rusted bars. As I tried to stand up, I realized I was tied to the beam behind me. The brig. I rolled my eyes in annoyance. I hated briggs, which was sort of the point. Still the bars and the rope seemed a bit excessive. My eyes scanned the room, and I noticed Edward in the corner of the room. He realized I was awake and walked over to me, standing on the other side of the rusted bars.

"Good morning," he murmured through the bars. I must have only been out for a few hours – he was still calling the day morning. "You put up a good fight, but not good enough," Edward continued. "The stunt you pulled today, it was not enough to spoil my plans, rather, it strengthened them." I stiffened defensively, and I tried to stand up, momentarily forgetting about the rope around my wrists. Edward laughed at me, fueling my frustration. With all the strength I could muster, I shoved myself up. I heard the ropes rip as I tried to stand. With one more tug, I was free. Edward's eyebrows raised, and his lips formed a half-smile. I approached the rusty bars. Edward took one step back. I put my face against the bars so that I could peek my nose through.

"Let me out of here. Now," I said with gritted teeth. The half-smile disappeared from Edward's face.

"I will not," he replied. Then Edward jumped forward and grabbed the collar of my shirt, and pulled me even closer to the bars, cutting my cheeks against the rusted metal. "You listen to me.

169

If you say that you love my son, I will let you out." Then he shoved me backward. I quickly regained my balance. I faced him again, but he was already turning around to leave. I walked back into the corner and sat down. I was alone. I tucked myself into a ball and rested my head on my knees. I sat there for who knows how long; the thumping in my brain wasn't a good time keeper.

Eventually, I heard a door open somewhere, and I lifted my head to see who was entering the brig. Immediately, I spotted Samuel's worried face. He ran towards the cell I was locked in. I stood up, brushing myself off.

"Carter! What happened?" he exclaimed. I shrugged my shoulders. Samuel rolled his eyes. "Obviously, something happened! There was a knife in your hand – my knife! And you were passed out in the middle of the hall…And you have cuts on your face! And you're just shrugging?" He slipped some wrap, clean rags, and a bottle of a liquid – probably alcohol – through the bars. Instead of picking them up, I bit the inside of my cheek in anger.

"Samuel, you don't know what has happened to me in my life. You wouldn't understand because your father has lied to you all of your life. You didn't have to go through what I had to go through!" I yelled at him. He stepped back in surprise. My eyes were on fire with rage. *How dare he come in here and treat me with such pity.*

"Why don't you explain it to me then?" he asked calmly.

"Because you would go off and tell your father! Edward has threatened me with my life, Samuel. I could lose my life just by shouting at you right now!" I continued yelling, clenching my fists in anger.

"He what?" Samuel exclaimed. I stopped in my tracks and faced him, pointing my finger at him.

"See, you think your father is just good and kind and has the best interest of everyone in mind. Guess what, he doesn't. My mother was terrified of him, and if she hadn't died giving birth to me, I can only imagine what he would have done to her. He threatened to kill my captain if I didn't comply with him. And you know what, I bet he hasn't even told you any of this. Well, I'm not surprised." I finished, crossing my arms. Samuel's jaw dropped.

"Don't you dare talk about my father like that. You must be mistaken. There is no way your mother would fear my father. They were friends! She must have-" Samuel began, but I cut him off.

"Oh, so my mother got it all wrong?" I laughed. "'Carter Ellen, I came for your mother, and I will come for you too'. That is what your father wrote to *me* in the back of *my mother's* diary. Now, do you think my mom got it wrong?" I questioned him. For the first time since Samuel came in, the brig was silent.

"I'm sorry," I eventually whispered. I realized I had gone too far. It must have been a lot for him to take in at one time. He hadn't ever intentionally hurt me, only his father had. Just the opposite; he had tried to help me here. He didn't deserve my rage. Being cruel to him would only make me as horrible as Edward.

"No, I'm sorry," he said looking at the ground. Then he faced me. "You said I wouldn't understand the things you have gone through. I think I can. I know I can at least try. Would you be willing to tell me what happened that made you so..." Samuel trailed off. I lowered my eyebrows, waiting for him to finish, imagining the words he would use to finish his sentence. Cold. Angry. Savage. "So strong," Samuel finally finished, and made me smile. It was the right word.

"On one condition, you don't tell your father anything I tell you," I stated. Samuel nodded. I sat down next to the bars and he did the same.

"Where do I start?" I sighed. Samuel reached through my hand through the bars, and I looked up at him.

"At the beginning," he begged. I nodded. I pulled my hand out from under his and began my story. I started with my father getting captured by pirates and went from there. And I didn't leave out anything. Never had I shared my experiences with Jonathan just before the storm, or Aaron after he discovered I was actually alive, in the same story. I was always afraid that someone would end up hurt. Not this time. In this cage, there was a tiny glimmer of freedom I hadn't known in a long time. Telling the story took a little over an hour. But I felt more open than ever. Someone deserved to know the whole thing. All the while, I used the small gifts Samuel had brought me to clean the scratches on my cheeks.

"Carter," Samuel breathed once I finished, "You have

survived the impossible. I can't believe – I mean – how could you even live with truths like these? Your life is literally a miracle in itself." He was right. The fact that I was here, alive, after everything I had risked, truly was a miracle.

"Thank you, I think," I replied, rousing a small chuckle from both of us.

"You know, it's nice to hear your voice. It's beautiful. You should talk more often," he said smiling. I smiled, and I couldn't decide how to react. I looked down. His hand slipped through the bars and squeezed mine. I shot him a tight smile and pulled out of his grip. Instead of retracting, his hand slid higher up my arm. I tried to pull away, but his grip tightened ever so slightly. He pulled me ever so slightly closer to the bars and when I looked up to face him, he pressed his lips to mine. I immediately pulled away, stumbling backwards.

"W-What? Samuel?" I stared at him, confused and shocked.

"It just felt right," he replied. My mouth hung open with astonishment. I didn't know what to say. He used me; tricked me into opening up, then abused my vulnerability.

"You're just as disgusting as your father," I snapped at him, angry, but even importantly, hurt. He winced at this jab. He didn't want to be Edward, at least, that's what he claimed, but his actions said otherwise.

"I wish I could say I am sorry, but I can't," Samuel mumbled. Then he stood up. I scooted back against the wall.

"After everything I said, everything I just told you, you still…" but words failed me. Anger, confusion, rage, and sadness filled me, leaving me speechless.

"I'm not sorry," Samuel said more confidently this time, "It was a perfect kiss." And with that, Samuel left the brig. I stood and yelled his name angrily, but he ignored me, which was a first for Samuel. After a few shouts I changed the way I channeled my energy. I slammed my fists onto the back wall of the brig. Then I sat back down in a corner, realizing more than I had before how much I wanted to get out of here. Not just these bars, not just this brig, but this ship as a whole. I wanted out.

CHAPTER 33

Run

I sat there in silence. How would my father have gotten out of this crazy mess? *He would find a secret passage.* Reminders of my father's amazing ship capabilities floated to the forefront of my thoughts. I never cared enough to learn his genius. How would my mother have gotten out of this situation? *She would write about it.* Well, all of the supplies I needed were far out of my reach, so that wasn't an option either. I frowned. For the first time, I had to figure out how *I* would solve the situation. What was my way of fixing problems? *Getting injured,* I thought to myself. It was true, most of the time I found myself in trouble, I ended up bruised, bleeding, and broken, but free. Pain was the only option left.

I scanned the edges of the bars, looking for a break. I spotted a few screws of some sort. I tried to twist them out, and while I couldn't pull them from place, they did loosen. I slowly walked to the back of the room and launched myself straight into the bars. They didn't budge. I did so over and over until I felt the bars begin to slip out of place. I took a few deep breaths, then I charged at the bars. The wall of rust fell to the ground and I toppled down with it. My head would pay for it later, but there wasn't much time to recover.

I lifted my head to an unwelcoming sight. Two men were running down the hallway, eyes locked on me. I sighed in annoyance and forced myself to stand up. I ran to my right, towards the hallways. I quickly gained speed, but I had no earthly idea where I was going. *That stupid blindfold.*

"Come back here girl!" yelled a gruff voice from behind me. I ran faster.

"You can't get away from us, Carter!" the other man yelled. The voice clicked somewhere deep in my head. *Who is that?* At that moment of confusion, I ran straight into the wall in front of me. Dazed, I tried to regain balance, but I was shoved onto the ground by one of the men chasing me.

"You're in big trouble young lady," stated the man with the gruff voice. I almost punched him in the face, until my eyes landed on the other man that was chasing me. How could those spring green eyes be staring at me right now? And why were they chasing me after I escaped?

"Aaron?" was the only word I could manage. For a moment, I thought I saw his love in his eyes, but a moment later, they hardened again. It couldn't be him, could it?

"What did she call you?" the man with the gruff voice. Aaron stumbled, but then he regained his words.

"She must be going insane. Too many hits to the head," he muttered. My eyebrows lowered at his suggestion. The man with the gruff voice rolled his eyes.

"Fair enough," he said. This time I did punch him. He jumped back, his hands covering his face immediately. I got up to make a run for the hallway, but someone grabbed my wrist. I turned to face Aaron, refusing to let go.

"Aaron! What are you doing?" I asked him in disbelief. He just stared at me as I resisted his grip on my wrist.

"I have to do my job," Aaron said, his words almost regretful. He tightened his grip and pulled me closer. I tried to squirm away.

"Aaron just let me go," I begged him, tears blurring my vision. I thought he appeared here to save me, not stop me.

"I'm sorry Carter, but I just can't do that," he murmured under his breath. In an instant, his fist connected with my temple and everything went black. But I was fighting him, and the darkness, and the overwhelming pain. My heartbeat was thumping in my head from the blow, begging me to let the darkness take control. I refused the offer of comfort and vulnerability. I pressed my eyelids tightly together. The pain was beyond compare, but I eventually opened my eyes to see Aaron's green eyes lined with tears and I watched as he bent down to pick me up. As he did so, I resisted him. Aaron had just tried to punch me unconscious and now he wanted to pick me up, drowning me in his tears of anguish. No way. He would pay the price for what he had done to me. I pressed my hands against his chest as he lifted me off the ground, but Aaron only pulled me closer to him. I tried to press away from him again, but it was too late. I felt so at home. The warmth of his body surrounded me. But I didn't pull him any closer. I was still angry with him.

He carried me through a series of hallways until we ended up on the main deck. Somehow, he knew these halls better than me. My eyes kept opening and closing as I tried to fight the black. My head pounded so loudly that I couldn't hear half of the commotion on the main deck. I knew Aaron was strong, I just never expected to feel the power of his strength myself. I bit down hard on my bottom lip, barely holding in a groan of pain. Aaron opened a door and slammed it hard behind him. In this moment, I shoved myself away from him, falling onto the ground, escaping his grasp.

My eyes scanned my surroundings, keeping my distance from Aaron. Captain's quarters. He had brought me into the lion's den. And Edward was there waiting for me. I couldn't even look at Aaron. He had carried me straight to the enemy. *How could he?*

"Mr. Harrison, thank you for bringing her. What is her condition?" Edward asked Aaron. *Mr. Harrison?* Aaron glanced down at me. Our eyes met for a second, but I quickly turned away. He didn't deserve my attention.

"I attempted to knock her out, but she was strong enough to resist the blow, which was… surprising," Aaron replied. I could feel his gaze resting on me. *Surprising? Surprising is when Aaron Getty magically arrives on the ship of a family rival and tries to knock you out! That's surprising.* But I wouldn't ever be able to tell that to him, not now, not ever. Somehow, he got onto this ship, for me. After rejecting him, lying to him, and giving up on him, he came back for me. I should have been happy that I wasn't alone. But he also tried to knock me out. My head was hurting so badly that I couldn't keep my thoughts straight. Whatever was happening, however he managed to stay here, it was far too confusing for me to understand at the moment. Still, Edward's words rang in my ears: 'He is stealing your heart in pieces because the last time he tried to steal it all at once and he failed. Slowly but surely, he thinks he will re-win your heart'. Was that what Aaron was trying to accomplish? Or was he living up to the final conversation we had before he was supposed to leave? Was he going to be my hero?

C H A P T E R   3 4

Replacing Fear

"You can leave us now, Mr. Harrison," Edward commanded Aaron. It felt so odd, so wrong, to hear Edward call Aaron by a different name. Aaron glanced down at me, but only for a moment. I ignored his gaze.

"So, Harrison couldn't knock you out. It looks like it was a painful punch," Edward began, staring at my temple. It must have swelled up or turned red because even Edward seemed shocked that I was still awake. I squeezed my eyelids together then looked up at him.

"It would be more painful to give in," I replied, and it was true. Edward raised his eyebrows, and a smirk crossed his lips as he watched me writhe in pain. He had such low expectations of me; it made my chest boil with fury. And yet, a glimmer in his eyes revealed something different. Pain, longing, and an anger of his own.

"How *exactly* did you get out of that cell?" he questioned me after some silence. I paused before I spoke, leaving my thoughts about Edward to formulate an answer to his question. I didn't know if I should answer him or not.

"My way," I replied. Vague, not telling him everything, avoiding the truth. Jonathan hated those kinds of answers. For a moment, I smiled, remembering how just the other night he was upset with me about avoiding the answer he wanted me to give. It already seemed so long ago. I had lived a whole other life in a single day. But the smile caused me more pain than it was worth, and it fizzled away in a matter of seconds.

"Interesting answer," Edward stated in reply, half to himself. I hoped that it actually was a good thing, but more than likely, it meant more torture. *Is it not torture enough to be punched in the head by a man that you love?* I wanted to ask this to Edward, but I held my tongue. Love.. I couldn't use such a word around Edward. He would only distort it in some wicked way. Despite my body's protests, I forced myself to stand up. Pain screamed in my head, trying to distract me, but I still stared into Edward's cold eyes.

"You must return to my ship eventually, and I assure you, when that day comes, I will not be married to your son," I stated clearly and proudly. Edward slammed his fists down on his desk and slowly stood up. For a moment, an odd look of vulnerability entered his gaze as it fixated on me. What was he thinking? But, once again, his blue eyes turned ice-cold before I could figure it out.

"If we return to your ship and you have not yet agreed to marry my son, I will force you to watch as I blast my cannons at your precious *Adventurer* and sink her with all of her crew. How does that sound?" he snapped through gritted teeth. I stared at him; not a word left my mouth, but fear was filling my mind. My crew dying because I would not marry someone? Though it sounded absurd, I didn't doubt Edward. He had the firepower, and he had the gumption. He was also insane enough to do something so foolish and cruel. When I looked back at him again, Edward was sinking back into his chair.

"By the way, something about Mr. Harrison seems," he paused, thinking of a word, "familiar." Then Edward looked at me with a sly smirk on his face. But he soon returned his gaze to the papers on his table. I stood there for a few moments, staring at him in shock. I wanted to vomit. He knew about Aaron, yet he was letting him stay here. I wanted to warn him, but I knew that Edward would find out. All the thoughts running through my head made the pain more difficult to bear. I soon collapsed on the floor again; my legs were not strong enough to carry me anymore. My body wanted me to close my eyes and give in to the pain. Edward stared at me intently, seeing what I would do next.

I blinked once; the pain was unbearable, but I fought, opening my eyes, and kept my gaze fixed on Edward.

Soon my body wouldn't care if I closed my eyes or not. My vision began to blur and darken. A few minutes passed and I couldn't make out Edward's face. But I watched as his figure stood up and came close to me. I watched as his form bent down, and I felt his lips brush against my ear.

"Give in girl," he whispered. I tried to hold my eyelids open, but Edward gently forced them closed.

"Aaron loves you," he whispered in my ear. A small smile formed on my lips. I didn't care if Edward knew he was here. Aaron did love me; that much was true if nothing else was. I tried to open my eyes again; I wanted to see Aaron. But Edward kept his fingers pressed on my eyelids. I kept resisting him while the darkness continued to call for me. When he realized I wasn't giving in without a fight, Edward stood me upright. He took his fingers off of my eyes. It took me a moment to open them, but a moment was too long. Edward didn't stand me up to help me; he stood me up to bring me down. He punched my temple again. Immediately, I was out.

***

I woke up in a familiar position, one I felt when I was on the pirate ship. Tied to the main mast was a feeling I would never forget and, now, always recognize. When my eyes flickered open, I was surrounded by the stares of some of the most important men on this ship. Before I even looked up, I felt their gazes on me. I didn't dare to meet them.

"What a lovely girl. It's a shame you are tied to a beam such as this," I heard Edward say once he noticed I was awake. How he could tell was beyond me.

"It's not the first time," I muttered a little louder than I had planned. Suddenly, Edward's fingers were forcing my face up so that I was staring him in the eye. I couldn't read his expression.

"You said what?" he growled. My eyebrows raised and then I shrugged my shoulders, deciding to play up on pretending this whole situation was a breeze.

"It's not the first time," I repeated. He visibly clenched his jaw. If he thought tying me to the mainmast was going to 'break me', well he was dead wrong. That theory was already tested, and it failed.

"First mate," he mumbled to the man next to him loud enough for me to hear. I swallowed. Edward was smart; if he wasn't whispering, it was purposeful. He wanted me to know what dangers I was about to face. "Get the swab buckets up here as soon as possible," Edward demanded. But I didn't think he would ask me to swab; I feared that *I* would be what the swab would be cleaning up.

"Yes sir," replied the first mate. I recognized the voice almost immediately. It was Henry, the man who saved me from Edward's shove the day before. Before I knew it, I had called out his name. Henry turned around, and I met his surprised eyes.

"Thanks," I breathed, glancing at Edward for less than a second. A small smile formed on his face; he had gotten the message. Soon after, I saw a hand fly at my cheek. Edward slapped my face, forcing me to meet his unyielding gaze again.

"Do not talk to my crew," Edward stated behind gritted teeth. I didn't reply. I was confused. *He forces me to speak, and then when I finally feel comfortable enough to talk, he silences me! He needs to make up his mind!* I didn't dare say it out loud, though. Over the past few months, I had learned it was not always best to speak my mind.

He pulled my hair so that my head would be forced to come closer to his. I wasn't scared. I had gone through this whole scene before. I knew how to get through this situation. That didn't mean I wasn't immune to the pain. But knowing I had an upper hand helped – a glimmer of a smile crept onto my face. Edward noticed, and his grimace tightened. He slapped my face again. Edward was a cruel captain, but he was no pirate.

"I will slap that smile off your face," he spat through gritted teeth. I only smiled bigger.

"Try and you will fail," I replied. Edward slapped my face again, just as I predicted. I continued to smile, just to prove a point. Edward closed his eyes and rubbed above his eyebrows, then he moved to stand behind me. I didn't feel strong and safe anymore. I listened as a knife began sawing through the rope. This time, I would be slamming my face against the boards of the main deck. There was no way to avoid it. I already began to brace myself. After a few seconds, I heard the rope snap, and my face was flying towards the boards. Sadly, my feet were still tied to the beam, and my hands behind my back.

"Is that smile off your face now?" Edward yelled, though, I could barely hear it over the ringing in my ears. I closed my eyes at the sound of his voice. *It's too loud. It's all too loud.* But I managed to make a weak smile. I was a professional at getting on his nerves. I was professional at getting on a lot of people's nerves. It was by God's will alone that I was still alive.

Edward shouted his frustration up into the sails. The main deck was silent. I had never heard a man yell so loud in my life. Edward kicked my side, and I bit down on my bottom lip to hold in a scream of my own. Then Edward chopped off the rope on my feet. I began to stand up.

"Don't you dare stand up," Edward threatened as he pulled out a gun. I gulped. Suddenly, he was no longer Edward, he was Gargan, threatening to kill me, pressing the barrel against my head, stabbing me in the arm. Uncontrollable tears shimmered in my eyes. I wanted to beg him not to kill me, not to shoot. A little lonely girl fought her way towards the surface of my heart. His finger was on the trigger. Edward saw my fear, and a smirk replaced the grim expression on his face. There was no sympathy for the child still in me.

"Do not move," he ordered me again, this time smiling. "Listen to my words, closely and carefully. You are going to stand up and walk to my quarters. You will sit there and wait for me. You do anything else - keep in mind, this gun is pointed at your back. You can be dead in an instant." *Thanks for that reminder,* I thought. My legs shook as I stood up. Flashes of memories of the pirate ship interrupted my reality, where I desperately needed to be present. Then the thought hit me, I had no idea where exactly his quarters were. I had been nearly unconscious the last time I found myself there. Not only that, this ship was so massive, so different from my own. I breathed in deeply and faced Edward.

"Where exactly are your quarters?" I asked Edward innocently. Edward's eyebrows raised and his fist tightened. For a moment, I believed he was about to pull the trigger. Then he pointed the end of his gun towards a door in the back corner. I nodded and slowly walked towards the door. As I walked, I spotted Aaron near a mast. His eyes reflected the fear I was experiencing. But whenever I felt like being sad or scared, I replaced it with anger and confidence. I saw words forming in his mind, just by the look in his eyes. 'No', I mouthed, but Aaron ignored me, as always.

"Captain, do you truly think that she needs to have a gun on her back? Has she not gone through enough today?" Aaron questioned Edward. I wanted to punch Aaron in the face for his words. He, of all people, should know how to keep his head down.

"Mr. Harrison, one can never be positively sure that enough is enough. In fact, I believe I have much more planned for this girl. All of it, she deserves to the fullest. So, I recommend that you watch your words, or you just might understand what it feels like to be Carter Ellen Key," Edward replied, gun still pointed at my back. Aaron only nodded and continued his work on the ropes. I breathed a sigh of relief. At least Edward didn't shoot him. Then I reminded myself that he has a reputation to live up to, a good one at that. While he treated *me* poorly, he was no pirate. Everyone thought that Edward was a great captain. He led his ship well. His son even saw the best of his father. It seemed that I was one of the few that knew the truth.

I continued walking toward the door. Edward followed and pressed the gun on my back, and I began to move faster. In a few moments, I was opening the door to his quarters. I walked into the room, but Edward shut the door and did not enter. I stood awkwardly, worry growing in my chest.

"Mr. Harrison," I heard Edward yell. I tensed up. I heard a single gunshot and a shout of pain.

"No!" I screamed and then covered my mouth. Tears rolled down my cheeks. I could only imagine what had happened just outside the door. I wanted more than ever to replace my fear and sadness with something else. But I couldn't. The mere thought of Aaron dying sent me weeping. *He wouldn't. He couldn't.* My whole body shook with my tears. "No, no, no, no," I cried between sobs. Edward swung open the door and entered the room. I tried to peek outside, but he slammed it closed.

I had never seen such an evil smile in my entire life. He walked over to me, but I didn't even realize it until it was too late. I stepped back when I realized how close he was, desperately trying to control my tears, but I couldn't.

"Poor Mr. Harrison," Edward whispered in my ear as he wiped a few tears off my cheek. He touched me with so much kindness, it nearly shocked the tears out of my eyes. *How dare he pretend to care!* "I didn't know you even cared for him that much." He began to wipe another tear, but I grabbed his wrist with a grip no one could break. My knuckles turned white as my grip only grew stronger. I thought I had known pain. Edward thought he knew me. Both of us were wrong.

"Don't act like you don't know," I cried angrily through gritted teeth. "I heard you whisper his name in my ear. You know that it was him!" I continued. Edward tried to pull away, but he couldn't. He wasn't walking away from this. He couldn't kill Aaron, *my Aaron*, and get away with it.

"You must be mistaken," he replied, almost laughing. But this laugh grew more worried as he realized I wasn't letting up.

"Don't lie, Edward," I replied.

"I'm sorry, Carter. But some people can only be changed one way."

CHAPTER 35

Iron Grip

"No," I whispered. My grip on his wrist loosened and Edward twisted out of my grip. He confirmed what I never thought would be true. I knew for a fact my faint whisper was not heard by Edward, but he read my lips all the same.

"Yes, now that you point it out, Harrison does resemble Aaron," Edward continued, the words forming a larger smile on his face. I shoved him away from me, but he grabbed my arms, keeping me close.

"Can you just stop acting like you don't know? Edward, stop!" I screamed. The tears came down harder. Edward raised his eyebrows.

"So, you actually did love this Aaron?" he urged me on, squeezing my arms tighter.

"Of course, I loved him!" I screamed at him, raising my hands, twisting out of his grip. And I listened to my words. I brought my hands back down to my side and stepped back until I reached a wall. I let the wall guide me down to the ground. And I sat there, looking at the ceiling. "Of course, I loved him," I whispered through the tears.

"Are you saying that he won your heart in the end?" Edward questioned me. It wasn't fair of him to ask these kinds of questions now. My head snapped to face him. But as I did so, I thought about my first kiss. I reminded myself of Jonathan's lips pressed against mine. And at the same time, Aaron's powerful emotions that flooded me when he kissed me on the pirate ship filled my body with grief. That man was gone.

"Is this all you want Edward? To live through Aaron? To see if my mother would have chosen you if you were killed? Is that why you let him stay on this cursed ship? Is that why you made sure to send him when I tried to break out? Is that why? Are you getting the reaction you want? Because that question has never been harder to answer than right now. Is that what you wanted?" I screamed at him. I stood up and grabbed his shoulders, preparing myself to shove him against the wall. Aaron's beautiful voice entered my head, asking me that question I never answered: Can you? I closed my eyes and loosened my grip on Edward's shoulders.

Tears soaked my eyelashes. There was no one here to mourn with me. There was no one here to share this pain. I thought someone had come to join me, pull me out of this loneliness, but just like that, he was gone. My legs shook, weak from the tears that were still rolling down my cheeks. I wanted to collapse, but Edward's iron grip on my arms forbid me from doing so. He wrapped his arms around me like my father used to do when I woke up from a bad dream. But this man wasn't my father, he was a killer. And this wasn't a bad dream, it was a nightmare come to life. Edward's arms were a cage, refusing to let me escape.

"That is not what I wanted, Carter; I told you that in the beginning. But some people can't step down, some can't let go, some people love too much. Too much of anything, as you now know, can get you into trouble. The power of a man in love is unstoppable against the power of a man's revenge, so I had to eliminate the threat.

"Your mother would not have reacted the same way, for you are nothing like your mother. She was brave, but not like you. She was strong, but not like you. She was raised by her mother, not like you. So many things make you different from her. Honestly, it is difficult to even compare the two of you," Edward explained, his tone growing rougher and more vengeful as he spoke. Then he shoved me away, releasing my arms, and I nearly collapsed. I forced my breathing to slow and my tears to weaken. I took a few steps back, sitting down and leaning against a wall; my knees curled up close to my chest. All I wanted right now was to hold

Aaron's hand and tell him that everything would be okay, that everything would work out in the end. Like it was supposed to.

"Then why all of this? Why are you trying to live through Samuel?" I asked him, wiping away the slow silent tears that continued to roll.

"Because," he began, "you are enough alike." He sighed, almost as if he felt sorry for me. I wanted so badly to punch him, but I forced myself back into my silent state. With that, Edward walked out of the room. I tried to push myself up, but I was weak from the tears. I decided not to move. I began weeping again.

"There are lots of tears, Mother," I cried out between sobs, rocking myself back and forth. "I hope I will have the victory in the end." I cried until my clothes were damp with tears and I began to drift to sleep, and even in sleep didn't stop my crying.

"Aaron!" I screamed in my dream. Edward was pointing the gun at him. No matter how loud I screamed, Aaron could not hear me. I watched helplessly as Edward fired the gun and the bullet sunk into Aaron's flesh. I listened to Aaron's agonizing scream of pain.

"Or is it disappointment?" asked Edward's voice. It echoed around me, and I was forced to hear the question over and over. "He didn't win your heart in time." Then he began to laugh. The evil in the man's voice made my skin crawl and pierced my heart with fear. But how could it? I was asleep, this was a dream.

"Go away Edward," I screamed, and slowly, after many times of repeating it, the sentence turned into a mere mumble. My eyes blinked open. Somehow, I had ended up in the room Edward had given me. I glanced out the porthole and realized the sun was rising. I had slept through the night, which was a miracle in itself. I propped my elbow up on my pillow, realizing it was still damp with tears.

I slowly shoved myself out of the bed. I walked over to my cracked mirror. There was no brush or comb, so I used my fingers to brush through my hair. After a few minutes, I tied it up in a bun with a loose piece of twine I had found. With that, I walked out of the room. Since Samuel's room was, sadly, connected to mine, I had to walk through. Even more unfortunate, Samuel had not left his room yet.

"Carter, I heard about your reaction to Harrison's death," he began. I continued walking, ignoring him. I didn't reply to him. I had told him about my relationship with Aaron, and he had dishonored all of it with that kiss. The least he could do was respect my mourning. No doubt Edward had told him "Mr. Harrison's" true identity. I bit down hard on my bottom lip in anger as I opened the door and walked out of the room.

"Carter, wait!" he chased after me. I didn't even pause. Then, I felt him grab my wrist. My body jerked around to face him. "Carter, I'm sorry. I know you are mourning. I just wanted you to know that if you need to talk to anyone, you can talk to me," he breathed. I tore my wrist away from him and I shook my head. I had already learned my lesson. Talking to him was a trap. Nothing more. *Like father, like son.* I continued walking towards the sounds of commotion. I wanted to go up to the main deck. There was no such thing as danger anymore.

Finally, I reached the main deck. The early morning busyness surrounded me, and yet I felt more alone than ever before. I looked up the mainmast, larger than any I had ever seen. That's where I wanted to be, atop the crow's nest, higher up in the sky than I had ever been. The first beam of the mast was higher than at home. I grabbed a loose rope and began to climb upwards until I reached the first mast. From there, I moved from the beams to the ropes until I reached the top.

Henry was at the top.

"Ms. Key, what are you doing up here?" he questioned me. I refused to reply, even with Edward's warning ringing in my ears. I held my hand out, asking for the telescope. Henry seemed to understand. He handed the telescope over tentatively and began his climb down. I sat on the edge of the nest, looking out at the sea. Maybe my home was out there, coming back for me. But this was only my second morning here, the start of my third day. They wouldn't be coming for me yet. Had they already realized Aaron was gone? Or had he told them he was leaving? They thought he would be alive; I was the only one that knew he was dead. Dead. Forever. Never coming back. I shoved the thought out of my mind. It was too heavy to handle alone. I focused my thoughts on the sea.

"Key!" I heard someone yell below me. I immediately looked down to face Edward. I rolled my eyes but refused to speak. "Get down here Carter!" he yelled. I refused to listen to him. I stayed at the crow's nest. The sea was my only source of comfort; I wasn't going to leave it because of four little words. I held the telescope up to my eye again and stared at the ocean waves. I heard a man making his way up to the crow's nest. I didn't care. He would have to drag me off this position. That's exactly what he did. The man grabbed my wrists and tied them together. The man pulled me down the beams and carried me as he swung on the ropes. When we finally reached the main deck, the man dropped me in front of Edward. I quickly forced myself up without my hands, having already learned how to do so when Gargan had done the same thing to me.

"Deliberately ignoring your captain's orders is a punishable offense," Edward warned. I gave him a look that said "Yeah and you think I care?", but I refused to say a word.

"Do you think that the rules do not apply to you?" questioned Edward. I shook my head innocently. Edward pursed his lips and shook his head. He nodded his head to two men behind me. Both grabbed my arms tightly and pulled me backward.

"You will soon learn what it means to feel pain."

CHAPTER 36

Pain

THE TWO MEN PULLED ME and shoved my head down. My hair was ripped out of its bun, falling in strands over my face. Suddenly, the men stopped, and I heard heavy footsteps coming towards me. I watched as Edward's hand moved my hair off my face. I lifted my head just enough so that I could see his eyes.

"Harrison was only the beginning. Tell me the words I want to hear, and I will make him the end," he whispered in my ear. I jerked away from his face, but Edward grabbed my chin and pulled my head closer to him.

"Tell me, for the good of Mr. Harrison," he barely breathed. His lips hovered over my ear. This time, I yanked my head away from his hand and whipped around to face him.

"Quit calling him that," I spat in his face. "What makes you think that Aaron's death will change my decision?" I lifted my chin in confidence. "His death only strengthened it. I cannot and will not love or marry Samuel Jacobs." I had never been so sure of anything in my life. Edward, in return, slapped my face. He was running out of ideas. I spat on the main deck and looked up at Edward once more.

"For the sake of Aaron Getty, I will not," I replied. With that, the two men forced my face down to the ground again. They continued pulling me backwards. I didn't care. All I could think about was the look on Edward's face after I left him with my final words. Anger was the first thing I noticed. His eyes were a pit of rage. I, his only prisoner, had dared to stand up to him. But the more I thought about it, I noticed somewhere in there was awe. My audacity amazed him. I had dared. And I knew I would pay the price. Thankfully, I was willing. No pain could compare to the feeling of a fatal bullet. Aaron did not deserve death. I did.

The two men dragged me down into the brig, untying my wrists as they locked me in the cage. This time they didn't leave me there alone. The two men remained in the brig to guard me. I had proved stronger than Edward had first believed. The men were hardly a restriction. Still, I needed to let my emotions out somewhere. I refused to cry in front of these two strangers. Instead, I began to mumble beautiful words my father had once said.

"'Look out onto the ocean. It's so wide and so deep; it can never be fully explored. I dare you to try one day. I don't think you can do it. Think of every person like the ocean. You will never know everything about them. You can try, and you will fail. But the goal is not to learn everything, it's to learn anything - anything that a person tells you or gives you or shows you, that's how you make a friend. Or an enemy.'" I whispered. In my head, I heard a six-year-old me ask: 'But you know everything about me. And I know everything about you, right?'

"'No, Carter. I don't know everything about you. I don't know your thoughts or dreams. I will never comprehend your emotions the same way you do. I don't know what the future holds for you. And as for me, I hope you don't know everything about me. Not every chapter of my story is worth reading.'" I wondered if every chapter of me was worth reading. I wondered if parts of my life were worth skipping over. I stopped to ponder –

"Please keep talking," requested one of the men. My head jolted up at the sound of his voice. I swallowed. These words weren't just helping me. I wasn't alone in my pain. So, I kept talking. But I switched from my father to my mother.

"Teardrops come through anger and right before bravery. They trigger sadness to prove you have a heart. They are a sign of courage because you know there is something better than the moment. So, the next time a tear drops from your eyelashes, you know you've won the war." I stated. But now they weren't just my mother's, but my own. I breathed for a moment or two. I refused to cry, but I was reminded of Aaron's death. I breathed in deeply.

"Who told you that?" the other man asked this time. I stared at him in awe. Why were these men so interested? I was their captain's prisoner; if anything, they should be insulting me, or avoiding conversation with me altogether. Maybe I had judged them too quickly. On the pirate ship, everything seemed so black and white. But here, these were honorable, hardworking men following their captain's orders. If I had grown up here, would I have done the same thing?

"My mother," I choked out. Silence filled the room. How much did this crew know about me? Did they know my parents? Did they know why I was here? Did they even know who I was? Or did Edward leave them in the dark, as he had done with his son? As these questions ran through my mind, the devil himself came down in the brig to see me.

"How has she been?" he asked one of the men. He only nodded. Edward stepped closer to the bars that separated me from the rest of the ship.

"It's time," he said to the other man. This time when the man turned, he did not face Edward; he faced me.

"It will be fine," he assured me. I ignored him, pretending nothing had happened. I could not be vulnerable in front of Edward. I lifted my chin as the two guards walked into the cell and grabbed my arms. I let them. They dragged me, following Edward back up to the main deck. They brought me to the main post and turned me around, so my head was against the post, and I hugged it with my arms. That was when I realized what was going on.

"I understand," I whispered to myself. One of the men nodded.

"Fifteen lashes," the other whispered in my ear. I heard a crack of the whip as a warning and swallowed hard. Most ships used this form of punishment. It was a miracle I had never experienced this on the pirate ship and a blessing that none of the captains of the *Adventurer* ever practiced it. I had heard that Americans captured on English vessels had been whipped to death. I told myself I should be grateful that I was only to be given fifteen.

"Are you ready, Carter?" Edward questioned.

"Always," I replied with confidence. It began. The first lash. The crack of the whip followed closely by sharp pain. It ripped through the fabric of my shirt. I groaned in pain and steadied myself for the next. The men who had guarded me adjusted their grip – holding me up when I so desperately wanted to let go of the post and run away. I couldn't dwell on the pain; doing so would only make it worse. By the fifth, I could not hold it in anymore. I screamed. My heartbeat thumped in my ears. I felt my shirt turning to shreds and blood dripping down my skin. On the tenth lash, I felt tears in my eyes. Or maybe they had been there the whole time, and I hadn't felt them until now. I was not going to cry. Not here, not now. On the twelfth lash, I could no longer hold myself up; my legs shook under the weight of indescribable pain. My two guards held my body up. Edward paused to let them situate themselves. There was almost nothing left of my shirt; the sleeves were slowly sliding down my arms, barely managing to cover my torso. I watched as pools of blood formed on the deck, growing sticky in the sunlight. I breathed in deeply; there were only three more left.

"You cannot break me," I whispered with the little breath left in me. The whip cracked against my back again. Thirteen. I breathed in. Another lash. Fourteen. I breathed in again. My eyes slowly blinked. My body was exhausted and losing blood quickly. I felt like passing out. Fifteen. Immediately, the two guards dropped me on the ground, and my feet did not catch me. Blood covered my back and it dripped down my sides. I tried to hold myself up on my hands and knees, but I collapsed. I crossed my arms over my chest and my legs curled up, trying to find safety.

"Do you want someone to help her Captain?" asked one of the guards. I breathed in deeply and imagined how good it would feel if someone could at least help me up. My eyes closed briefly, hoping – praying. *Please, Lord, be merciful just this once.*

"No, she will do fine on her own," countered Edward. Disappointment sunk into my chest like a corpse in the waves. It was silly of me to hope that a man who killed someone I loved would take pity on me. One of the few times I had been willing to accept someone's pity, it wasn't even offered. Ironic, in the cruelest of fashions. I kept my eyes closed to hide the oncoming tears. I heard someone running. Then I heard a gasp of a man I *really* didn't want on the main deck.

"Father!" Samuel exclaimed in shock. My eyes flickered open.

"It is the punishment, you know that," Edward snapped back at him.

"Have you lost your mind?" Samuel argued, "Look at her. You refuse to even offer a hand?" For a man who loved his father, he had no issue publicly arguing with his captain – on my behalf, at that. I hated all the gazes on me; I felt so helpless. Samuel's eyes met mine for a moment. I could not let his hand touch mine again. I forced myself to stand up, and I let out a high pitched sound of pain. Breathing in deeply and crossing my arms back over my chest, I forced the remnants of my shirt and undershirt back into place. I turned around to face Edward and Samuel. Many of the other crew members turned away, out of respect for my privacy – something Edward and Samuel Jacobs knew nothing of.

"I'm fine," I insisted. I gave a curt nod to Samuel, but every move I made caused a sharp pain in my back.

"Really now?" questioned Edward as he approached me. I stumbled backward, knowing his next move. But I wasn't fast enough, or strong enough to defend myself. He shoved me down onto the ground again. My back slammed against the bloodied boards of the main deck. I let out a piercing scream. The sound echoed around us. Silence followed. It was as if even the waves had stilled. I breathed heavily, knowing that I would not be able to stand. The pain was all I could think about now.

I shut my eyes, holding in tears. Agony overwhelmed me. My whole back was on fire, and I couldn't force myself to even sit up. I was fading away. I heard Jonathan's voice.

"You won't die, I can feel it," his voice whispered in my mind. Suddenly, that whole scene replayed in my head. I had finished reading my mother's diary. I had just explained everything to Jonathan, and he assured me that it was okay to cry. That's when I told him about Edward's note at the end. He held me in his arms and tried to convince me that I could be safe. And I felt so safe in his arms and the quick kiss brought comfort to my conscience. Could he feel this? Could he have ever foreseen this? I breathed in deeply and slowly let it out. But what was only supposed to be a quiet breath came out as another scream, or rather, cry of pain.

I breathed in deeply again, this time, it was Aaron's voice.

"Aren't friends supposed to help each other in times of trouble?" he had questioned me. He was in my room, reading the dairy without my permission. I had gotten so angry with him; I didn't want him to get hurt. Why didn't I try harder? *Maybe if I had tried harder, he might still be alive.* I couldn't think about that. *But what else am I supposed to think about?* Pain interrupted my thoughts for a moment. *Get up.* I breathed in deeply and used my hands to shove myself up to a sitting position. I breathed again, staring right at Edward. Most of the crew had returned to their positions but were glancing my way often. Others, like the two guards, had stayed by my side. I wished that I knew their names. Samuel stared at me, a clear sense of fear in his eyes. Edward looked at me approvingly. I forced myself to a standing position. I moaned in pain and bit the inside of my cheeks, holding in a scream. The two guards immediately turned to Edward, begging him to let them help me to my room. Edward only shook his head. I rolled my eyes. Samuel stomped over to me and picked me up, ignoring his father. I opened my mouth in pain but forced myself to be silent.

"Samuel, you still managed to hurt her," Edward retorted, as if he actually cared about my well-being. Samuel ignored his father. I glanced down at the boards I had laid on. They were covered in blood. My blood.

The rest was a blur. Samuel carried me down to my room, laying me face down on my bed. I took a quick glance at his arms, stained red. It was the last thing I saw before I drifted asleep.

I heard the crack of a whip ring around me. Pain pierced my back at the mere sound. Someone kissed my lips, but I didn't wonder for long. Aaron's kiss was so filled with emotion; it gave me the strength not only to endure but to fight back. I turned around to catch the whip with my arm, prepared to fight Edward. I stared at the man who had been holding the whip. It was Aaron.

C H A P T E R   3 7
Twisted Lies

"No!" I SCREAMED, jumping awake. Immediately I winced in
pain. I glanced out my window. Based on the sun, it was soon to
be evening. I breathed deeply. I felt a cloth soaked in saltwater
on my back. Although it stung terribly, I knew it would help my
condition. I wondered how long it had been there. A dress was
laid out for me to wear since my clothes were shredded. A dress.
I tried to think of the last time I had worn a dress. *Oh wait, you
haven't*, I reminded myself. I wasn't going to start now. Instead
of my shirt, I was wrapped in thick, white cloth from my waist
to just below my collar bone. My shirt, in pieces, was thrown in
the corner. I moved my legs over the edge of the bed, but I heard
someone approaching the door and lay back down.

A young girl with black-brown hair and hazel eyes walked
into the room, wearing a dress similar to the one that was laid out
for me. She placed a hairbrush on the desk under the mirror. She
glanced over at me, and her eyes widened when she noticed I was
awake.

"You're up," she mumbled, half to herself. She nodded to the
dress. "Samuel asked us to find you something to wear and clean
you up. Here's a dress for you," she explained.

"Wait, who's us?" I asked the girl.

"Owen, he's the doctor, Eva, she's my sister, and me, Vivian.
Eva and I both help Owen with his work," Vivian explained. I
nodded in understanding. After some silence, I nodded at the

dress.

"Thanks for everything, but I am not going to wear that," I stated. She gave me a questioning look. Then she shrugged her shoulders.

"I'll go try and find another one, but," she began but I had to interrupt.

"No, I mean I am not going to wear a dress," I clarified. Vivian was flustered. Then she just shook her head and faced me again.

"I'll see what I can do," she mumbled. I began to push myself up, fighting the pain, but Vivian rushed over to me and gently pressed me back down on the bed.

"Try to rest," she urged. I nodded and she walked over to the door to leave.

"Vivian," I caught her before she walked out. "How old are you?" I asked. I didn't know why that was the question that escaped my lips, but it was. She sighed in frustration. I could tell that she was annoyed by my curiosity, but I couldn't help but search for a friend in this prison.

"I'm sixteen, Eva is seventeen, nearly eighteen," she answered, and with that, she walked out the door. I breathed a sigh of relief. While I had enjoyed the company, I hated being so vulnerable among strangers. I wanted to be alone. The stares she gave me were too similar to the stares the crew had given me a few hours ago. Despite this, I had more questions for Vivian whenever she came back in. Loneliness was part of the torture this ship came with – maybe these girls could help me escape that torture. But deep down, I knew they couldn't. The hole that needed filling was far too large. Aaron was gone. *Gone.*

I breathed in and forced myself up. I held in every noise I felt like making. If I made a sound, someone would come running into the room shoving me back on the bed. I slowly walked over to the dress lying on a chair. I let the fabric slide through my hands. The gray dress was simple, but it didn't change the fact that it was a dress. I sat down and looked at myself in the mirror, then carefully began running my hands through my hair, combing through the knots that had formed. It was a more painful task than I had expected. I looked at myself in the mirror then turned around to get a glance at the condition of my back. Even with the mirror shattered, I was able to see how badly my back had been ripped apart. The blood had seeped through the fabric that had been wrapped around me. Suddenly, I heard someone approaching my door again. I assumed it was Vivian, and I tried to get back to my bed, but I wasn't able to move that fast without being in pain. The door opened and another girl walked in. She dropped the tray of herbs and medicines she had probably planned on using to help cure my back.

"Are you Eva?" I asked her quietly as she bent down to quickly pick up her things.

"Yes, in fact, I am. Now, how about you tell me why you decided it would be okay for you to get out of that bed and walk around?" she questioned. Eva was almost two years older than me, according to Vivian, but she spoke with so much more authority than I could muster in a moment like this. She knew her place, and since I was injured, she knew she was the one in charge. I sighed.

"I'm sorry, Eva. I know how frustrating I probably am to all of you, but I am not good at just lying around," I apologized. Eva shook her head with a smile on her face.

"Carter, you aren't frustrating. Just use your head," she replied, her voice kind and gentle. I smiled and Eva guided me to the bed. I laid down with my face on the pillow. Eva slowly unwrapped the white cloth and smeared a variety of juices over my back and talked to me about life on the ship.

"I bet you have guessed, but to reiterate, Edward is a harsh captain. I mean, he's normally not *this* cruel, but he can get a little over the top every once in a while. Somehow, you've managed to pull his strings multiple times in the past two days. I understand why he does what he does, but it doesn't make it right. When Samuel was seven, Edward's wife died, and-"

"What was his wife like?" I interrupted.

"I never met her. My father, Henry, did," Eva explained as she rewrapped the white cloth. "She was an exceptionally beautiful woman, with a very kind personality, but it often seemed that the couple was distant, like the two pretended they were married but didn't live it out. That's what my father said, at least. Which is common. Anyways, his wife died, and Edward seemed to burst. Samuel was left with no mother to care for him, so he was under the care of his father. Edward always spoiled Samuel, giving him the best of everything, promising him that someday he would marry the most perfect woman in the world. But to everyone else, he enforced his rules harder than ever. Beatings like this were common the first month or so, but they eventually died down. The crew had realized it was best if they kept their mouth shut and did as commanded. Especially with the war on the rise. Once we were called to defend American ships, everyone's priorities finally seemed to be aligned, for the first time since Edward's wife's death.

"Then you came along. He hasn't really told the crew why you are here, but I think I have a pretty good guess." Eva paused and the two of us glanced at each other. Then I returned my gaze to the wall in front of me. I didn't feel like explaining my end of the story just yet. Eva sighed and continued. "It was wrong of Edward to torture you with the blindfold and secrecy like that. Or shoot that man, Mr. Harrison. I heard you reacted with, um, great emotion. That's what my father told me. He said they heard you crying from outside the captain's cabin. And then, when Samuel moved you after you finally passed out, father said you were still shaking and crying. All over a man you barely knew…" Eva trailed off and treated my wounds. I clenched my jaw tight as tears stung my eyes. I sounded so weak and pathetic from this point of view. As if Eva had noticed in the silence what I was thinking, she spoke up again. "I found your reaction rather…admirable. To care so much about someone's health and well-being, it's human. And you were very brave for being so honest. If it eases your conscience, he is recovering well."

Wait.

"He's what?" I exclaimed in shock. I felt Eva jump in surprise to my reaction.

"He's recovering well," she repeated. I sat up and turned around to face Eva. She reached out to force me to lie back down, but I just grabbed her hands. I took note of the fear and worry for me in her eyes, but I couldn't feel the pain anymore.

"You mean, he's alive?" I asked her again. Eva only nodded. I started laughing and pulled myself out of the bed. Eva grabbed my wrist, but I was much stronger than her, even recovering. I slipped out from her grip with not so much as a tug.

"Carter, wait! Don't hurt yourself!" Eva exclaimed as I walked towards the door. I turned, feeling nothing but pure joy. I was speechless. What could I say? Aaron was *alive*, and I had thought he was dead! No words could explain this feeling. I thought I had lost him forever. I felt like running to him. I wanted to see his face. I wanted to hold him in my arms. I opened the door and walked through Samuel's room. He wasn't there, so nothing was stopping me. Eva ran up to me and turned me around to face her. I felt no pain. Happiness had numbed me.

"Carter, please. Don't exert yourself like this," Eva begged. I ignored her warnings. There was only one thing I wanted to know.

"Where is Harrison?" I asked Eva, so stern even I wouldn't recognize it as my own voice. Eva stiffened, and then guided me to the room, at a pace that wouldn't allow me to run. Despite my demands, she held to her word. She wasn't going to let me get hurt. In a way, I felt cared for, but these thoughts were overpowered by my need to see Aaron. Alive. As we arrived, she slowly opened the door.

A man I assumed was Owen was hovering over Aaron. His eyes were fixed on Aaron's shoulder, slowly unwrapping the white cloth that matched the cloth covering my torso. My heart rate went up. I bolted over to Aaron, grabbed his hand, and began to cry tears of joy. Aaron opened his eyes and looked straight into mine. His smile contained more emotion and power than the ocean itself. Even the sea seemed still in comparison.

"Carter, why are you here?" he asked me, using his other arm to place a strand of my golden hair behind my ear, then cupped my cheek. I couldn't even think of words. "Please stop crying Carter; it makes me feel like something bad is happening," Aaron urged. I managed a laugh and wiped the tears of joy from my cheeks.

"What happened to you?" he asked, realizing that I had exchanged my old, worn clothes for bandaging. His hand moved down my back. I grimaced, but that was all. It was just enough for Aaron to notice the pain. He brought his hand back up and rubbed my cheek with his thumb. "Carter, what happened?" he asked me with more seriousness this time. I squeezed his hand with both of mine and shook my head.

"It doesn't matter. You're alive, that's all I care about right now," I replied. Then I pressed my lips against his knuckles. I forgave and forgot the incident where he faked being a crew member here, chasing after me. I was just happy he was alive. It was as if all the hardships that this ship had forced me to experience in just a matter of two days had been picked up and taken with the ocean winds. I felt safe in the middle of this dangerous ship. But Aaron pulled his hand away and placed it back by his side.

Owen returned to Aaron's side, giving me a confused glance every once in a while, making me more aware of how immodest my choice of clothing was, then he glared at Eva behind me. I glanced back at Eva. She managed to find an old shirt and helped me put it on over the cloth that had been serving as my shirt until now. I stood up; the pain was beyond words, but still better than this morning. Half of the pain I had been bearing was emotional, and now that weight had been lifted. But Owen and Eva didn't understand that. Judging by the glare Owen had given Eva, I owed her an apology for my seemingly unexplainable actions.

"I'm sorry Eva, I just…" I trailed off. My words failed me as I glanced over at Aaron. He still looked to be in so much pain. I wished there was a way I could help.

"Yeah, I think you owe me an explanation, but after you get back in your room. You aren't ready to be *running* through the halls," she retorted, but there was a smile on her face, assuring me that she wasn't too mad at me. Owen, on the other hand, still wasn't smiling.

"Yes," Aaron agreed from behind me. I glanced back his way, but only for a second. My happiness waned as reality sunk in, and now my pain was more prominent. "The next time I see you, I would like it if you had *actual* clothes on," he exclaimed. This time it was Aaron receiving Owen's disapproving eyes. I blushed a deep red at his words, but the sound of his voice was music to my ears. *He's alive.*

I walked towards Eva and she opened the door. The two of us walked in silence. I fiddled with the ends of the stranger's shirt I wore. I guessed Eva was thinking about what she had just witnessed, going through a series of events that ended up with her patient running to the arms of some crew member, crying tears of joy. My thoughts could be summed up in one word. Aaron.

He was alive. Everyone had convinced me he was dead. But I just held his hand. He just touched my face. Aaron was *alive*. When we finally reached the door to Samuel's room, Edward was blocking our way.

"What on earth are you doing out?" Edward questioned me, anger in his tone, his eyes revealed a different emotion: amazement. Eva quickly stepped up.

"Sir, I can explain," she began. I put a hand on her shoulder and moved her aside. This wasn't her battle to fight. A sharp pain moved through my back as I stepped up to stand face to face with Edward, but I was filled with a new emotion now. Anger.

"You lied to me," I exclaimed behind gritted teeth. He watched as I cried out my heart when I believed Aaron was dead. He watched as if it was a show to enjoy from balcony seats at a theatre. I wasn't an actress, and this wasn't a play. This was my *life*.

"About what?" he snapped back as if he didn't know what I was talking about. But the way his lip quivered after he finished speaking proved that he knew I had discovered his little secret.

"When did you plan to tell me?" I questioned him. Eva's eyes widened as she saw the argument escalate. Now it was her turn to put her hand on my shoulder and move to stand between Edward and me. For a split second, her eyes met mine, filling with fear. She was scared Edward would try to hurt me again. I was her patient; she wanted me safe. I gave in to her fearful eyes. I couldn't make trouble for Eva, no more than I already had. She nodded and then turned to Edward.

"We are sorry we disturbed you, Captain Jacobs. She needed a breath of fresh air and has been seeing things all day. She woke up screaming from an insane dream,"-at least that part was true- "and can't keep herself still. I thought a walk would do her good. It seems I was wrong," she finished, glancing my way only for a second. I thought I had developed the best lying skills by living with pirates, but this woman was a natural. Even I believed her story.

"It seems so," Edward mumbled angrily, as he stepped out

of our way and we walked through the door. Eva shut the door and we walked into the room. We walked through Samuel's space, then opened the second door that led to the room I was staying in and she helped me lay down on the bed. She and I breathed a sigh of annoyance at the same time, but not for the same reason. Her annoyance was directed at me, while mine was directed at Edward. It didn't matter, I was still the one injured, so she was the one with authority.

"Get some rest," she said. I nodded, even though I knew it would be so hard to sleep with so many thoughts running through my mind. "When I come back, I want an explanation for… whatever just happened right then. That was a string of unnecessary events that nearly ended up with me in your position. It better have been worth it," she exclaimed, trying to act angry, but she was scared. The way she bit down on her bottom lip and stared at my back gave it away. My actions were rash and selfish, and I didn't realize how it may have impacted Eva. As I began to force myself to sleep, I prayed that Eva would not have to face the bloody, painful whip. I prayed that I would not be the cause of anyone else's pain except for my own.

CHAPTER 38

The Dinner

His hand slowly slid under my shirt, resting in the small of my back. It was rough from the years of life on the ship, but every time they moved, I felt comfortable. The other slid around my waist pulling me closer to him. My hand wrapped around his waist while the other was pulling his neck, then moved into his soft, dirty blonde hair. His lips were gently pressed against mine.

Jonathan.

"Get up!" Eva whispered in my ear. My eyelids fluttered open. As my vision cleared, I saw Eva sitting next to me, her hand tapping my shoulder lightly. It was the middle of the night, and the stars glistened over the black ocean just outside the porthole. My room was filled with the light of oil lamps. A golden gown was laid out on my chair. I sat up quickly, but a piercing pain in my back reminded me of my weakness.

"Eva, I told Vivian that I…" I tried to explain to Eva as I slowly sat up.

"I know," a voice interrupted. It wasn't Eva. Vivian came out from the corner of the room. My eyes widened in surprise. Her hazel eyes glared at me and, for some reason, they seemed to tear me apart. Eva's hands shook as she stared at Vivian. Eva may have been older than Vivian, but Vivian was the tough one of the two.

"We have orders from Captain Jacobs that you will meet Samuel on the main deck wearing this," Vivian continued, an angered tone filled her words. "I don't try to make people unhappy, but no one else wants to be the bearer of bad news, so that job happens to fall on me," Vivian stated when she noticed I had raised my eyebrows. Part of me wanted to believe her, but I could tell she was hiding something from me. Something in her tone was off.

Eva took my hand and she and I walked to the chair. She steadied my body as I leaned back, wincing as my back made contact with the chair. But I needed to overcome my pain. I decided to think about my dream. A dream filled with passion and love, emotions I would never feel aboard this ship. Eva combed through my hair and made two small braids and tied them together in a bun behind my head. It was so simple, but stunning at the same time. I stood up. Eva and Vivian helped me into the dress, tying it tightly around my torso. I ignored the pain in my back once again. Soon, by ignoring it, the pain from the lashes went away altogether. Something else was going to happen. I had to step away from the pain of the past so that I could bear a new pain, though I had no clue what it would be. Vivian straightened the creases in the dress. I looked stunning. I wasn't used to looking like this. If someone painted a portrait of me now, I would find myself unrecognizable. Night three on this ship and I no longer recognized myself. The dress felt heavy, and, between the lash wounds and the corset, I could barely breathe. Eva stepped back to look at me and, a few moments later, she began to cry. My eyes widened in shock. I turned around quickly and moved toward her.

"What's wrong?" I asked her. She shook her head.

"Carter just don't get into trouble. I am not kidding. Edward always has his gun on him, and lately, he hasn't been afraid to use it. He threatened me that if you didn't get your act together, he would shoot you tonight so that the most beautiful night of your life would be your last," she sniffled. I shook my head with a half-smile, but inside I was feeling a twinge of worry that I quickly shoved away, for Eva's sake.

"He's got it all wrong, Eva. Tonight will be one of the worst nights of my life; so clearly, he's not talking about tonight," I replied. Eva merely nodded. Vivian gave me a look of approval and guided me down the hall. She carried a weight in her eyes that made her seem older. Like pain. Eva stayed behind in my room, cleaning up around the bed. I caught her eye and mouthed 'goodbye' then faced forward.

Samuel was not in his room. What was I expecting? I had already guessed what was going on. It was just another one of Edward's setups to see if I would say I would marry Samuel. But I spotted Samuel's knife, the same one I had picked up before, lying on his desk. *He will never learn, will he?* When Vivian wasn't looking, I picked it up and hid it under the folds of my skirt. The only thing dresses seemed to be good for was hiding things in plain sight. Pain, knives, truth – all could be lost in the waves of a dress's skirt.

We walked through the hall until we approached the final staircase to the main deck. Silver moonlight mixed with golden candlelight to illuminate the steps as I walked up carefully, trying not to step on the dress. In the center of the main deck was a small table set for two. Candlesticks sat in the center of the table, the wax already dripping down the sides. Samuel was already seated, dressed in his best, same as I. Slowly, I approached the table and glanced around the main deck and spotted two silhouettes, one standing, one crouching, but I couldn't make either of them out. I gave up and continued to follow Vivian closer to the table.

Samuel stood up and nodded to Vivian. He gave a weak smile, but something in his eyes said much more. It was a look of longing and begging for forgiveness. Pain glistened in Vivian's – the same pain I had seen in Aaron's eyes when…I was barely able to keep my jaw from dropping. She loved Samuel, and maybe once he felt the same towards her, but Edward's plans had ruined that. In the candlelight, I noticed the tears shimmering on her eyelids, but her jaw was clamped shut, either in anger or by order of her captain. I thought my pain was great. Vivian had lost everything to a tortured stranger that she was forced to care for. My stubbornness probably only made things worse. Samuel moved to take my hand, but I kept it out of his reach until he gave up.

"I can seat myself, thank you," I said kindly, but with an edge to let him know that I was still mad at him. Both of us sat down and stared at the table. There was no food or water. Just silence and candlelight. *Not much of a dinner.*

"Carter, please, let me explain," Samuel eventually said, but there was nothing left to explain.

"Explain what?" I questioned him, "Explain that you have been lying to me for the past two days about Aaro-Mr. Harrison? Or that, after I explained my entire life story in detail, you decided it was okay to kiss me? Where do you want to start, Samuel? When do you feel like there are too many secrets floating around?" I didn't care if those two silhouettes were here to kill me if I dared to say something like this. The truth had to be said.

"About Mr. Harrison, well, I can't really…" he trailed off. I rolled my eyes. Then I leaned over the table, closing any gap for his escape. Samuel stiffened in his seat, but it didn't phase me.

"Can't you see Samuel; I am tired of not knowing. Just tell me," I begged him. He bit the inside of his cheek and glanced at the two silhouettes. I followed his eyes. I figured out one man over there; no surprise, it was Edward. Then, he returned his gaze to me.

"There are more secrets on this ship than you can even imagine, Carter. I only know a select few," he eventually replied. I sat back a little.

"Tell me the ones you know then. Anything can help me right now," I urged. He sighed and almost smiled.

"This is supposed to be one of those dinners where you fall in love," he stated, half to himself. I rolled my eyes.

"Samuel please. There isn't even food on the table. This wasn't meant to be a dinner. Just be honest with me," He glanced over at the silhouettes again.

"I can't, for your own good," Samuel replied, not even looking at me. Angered, I pulled the knife from the folds of my dress.

"Samuel," I stated behind gritted teeth, stabbing his knife into the table. At the sound, Samuel quickly turned around and stared in awe at the knife in the table.

"How did you…?" he questioned me. A wry smile formed on my face and I shook my head.

"As you said, there are many secrets, I only know a few," I snapped. I pulled the knife out of the table and pointed it at him.

"Yet, there are many you don't know, Ms. Key," said Edward's voice coming from the corner of the deck where the shadow was hiding his face. He bent down and grabbed the wrists of the man who was hunched over. I realized the man was tied up. Edward dragged him into the light. As he came closer, I realized the man was shirtless and his back was covered in blood. Lashes. As he came completely into the light, I recognized him. I dropped my knife and rushed over to him.

"Jonathan? Jonatha! Are you okay? Can you hear me? Jonathan, please speak to me." I moved some of his blond strands of hair away from his face. I watched as his eyelids blinked open to reveal his beautiful blue eyes. I breathed a sigh of relief and almost smiled. He slowly forced himself to sit up. I didn't stop him. He wouldn't have stopped me. I held his face in my hands.

"Why are you here?" I asked him, almost crying. I moved to untie the rope that was keeping his hands together behind his back, then moved back in front of him. He glanced up at Edward for a moment, and then returned his gaze to me.

"I was convinced," he replied. I shook my head. I glanced at his back, but I already had guessed. I ignored the world around me and placed my hands on his neck. Jonathan understood perfectly. He wrapped his arms around my waist and pulled me closer to his chest. His lips gently pressed against mine, delicate and careful. I wanted to pull him closer to me, but his back was covered in blood, and I knew he was in pain. But this kiss reminded me why I told Jonathan when I first read the diary, why I chose him over Aaron, why I picked him for my final goodbye. He pulled me closer, I felt the warmth from his chest, and I immediately felt at home. His lips pressed harder against mine while one of his hands moved up my back, but I didn't even wince. Our lips parted only for a moment; somehow Jonathan managed to whisper: "I love you." But then the reality around us came into full view once again.

"Interesting, don't you think so Aaron?" Edward announced. In shock, Jonathan's lips left mine and I immediately turned in the direction Edward was facing. I hadn't even seen him lurking in the shadows.

"Aaron?" I asked, standing up. Jonathan stood up relatively quickly behind me.

"Carter," he stated. I heard a mixture of sadness, disappointment, and maybe even happiness in his voice.

"Aaron, please let me explain. I'm sorry, I just, Jonathan and I…you and I…," I got lost in my own words.

"No, Carter. I understand; it's okay," he assured me. I glanced at Jonathan and then began to walk towards Aaron.

"I am so sorry," I whispered as Aaron took my hands.

"No, you aren't," he said, lifting my head to face his. There was a smile on his face. "You're just saying that. You wouldn't have been apologetic if I weren't here. But it's okay, I think I finally figured it out.

"At first, I thought there was no such thing as 'in between' because I grew up only seeing hatred and evil. I was wrong. I think that there is a spot where one can be more than just a friend, where you love them with all of your heart, but your heart doesn't belong to them. It's a place with no name, a place of constant guilt, constant regret, constant revelation, and constant love. I don't know what it is, but I found it. I'm sorry for pulling you away from Jonathan. You both love each other so much…" My jaw dropped. He curled my hair around my ear, and I grabbed his hand and held it tightly. I pulled him closer to whisper one last sentence in his ear, one I didn't want certain people around me to hear.

"Be my hero," I whispered. I felt his cheeks rise in a smile.

"I would love to be your hero," he whispered back, his smile growing bigger. *Is that even possible? Did he really just say that to me?* I thought to myself. I had never been more relieved in my life.

"You will be. No more, and no less," I whispered in his ear one last time.

CHAPTER 39

Rage

"Well, Carter, now that you have finally solved the problem your mother couldn't," Edward began, and almost immediately pulled out two guns, pointing one in Aaron and I's direction and the other at Jonathan. My eyes should not have widened with surprise, but they did. Samuel came in between Aaron and me and got down on one knee with a simple silver band carefully balanced in his fingers. I shook my head.

"Samuel, why are you doing this?" I asked him, but I was screaming. I wanted to know the real answer this time.

"Because I love you, Carter," he replied. In the corner of my eye, Edward was giving a nod of approval to his son. It's what he wanted Samuel to say. His son was just a puppet, an actor reciting lines he was forced to memorize. I was determined to change the story.

"No, you don't; you love Vivian. I saw that look in your eyes when she glanced your way. It's why she is constantly angry at me. Before I came along, you loved her. But I'm here now, and you can't anymore. Because your *father* said so," I snapped back. Samuel glanced down on the ground, but he returned his gaze to me.

"That's not true, Carter," he fought back. I groaned, rolling my eyes.

"Stop being a child! Your father can't tell you who to love or who to marry!" I replied harshly. But he ignored me and kept on.

"Carter, will you marry me? Not just for the good of your own heart, but Jonathan and Aaron's as well," he continued. He was threatening me. Just like his father. It was either I marry him, and Jonathan and Aaron live, or I don't, and they die.

"I want you to know that I will never love you," I muttered angrily at Samuel. I glanced at Aaron, he looked like he was about to punch someone, and I looked at Jonathan. He closed his eyes for a moment, holding in tears. This moment was meant for him. The ring. My hand. Down on one knee. Underneath the stars. I looked at Samuel and nodded. I wanted to punch him or cry or both. If the guns weren't pointed at Jonathan and Aaron's heads, I would have punched him, and I wouldn't have agreed. But that wasn't the case. And the cold metal ring slipped around my finger, binding me to a promise I didn't want to keep. As he stood up, I walked away from him. Aaron tried to say something to me, but I ignored him. Something more powerful than rage consumed me – defeat.

As I walked through the hall to the room Edward had given me, I ran into Vivian. Her eyes widened in shock as her gaze caught on the sliver on my finger. I glanced her way then stared down at the ground.

"I am so sorry this had to happen to you Vivian," I said to her as I walked away. Even if she fell in love again, there was no doubt in my mind that she would ever forget the day when the man she loved so much was stolen from her by someone who didn't even want him. I didn't want to be that someone, but Edward had given me no choice. I stormed into my room, slamming the door behind me. I stared at the shattered mirror. I wanted to fix it so I could shatter it again.

I looked down at my dress. I wanted to take it off and wear normal clothes. I wanted to wear a worn shirt and patched up pants, not a princess dress. I walked over to the corner where my shirt lay, with my pants neatly folded next to them. In pain, I attempted to untie the top of the dress, letting out a wail of pain. It wasn't fair, I wanted out of this dress. I wanted out of this engagement. I ripped the skirt, but it only fueled my anger. The tight corset, this dress, it had to get off of me. Another shout of frustration. I stared at myself in the broken mirror, helpless in this tattered dress. I wiped my eyes, but I wasn't crying. Then I heard someone come running down the hall, no doubt running after me. I prepared myself for the worst. I heard someone open the door to Samuel's room and pause. Then, whoever it was continued running towards the door that connected his room to this one.

Jonathan came running into the room.

I breathed a sigh of relief. Now tears shimmered at the edge of my eyes.

"Jonathan, what are you doing here?" I stared at him -- both confused and worried. The blood was drying on his back and he needed to be cleaned up. He should not have been running. But I reminded myself of my reaction when I learned Aaron was alive. Pain becomes obsolete. I blinked away the tears. He looked at me, my braids now a mess and the skirt of my dress ripped. It was embarrassing. This wasn't me.

"How can you still look so beautiful?" he whispered and smiled weakly at me. I shook my head with a sad smile.

"So...this is my first time wearing a dress and I am learning I can't take one off," I replied, sniffling. He chuckled a bit and walked over to me. Both of our lives – our dreams – had been destroyed, and yet, here we were, smiling and laughing with each other, pretending I wasn't engaged to an insane man's son.

"Do you want some help?" he asked gently. I gave him a weak smile and nodded. "Don't worry, I will just loosen it, you can do the rest on your own," he assured me. Privacy, and someone who actually respected it. On this ship, such a concert didn't seem to exist. I turned and he untied the back of the dress and revealed the corset, which he then loosened. I could finally breathe. He paused for a second. I didn't turn to face him; he didn't move to stand in front of me. His fingers gently touched the top of the white cloth that covered my wound. I sucked in a breath and bit my lip.

"Carter?" The way his voice quavered when he said my name, though it might have been a question, he already knew the answer. The sound broke my heart. I turned to face him, biting my lip.

"He hurt us both, Jonathan," I whispered and gently traced his jawline with my fingertips. "In more ways than one." He took my hand gently, lovingly, and moved it from his face. He looked down and my gaze raked over his face. He had bags under his eyes from a lack of sleep and bruises on his cheeks from where he had been beaten. His face had thinned, making his bone structure more visible. Had the crew of this ship known? Had the crew of my home known?

"What happened?" I managed to whisper.

"When you asked me to come aboard, they didn't let me leave. They pulled me into a dark room and gagged me. I was fed once a day, and, if Edward was in a bad mood, he would let his anger out on me. One day, he was so happy, that he untied me, ungagged me, and let me roam around the room. They gave me two meals that day. It was a day or two ago, I think. I lost track of time," he explained. The day where he pretended to kill Aaron. The day he watched as my heart was broken in two. It was silent for a moment. Edward was so happy that he broke my heart. He thought he had finally broken me.

"What about you?" Jonathan asked me, breaking the silence. I breathed.

"I'm stubborn, and I know how to pull his strings. He's a strict captain and I broke his rules. The punishment was fifteen lashes. At the moment, I was more than willing to take them." I paused, my words softening. "No, I wasn't willing, I wanted them," I replied, half to myself. It was true.

"Wanted them?" he questioned me. I nodded. "Why?"

"That day when Edward was so happy, well, Aaron spoke up for me that day. I had warned him not to, but it didn't matter. So, Edward shoved me into his quarters and shot him. He told me that he had...killed Aaron. Samuel told me the same thing. Edward thought he had finally destroyed me that day," I explained, "He almost did." Jonathan moved closer to me. I looked up at him.

"I wanted to die, you know," Jonathan murmured. Now we weren't talking about days past; we were talking about tonight. The band on my finger grew colder.

"I couldn't watch you die," I replied.

"I know," he whispered in my ear. He paused for a moment and I met his gaze firmly before turning away.

"I hope everyone on *The Adventurer* is alright. I wonder what they think happened," I mumbled, changing the subject. I couldn't dwell on tonight's event any longer. But Jonathan wasn't ready to leave it behind.

"This is a fate worse than death. I love you and I want you to be happy. With you marrying Samuel, everything is in shambles. At least when you were considering Aaron, you would have been happy." He began to cry. I guided him to the bed and sat down. His face fell in my lap as he began to cry. I tried to remember the last time I saw Jonathan cry like this. But I couldn't manage to think of one moment as miserable as this. Even when Captain died, he still kept himself together. It broke my heart to see him this way. I gently rubbed my fingers in his hair, letting silent tears drip down my cheeks. It was my turn to be strong for him, but neither of us were strong enough for this.

We lost track of time. I didn't know how long we sat like that before two of Edward's crewmen came to drag him from my arms. He screamed and fought them, and I cried. He didn't escape their hold. It was worse than a nightmare.

CHAPTER 40
Talking

THIS WASN'T FAIR. None of it. Anger filled my brain as I stripped myself of the cursed dress. I shouldn't be engaged to a stranger. Jonathan shouldn't be suffering on this ship. Aaron shouldn't be recovering from a gunshot wound. All three of us should have been living our happy, mostly normal lives aboard the *Adventurer*. Once the dress was off, I grabbed the shirt and blood-stained pants and put them back on. I didn't care how miserable I looked, at least it was more myself. I was angry at Samuel. I was angry at Edward. They had stolen everything that I thought had belonged to me: my home, my friends, my life, and my heart. The one thing they had left me with was rage. They thought they could squash my fire, but they had been wrong. They had set me ablaze. I had to fight. I had defeated the pirates; I could defeat Edward too. And I would do so with dignity, unlike Edward. Just like on the pirate ship, I would escape. A mutiny. It was my last and final option.

I stood up and stomped out of the room and into Samuel's.

"I'm still awake," he stated once I entered. He turned up onto his pillow, facing me. "Is there something you want to talk about?" Samuel asked me innocently.

"Sure, if you want to tell me where you store your weapons on this ship, or where they are keeping Jonathan," I replied, walking past him, headed towards the exit. I couldn't even look at him.

"Not exactly the conversation starter I had in mind, but if you want to know, I will tell you if we sit down and talk like we were supposed to at that table. Speaking of which, why are you back in that old sailor's shirt again?" he asked. I ignored his question.

"The last time we 'talked', it didn't exactly have the best ending," I stopped, turned to face him, and crossed my arms. Samuel sighed and laid down on his back again. I rolled my eyes. I wasn't going to get anywhere at this rate, so I put my hand on the door. I didn't need his help. I could find things myself.

"You know, we are going to be married," he stated. I didn't know if he was talking to me or himself. I stopped and looked at him.

"I am aware of this fact, Samuel. It doesn't mean I am okay with it," I snapped back. He turned to face me again.

"It doesn't mean I'm okay with it either." This made me pause. "You were right about Vivian. She's a lovely girl and will grow up to be a fine woman. Just as Jonathan is a fine man. But both of us will have to come to terms with our losses," he continued. I rolled my eyes and pulled a chair up to his bed. If this was the only way I could gain his trust, I would do it. The more the merrier in this mutiny. This ship had a larger crew than the pirates. I couldn't win with only myself. Samuel sat up, almost stunned.

"I'll take you up on your deal. Let's talk," I stated. Samuel swallowed and nodded, surprised.

"Um okay then. Where do you want to start?" he asked me.

"Why would you listen to your father when he told you to propose to me when you knew that you were in love with Vivian?" I questioned him. Samuel nodded, but I could hear him gulp. *This is what he wants, isn't it?* If this question was too difficult to answer, maybe he would give up on this whole endeavor.

"Because my father convinced me that it would be best for me. He knew about Vivian, and he explained that our love was a fantasy, that it would never work out. He told me that Vivian would eventually return to land, but I would remain at sea. Our love would be a mere shadow of the past. I don't doubt my father's judgment; he knows me almost as well as I know myself. And he's already gone through this part of life. He doesn't want me to make the same mistakes that he did," Samuel finished, breaking away from my gaze near the end. I nodded, pretending to understand. I disagreed with him, but that didn't really matter.

"Okay, my turn," he exclaimed. I rolled my eyes; somehow, Samuel managed to turn whatever this was into a game. "How did you finally convince Aaron that the passion felt between the two of you was not love?" I smiled at myself, reminded of only moments ago when I promised him that he could be my hero.

"You've got it all wrong, Samuel. That passion *is* love, it's just not the 'I'm going to marry you' type of love. It's… a weird love. It's like he's my family, but I've only known him for a month or so. There's just some special connection that is without explanation," I explained. "Now, I can't explain how he finally came to accept our situation, but I am very glad he did." Samuel nodded. I realized that it was once again my turn to ask him a question. I breathed.

"How many girls have you actually 'fallen in love with' in the past?" I asked. He sighed and thought about it for a moment.

"Two, tops," he answered. "Jessica was the first. That was three years ago. She left the ship to work with her sister. Then Vivian, of course," he replied. I smiled.

"I knew you didn't love me," I muttered happily to myself. His head shot up.

"You said in the past," he countered. I rolled my eyes. It was his turn to ask a question, unfortunately.

"Hum, it's hard to think of questions since you've already told me everything about you," he explained after a moment or two of not asking questions. I was still bitter about that. Making such a statement was only rubbing salt in the wound. "Why couldn't you kill that pirate captain even though he was the man who killed your father?" he asked me. I was shocked that he could ever think of me doing such a thing. I was hurt. I knew that I had been an angry trouble-maker while aboard *The Cobra*, but I was no killer.

"Don't you see, Samuel? If I did that, I would be going against everything I believed. I would become the person I loathed. I would be going down to his level if I killed him!" I exclaimed, furious. I would never be able to kill anyone. I had seen the pain that death creates, felt it.

"Okay, okay, I'm sorry," he tried to calm me down. I just ignored his words. It was my turn, and I had a question.

"Why did you lie to me about Aaron?" I asked him. The room fell strangely quiet.

"We – I thought you loved him. I needed you to say yes if I asked you, but you only got more secretive. You tried to get on my father's nerves more often, getting you into more trouble, but my father blamed me. He wanted to kill you, but I told him he couldn't. He said I'd better get my act together, and I tried. I tried especially hard with the dinner, but my father had a plan of his own. If I failed, we would switch. And I did. You pulled the knife, and I was done. I didn't know my father had Jonathan. It angered me to discover this secret just as much as you," he explained. I seriously doubted that last statement. It angered him? It infuriated me. Tension weighed down on us. I was still upset with Samuel, his choices, his actions. But I pitied him too. He grew up with a father who never truly loved his mother, a father who dictated his life, a father who lived through his son, rather than letting his son live.

"Samuel, when are we getting married?" I asked him. Despite how much I wanted to avoid the question, this was the reality that plagued me.

"My father said tomorrow, but if that doesn't work for you, I can see what I can do," he replied softly. I gulped hard. Tomorrow? He couldn't be serious!

"Just give me one more night, Samuel. I can't bear it if I marry you tomorrow," I explained. He nodded. It was the truth, but there were other reasons as well. After tomorrow, there was a tiny chance the *Adventurer* would be back, or that I could pull a mutiny together by then.

"As I said, I'll see what I can do," he replied. I glanced out the window and wondered how late it was. Two, three in the morning? I stood up and began to walk back to my room.

"Wait, what about the weapons? And, and Jonathan?" he asked me. I returned a weak smile.

"Tomorrow morning, first thing." And I continued walking into my room. *Tomorrow. My fourth day on this ship.* So much had happened in these past three days. I was taken from my home. I had been beaten. I believed Aaron to be dead, then he was alive. I found Jonathan tortured and abused. And now I was engaged. Edward was right, he did coax it out of me. He pulled all the right strings to make me succumb. I glanced back at Samuel one more time before closing the door that connected the two rooms. I knew that he was probably wondering what I wanted with the weapons, or he might have already guessed. Maybe he knew and wanted it too, but he was just scared to admit it. All I wanted was to avoid getting married.

I fell into the bed. Almost immediately, the idea of comfort and rest surrounded me, and I fell into a dark, dreamless sleep. For the first time in months, I was too tired to be plagued by my nightmares. But it was so short. I only got to sleep for a few hours before the first beams of sunlight danced through the porthole and forced my eyelids to open. I realized that, if the Adventurer didn't come for Aaron, Jonathan and me, this mutiny would be the last chance I had to keep the name Carter Ellen Key.

CHAPTER 41

Weapons

I SHOVED MYSELF OUT OF THE BED. On the chair, instead of a dress, were pants and a clean white shirt, neither stained with my blood. I ran over to the chair. Normal clothes for my last half-way normal day as Carter Ellen Key. I held in the tears as the thought entered my mind. Carter Ellen Key, the name my parents had given me. If I ever thought of my name changing, never had I imagined the name Carter Ellen Jacobs. A note was left on top of the shirt. I picked it up and read it quickly.

You looked lovely last night, but if you insist.

-SJ

Lovely? Did I look lovely stabbing his knife into the table? Or when I was crying and reluctantly nodding yes to your stupid offer of marriage while the two men whom I care about most deeply about had a gun to their heads? My jaw tightened, and I threw the note back on the shirt. I asked him to help me find weapons and the love of my life, and he decided that the appropriate response was to call me *lovely*. I didn't change into the clothes. Not if Samuel gave them to me attached to a note like that. I tugged off my shirt and the white cloth that was covering my wounds. I wrapped myself in the new white cloth and pulled my stained shirt back over my head. It was gross and smelly and raggedy, but it wasn't tainted by *him*. And I walked into Samuel's room.

"Didn't like the clothes I provided?" Samuel asked immediately upon seeing me. I shook my head.

"These are mine, and those were yours. I like mine better," I retorted. Samuel laughed a little. I couldn't believe that joy was possible right now. Today was our last day as the people we wanted to be, and that was if Edward had agreed to delay the wedding.

"Are you ready to get your hands on some weapons?" he asked me a little too enthusiastically. I nodded, not even trying to fake a smile. Samuel swallowed loudly, realizing that his optimism was not appreciated. He opened the door, but I waited for him to walk through first. He raised his eyebrows but eventually left the room taking the lead. I followed closely behind him. My mind wandered, wondering if he had been able to delay the wedding, or if he had even spoken with his father since last night.

The weapons were located in a room a few levels below the main deck, somewhere in the quarterdeck. To be honest, I was quite lost. My first day and a half on this ship, I had spent blindfolded, and now, when I was no longer blind, I was realizing how large this ship truly was. But this tool room seemed to be in an awkward place. It wasn't convenient for an unexpected battle, in my opinion, but I hadn't grown up on a warship, so how would I know? He opened the door to the room. Guns of all shapes and sizes covered the back walls while swords and daggers filled barrels. My jaw dropped in shock. I couldn't wrap my mind around the fact that this ship could still float with all this weight. The guns scared me. I made my way to the swords where I felt safer.

"The guns would be your best bet, Carter," he mentioned, off to the side. He had already guessed what I was planning.

"Our best bet," I corrected him. He thought he understood all of my intentions, but I was not as self-centered as he assumed. He gave me a confused look. "Be honest with yourself, Samuel. You can't possibly be in love with me, even if you thought you were. You've lied to me and I've kept secrets from you. Your father can't stand me, but he loved my mother. You 'love' me based on your father's biased word. Besides, the look in your eyes isn't love, like it is when you see Vivian. When you see her, you long to be with her. Even when you were at dinner with me, she was the one you wanted to be with. When you look at me, it's like you're faking, or begging. I don't mean that as an insult. Just letting you know," I finished, leaning against the barrel of swords. Samuel only sighed.

"I guess you're right, Carter. I cared for you because of my father, and the look in my eyes when I see you is probably begging because I want to please my father so badly by conceding to his wishes, which you refuse to grant. I feel knots in my stomach when I look at Vivian, but…" he was silent for a moment. I didn't say anything. Whatever he was going to say, I wasn't going to try and force it. "But I think I want to love you. You are quite the character," he finished. I just shook my head and laughed. Yes, I actually laughed.

"Samuel, you can't force love! It just happens," I told him, "Trust me if I could control if I loved someone or not, I would never fall in love." Samuel managed a small smile and raised an eyebrow of curiosity. "Don't get me wrong. I love Jonathan with all of my heart, and I wouldn't trade that for anything."

He chuckled. "So, if you could control it, you would still choose love." I thought about it for a moment. I guess I was a bit contradictory.

"I guess you're right, Samuel. Now that I know what true love is, I choose to love Jonathan more every day. Choosing to never fall in love, that's something the old Carter would have said."

"The old Carter?" he asked with curiosity.

"Yeah, the old Carter," I sighed, not caring to elaborate.

"So, you're okay if I don't like you?" he asked. I laughed.

"Completely. You're not going to fall in love with every girl that lays eyes on you. And not every girl that lays eyes on you is going to fall for you," I laughed. He released a sigh and smiled. I assumed his father had told him something on the contrary.

"We will never forget this," he exclaimed and started laughing at the thought. I calmed my laughter and smiled at him. He was right, we never would. My thoughts twisted his words into a meaning darker than he had intended. The wounds on my back would remind me every day of the pain I suffered while fighting for my love. And if Samuel and I got married, it would all be for nothing. Those scars would serve as a reminder of the dreams that I lost. I shook the idea away. We would escape this fate. I glanced over at Samuel, who was collecting weapons, as I should have been.

"We can always be friends, Samuel," I told him. He nodded.

"I would like that very much," he replied. This moment was surreal – simply too good to be true.

"Okay, well, back on topic," I breathed heavily. "Guns. I can't hold one to save my life. Well, that's not exactly true, but I think you know what I mean. They are terrifying. If you want to use one, go for it. I just would rather not; I don't want to kill people in this mutiny, however naive that seems. It is your *father* we're attacking," I explained. Samuel nodded and pulled a pistol off the back wall. I pulled out a few swords to test the balance and length in accordance with my body.

"So, this a mutiny?" he asked me when I was on my third or fourth sword. I snorted. *I thought that much was obvious.*

"If we refuse to marry each other tomorrow, yes," I said.

"And you are prepared for the big no?" he said, almost laughing. He thought he knew the answer. But this question had floated in the back of my mind since Edward had spoken to me about the marriage. His threats were anchored in my mind.

"No," I replied softly, just loud enough for Samuel to hear my answer. He stopped looking at the guns and walked over to me. Yet another weight rested on the both of us.

"You're not? Why?" he asked me, placing his hand on my shoulder. I turned and moved his hand off my shoulder. Samuel was sweet and meant well, but I knew more about the happenings on this ship than he did.

"Your father threatened to sink my ship, kill my family if they came back before we were married. That's why this attack has to work. You want to be with Vivian, and I want to be back home," I explained. He nodded.

"When exactly is this attack?" he asked me.

"Well, I think I can get the manpower by tonight," I said, thinking aloud. He looked at me confused, but I didn't care to spell it all out for him. "You will show me where they are keeping Jonathan, right?" He nodded and I echoed the action. "I have a few other ideas about men that might help us. So we will attack tomorrow."

C H A P T E R 4 2

Convincing

"Tomorrow!" he almost shouted. I immediately rushed over and covered his mouth.

"Good grief, Samuel, are you trying to give us away?" I snapped. He pulled my hand off his mouth. He shrugged his shoulders to say "sorry" and that was enough for me. I grabbed the swords and a few daggers as Samuel picked up two guns for himself. With that, the two of us slipped out of the weapons room. After a shout like that, it was only a matter of time before someone found us. We both ran to his room. Miraculously, we arrived without being caught. We both took deep, frantic breaths. I stared at the weapons that we had dropped on the floor in our haste.

"So, that manpower?" he asked me between catching his breath.

"Jonathan, Aaron, Eva, Vivian, Owen, and Henry," I told him.

"That's it?" he questioned me, shocked, still trying to recover.

"Yes," I replied confidently. "Well, maybe a couple of other crew members, but I don't know their names. The ones that guarded me in the brig and brought me out to be whipped by your father. They took a liking to me. They might support us." Samuel rolled his eyes. Apparently, I had made a ridiculous assumption.

"How exactly do you plan on getting Henry on our side?" he questioned me, not even caring to acknowledge the possibility of guards.

"I don't. You're the one that loves Vivian, his daughter," I said, watching his face grow bright red. And I began to explain the plan in full detail. Whether the plan would work out or not, it was our only shot. An oddly reassuring thought. I was going to do everything I could to escape, even if it ended in my failure. My marriage.

"There are quite a few ifs," he mumbled as I finished. I crossed my arms.

"True, but I don't see you coming up with any better ideas," I countered. He sighed and reluctantly nodded.

"I'll do it, but only if Henry agrees to side with us," he replied. "Without him, we don't have a real chance." I bit my lip. I disagreed with him, but I took what I could get.

"What about showing me where they are keeping Jonathan?" I asked. Whether or not Henry agreed, I wanted to know where the love of my life was being kept. He looked at me then looked down.

"I will, just, not yet. After we talk with Henry," he replied. I swallowed hard. Why would he want to delay showing me? Did he not trust me? Was he using Jonathan as leverage? I tried not to dwell on it, but doubt had already taken root in the back of my mind.

"Fine. Let's find Henry then," I replied, setting the weapons down on his bed. Maybe he wanted to delay, but I didn't have that luxury. The sooner we finished this step, the sooner I would find out where Jonathan was.

"Wait, now?" He looked at me, eyebrows lifting, more shocked than confused.

"Yes. Now. We can't waste time." And I wouldn't. I headed to the door, and, with a groan, Samuel followed after me. We reached the main deck, and I realized how much of the day had passed. *Noon? Already?* How had it all gone by so quickly? I scanned the deck – which was so much larger than what I was used to – and spotted Henry at the helm. Samuel excused Henry from his post, while I tried to stay lost in the crowd so that Edward wouldn't spot me. Henry seemed confused, and it only increased when he saw me joining Samuel. Samuel led us to a different space, not far from the main deck, where I had never been before - at least, not that I had known. Maybe I had been there once blindfolded. New was dangerous on this ship. After my conversation with Samuel, my confidence had dwindled. But I knew that my plan was solid. I had faith in Henry. Samuel closed the door, separating the three of us from the rest of the ship, hopefully shielding us from Edward.

"What's going on Samuel?" Henry asked, with a hint of fear in his voice.

"I just...I need to tell you something that has been on my mind for a while now," Samuel explained calmly. His voice gave me chills, just as it had the first time he talked to me. The blindfold had been covering my eyes then, keeping me from seeing who his father had forced him to become. This voice was *his*. Gentle and kind but… determined.

"Does it have something to do with her?" Henry asked, nodding his head in my direction, speaking a bit more calmly this time. Samuel nodded then took a deep breath. I realized that I had no idea what he was going to say. We never practiced, there was no time; we just jumped right in. Headfirst.

"Mr. Peterson, I have been thinking about this for a long time. Your daughter, Vivian is a lovely girl and growing up to be an amazing woman. I love her, and I am not afraid to say that she feels similarly about me," Samuel explained. Henry's jaw dropped into a smile. A small smile formed on my face as I breathed a sigh of relief. Samuel wasn't tricking me; he was on my side. My eyes landed on Henry again. For a moment, I wondered how my father would have reacted in a similar situation. I imagined Jonathan telling my father that he loved me, asking for his blessing. My daydreams were halted by reality when Henry spoke.

"But the engagement?" Henry questioned Samuel, nodding my way. My head lowered.

"It was arranged by my father," Samuel stated, his voice lowering. It was silent as Henry figured out what was happening. We all glanced at each other. Henry's eyes widened.

"A mutiny?" he asked, shocked.

Both of us nodded in sync. Right then, the door squeaked open. I stepped back into the shadows almost instantly, fearing it was Edward.

"Father?" she called out with the door cracked open.

"Yes, Vivian, I am in here," he replied kindly to his daughter's voice. Vivian swung the door open. Her eyes widened in shock as she saw Samuel, but she quickly turned away when she glanced at me.

"Father, what's going on?" she asked, taking a few steps towards Henry. There was a confusion in her eyes. Like pain and hope had entangled themselves in her heart. Each had their own firm grip on it, refusing to let go. She looked to her father as if he could solve the struggle.

"A mutiny, Vivian. For you." Vivian's eyes lit up, her eyebrows raised. She looked doubtingly towards me, then shifted her gaze to land on Samuel. Silence rested on the four of us as Samuel took a few steps to stand in front of Vivian. He lowered his head and she stood up on her toes. The tips of their noses brushed against each other, and then the two kissed. I blushed deeply, knowing I should look away, but I couldn't. These moments were rare in life, even more so on this ship. Vulnerability and joy coming together to create nothing less than a miracle. Their lips parted for a moment.

"You're not playing games with me, are you Samuel?" she asked, her voice shaking. She still couldn't believe it.

"Never," he whispered in her ear. She breathed out heavily, her whole body sighing in relief. They started kissing each other again. This time, I did turn away, moving my gaze from Samuel and Vivian to Henry. He was staring straight at me. 'Thank you,' he mouthed. I smiled. 'Gladly,' I mouthed back. Henry held in a laugh. As I returned my gaze to Vivian and Samuel, who were no longer kissing, I was reminded how vital this mutiny had become. Samuel needed Vivian. I needed Jonathan.

"Okay, so you will help us?" Samuel asked Henry while holding Vivian close to his chest. Henry nodded. My smile grew. There was hope. I looked back at Vivian. Pain and hope still dwelled in her eyes, even as she was held in the arms of her love. One day, the pain might go away – she would learn to forgive him. And they would be happy. No more hoping for something better or praying for the pain to go away. Just pure joy. And love. *Jonathan.*

Henry left first. Vivian followed a few moments later,

shooting Samuel a look like a promise. When she was gone, it was my turn to face Samuel.

"They're in. Now you are going to take me to Jonathan." I told him. This wasn't a question.

CHAPTER 43
Finding Jonathan

He swallowed nervously, then nodded. I crossed my arms.

"What? You expect me to just watch you get to be in the arms of your love while I sit back, knowing mine is being beaten somewhere? Yeah, I don't think so. Besides, he needs to get better if he is going to help with the mutiny. We need all the help we can get." He opened his mouth to argue, but I cut him off. "We find Jonathan and get him to the infirmary, or we get married. Those are our two, and only two options." He shut his mouth. I nodded and he opened the door.

"Where do you think Edward is keeping him hidden? I mean, he kept Jonathan hidden from you, so he must be someplace secret," I thought aloud as we walked through the maze of hallways side-by-side. Samuel bit at the inside of his lip nervously. This time, I was the one who placed my hand on his shoulder. "We're going to be okay. Remember, this isn't my first mutiny," I said, trying to be kind despite the pressure we were under.

"Yes, well, it is mine. And it's my father we are overthrowing. So, forgive me if I am a bit apprehensive," he retorted. I stopped walking. It took him a few paces to realize I wasn't alongside him, then he stopped and turned around.

"Samuel, I'm sorry. I know this is difficult for you, and I won't pretend to completely understand what's going on in your head right now. But a mutiny is serious business. You have to be all in, or else it doesn't work. There are a lot of people counting on you... counting on us." I told him. He nodded. Then he looked up, gave me a weak smile, and nodded a bit more confidently.

"Okay, if I were my father, where would I hide my captive's lover?" he pondered aloud, giving me a playful smirk. I rolled my eyes with a smile. The only way to break up this intensity was with forced smiles.

"Well, it's a large ship with a large crew. It has to be in a place rarely used and rarely visited," I continued.

"So, neither his cabin nor his quarters. Nor the kitchen or food hold," he answered out loud. My eyes widened.

"You have separate holds just for food?" I couldn't help but ask. Before he could respond, I raised a hand to stop him. "No, don't answer that. We need to stay on task." Samuel chuckled. It wasn't funny, it was frightening. The more I learned about this ship, the larger it seemed.

"You might be onto something there, though," he replied with a small smile. "The last time we made port, we got new sails, so we wouldn't need to replace them or fix them anytime soon after. Jonathan might be in the sail-room," he suggested. I raised an eyebrow. Larger ships were strange. Everything we had was in one hold. But we also didn't have to store a spare sail. I nodded in agreement.

"The only thing is, we will need to go through the half-deck, which is where most of the crew stays. We have too large a crew to provide individual cabins for all of them. We will need to be careful. If someone spots us, they will tell my father," he explained. I suddenly felt guilty for having a space of my own here. Whose space had I been taking? Or did all of it used to be Samuel's? I didn't have time to focus on any of these trivial things. I needed to find Jonathan.

Silently, we made our way down to the half-deck. Since it was the afternoon, I assumed there wouldn't be as many crewmen down here. I assumed correctly, but there was still a decent amount of men in the mass of bunks. About ten, probably the night crew, trying to get their last moments of sleep before starting their day. I took a deep breath. The two of us silently weaved through the bunks, careful not to wake any of the crew, and stay in the shadows. Once we made it to the ladder that led below deck,

I let out a small breath of relief and followed Samuel down the ladder.

It was a maze down there. And nearly pitch black. I regretted not bringing a lamp. But Samuel had grown up on this ship, and if he was anything like me, he would know this place like the back of his hand. After running into a variety of hard objects, bruising my legs, and barely managing to keep up with Samuel, we made it to the sail room. In the back, I could see a faint light, a lamp most likely. The two of us glanced around for any crewmen, acting as guards. None. We slinked towards the light. The moment I saw him, I couldn't resist.

Jonathan had collapsed on the floor, passed out after having been whipped or beaten, or both. I rushed to his side, and I ran my hands through his hair.

"Jonathan? Jonathan, wake up. I'm here," I murmured in his ear. He didn't move. Tears silently rolled down my face. I pressed my lips to his cheeks and whispered again, "Jonathan, please wake up, we're here. We're going to rescue you." He groaned. That was enough for me. I turned to face Samuel, who had gone pale and stood motionless.

"Samuel, help me carry him," I begged him.

"I can't believe my father would do this," he barely breathed. I frowned.

"I know, but right now, we need to get him to Owen. Please, help me," I replied. Samuel nodded and rushed over to help me. I could no longer feel the pain of my wounds, only desperation to save the man I loved. Together we lifted him and got him out of the room. The two of us carried him through the pitch-black holds until we reached the half-deck, then weaved through the bunk beds once more, miraculously not waking anyone, or, at least, I hoped we hadn't. Once back to the quarter-deck, we made our way to the infirmary. Owen was shocked, either because we entered his space in such a rush, or by Jonathan's condition. He helped us lay Jonathan on a cot, then Samuel pulled Owen aside to explain the importance of keeping this secret. I knelt beside Jonathan and held his hand in mine.

"You're going to be okay, I promise," I whispered and kissed his knuckles gently. His eyes weren't open, but he weakly squeezed my hand. He heard me. I smiled, but the tears that were flooding my eyes reflected my true emotions. Jonathan could not die. It wasn't an option. We needed him. I needed him. Not just in this mutiny, but in my life. Without Jonathan, I knew I could never truly be happy.

Samuel had to pull me away from him, telling me Owen had to get started helping him now if there was even a chance that he could fight for us. I wanted to stay by his side. I couldn't leave. Suddenly, another hand rested on my shoulder. I looked up to meet Aaron's beautiful green eyes. He had almost fully recovered, but he still had white cloth wrapped around where he had been shot. I started to cry.

"You have to go, Carter. You don't want Edward to find you. I will watch over him for you," Aaron promised. I shook my head, my crying growing into wailing. "Carter, you have to go," Aaron repeated. Samuel started pulling me and I fought against him until he pulled me out the door and slammed it in front of my face, keeping me away from my love. I felt like collapsing, but it wasn't one of my options. Samuel wrapped his arm around me as we made our way back to the room. This time, I didn't move his arm away. I was overwhelmed and shocked at the state Jonathan was in, at the state that Edward had put him in. *How cruel could a man be?* I had already agreed to marry his son, why did he continue to abuse my love? I felt Samuel's thumb gently rub my shoulder, trying to comfort me in the ways he knew how.

We turned the corner and found ourselves face to face with Edward. Both of us froze. He shot us a wicked smirk. He looked like he knew that he had the advantage. But that wasn't true. We were the ones with a secret.

"That's quite the show you're putting on there," he commented. I swallowed hard, suddenly doubting my confidence in that secret.

"We are trying, Father, like you want us to," Samuel replied. I was glad he spoke; I was still at a loss for words. It was silent in the hall for a moment. Edward looked from me to his son, then his eyes landed on me. In a blink of an eye, he pulled a gun, and both of us jumped back. He aimed it at my head. I gulped, praying my tears away.

"A mutiny, huh?"

CHAPTER 44
Indecisive Heart

I DIDN'T KNOW IF I WAS SUPPOSED to respond to Edward's question. Samuel's arm dropped from around my shoulder. Now I was no longer alone in my shock. I searched my mind for the moment where we slipped up, where we told the wrong person, but no one who we told would have told Edward. And yet, he knew. Edward knew it was a mutiny. He didn't know when or where, but he knew why. I had no words. I wasn't ashamed of my actions, and I wasn't going to negate the claim. But I sure wasn't going to give him a reason to pull the trigger.

"Father, listen to me!" Samuel begged his father. With his gun still pointed at my head, Edward turned to face his son, erupting with rage, his face red with fury. Fear churned in my stomach. If he accidentally fired, I would be dead.

"No, you listen Samuel!" Edward interrupted. "This girl has talked you into loving some - some child!" he exclaimed. I chose not to point out the fact that Vivian was older than me. Samuel tried to interrupt, but Edward ignored his son's cries of protest. "She gave you reasons to 'fall in love' with Vivian and gave you reasons that you shouldn't love her instead. She told you to mutiny against your father, your only parent, the only person that will love you enough to tell you the truth." Samuel stared at his father in shock. My eyes widened. I stared at Samuel, praying that he wouldn't give in to his father's manipulation. *Not again.*

"Then you admit that Carter doesn't love me?" he snapped

back, seeing through his father's lies. I was proud of him; he had caught his father in his own words.

"She is merely blinded by the fantasy that surrounds her," Edward countered. I rolled my eyes. I was standing right there, and I so badly wanted to argue with him, but as long as that gun was pointed at my head, I held my tongue. Besides, this was a fight between father and son.

"Father," Samuel groaned in frustration, "Any romance that you do not approve of isn't real."

"Because I have seen true love first hand. It was like nothing I had ever witnessed before," Edward argued.

"Yes, when you fell in love with Carter's mother. I know, Father. You're still upset, you're still angry, but forcing Carter into this isn't the right thing to do," Samuel sighed frustrated. Edward's jaw dropped.

"How did you learn that?" he questioned his son. Samuel nodded at me. Edward's jaw tightened and looked at me with his hard, cold stare. I refused to shrink back.

"And did she tell you that she *chose* to come aboard this ship?" he questioned his son, even though his icy blue eyes were still chewing me apart. Samuel glared at me. I clenched my jaw. *Chose* was not really the right word. Technically, I chose to board his ship, after being threatened and convinced he was going to kill me if I didn't. But Edward took another step toward me, pressing the barrel of the gun to my temple. I swallowed hard, unintentionally making me look guilty rather than fearful.

"You what?" Samuel questioned me, so confused at the entire situation that his voice was becoming breathy.

"Oh, so she didn't tell you," he smirked, smiling evilly. I sighed in frustration. "Well, before she even left her ship, when she first met me, I gave her a choice. I asked her if she wanted to board my ship. She wanted to come; she and Jonathan made that decision together. They could have refused my offer, and yes, I would have been upset and I would do everything I could to try to bring her aboard, but if she refused, she would refuse. And I would have left. Now you see, Samuel, the little part of her story that she left out," Edward explained. Edward was making it sound like everything was butterflies and bluebirds.

"Why didn't you tell me that, Carter?" Samuel questioned me. I rolled my eyes and clenched my jaw. Despite the gun to my head, he needed to know what happened in the moments before I boarded *The Cobra.*

"Because I didn't really choose. Did I, Edward?" I countered Edward's argument. "He threatened me, and all I knew of this stranger was that he once loved my mother and went crazy when he was refused. If I refused him, I could only imagine what tortures I might have endured. You see what he does to me now, *and I said yes!*" Edward's grip on the gun tightened and his finger hovered over the trigger. I watched Samuel's eyes as he compared his father's words with mine.

"Please, see through this," I urged Samuel, glancing at him, trying to keep an eye on Edward...well, Edward's gun. Then I glared at Edward. He raised his eyebrows, shocked by the intensity of emotions that floated in my eyes. I'm sure it surprised him more than he cared to show. Anger no longer only filled Edward's eyes, but mine as well. I remembered how horrible Jonathan looked when we found him, how cruel this man who called himself a captain had treated the man I loved.

The more I thought about the situation, the more I realized, my plan for a mutiny was ridiculous. It wouldn't work. I was ridiculous for even thinking of it. With Edward being so devious, I would never be able to carry a plan out. Samuel was too gullible. I could already see it in his eyes that he was considering Edward's argument. His father knew what to say to flip him, to control, and bend him to his will. I, however, had only recently met Samuel, making things difficult. I still had to try.

"Samuel, don't think about me. I don't matter. Think about Vivian. She's the one you need to be worried about. You finally - publicly - announced your love for her, and with just a few twisted lies from your father, you're going to take it all back?" I challenged him. Grief and confusion filled his eyes. He didn't want to think about it. But the thought had crossed his mind before. I heard the click of Edward preparing his gun to shoot a bullet through my head. With every word I said, I was crossing the line. I needed to choose my words carefully. "Samuel –"

"Don't remind me of things I cannot have!" Samuel yelled in

a burst of unexpected rage. My eyes widened with shock. Never had I seen Samuel reach this level of anger before.

"You *can* have her. You can have love. If a heart can be swayed with mere words, not an action in sight, how can one even say love exists?" I muttered. He bit his bottom lip in anger and maybe sadness. Before I could let out another word, Edward spoke up.

"Samuel, you tell me. Are you going to marry Carter? It would probably be in your best interest to do so. Or will you merely let her walk off with her fantasy love and you stay behind with a broken heart?" Edward once again questioned his son. Samuel looked at his father, then looked at me. For a moment, it was as if he was searching -- searching me for another way out of this situation. And then it changed. His eyes were sad and sympathetic. I lost. I tried to think of something to say to persuade him back to my side, to the truth, but there was nothing that could trump his father. Samuel would no longer be my ally. He could no longer be my friend. Edward had once again changed his heart. He had once again convinced his son that the best thing to do was to marry me. I felt like crying and punching someone at the same time. And yet, I was silent and motionless, still pleading with my eyes. It was a lost cause.

"I am putting my trust in you, Father," Samuel began.

"Samuel, think of Vivian, please. Think of that wonderful kiss!" I whispered harshly. Never had I wanted him to listen to me more. Only moments ago, Samuel was helping me prepare for a mutiny so that we could both be free to love who we wanted to love. That Samuel had been taken away, shoved out of the picture by the same man who had shoved Jonathan into the sail-room to be beaten and whipped and left for dead.

"Yes, that wonderful kiss that couldn't be ruined by rusted bars. That wonderful kiss, Carter, that I will never be sorry for," Samuel replied calmly, touching my hand too kindly for my liking. Now Samuel was the one twisting my words. How could that be? *Like father, like son.* I pulled my hand out of his reach, and it was grabbed by Edward. I thought about Jonathan one last time. How I wanted to kiss him one last time.

"I love you, Carter," Samuel whispered in my ear. And

suddenly, he was softly tying the blindfold over my eyes. I tried to fight him off with my free hand, but it didn't take long for Edward to snatch that one too. That dumb blindfold again.

"No, Samuel, you don't," I could barely whisper. I nearly mouthed it. My anger and sadness had overwhelmed every other emotion. Edward kept a firm grip on my arms as the blindfold was tightened behind my head. I heard Samuel step away, Edward released my hands, then I felt the cold metal barrel of the gun against the back of my head again.

"Father, I want to marry Carter Ellen Key tomorrow morning. She has said things that have made me stray, but I have returned. I want to do what is best for me, what is best for us," he proclaimed. I pictured Edward nodding approvingly at his son. Samuel reached for my hand. I flinched and closed my hand into a fist.

Samuel pressed his lips tightly against mine. Immediately I pulled away, not only because I couldn't see it coming, but also because I didn't want it to come. I felt the gun slip away from my head. The opportunity presented itself, and I had to take it. I kicked behind me, where I believed Edward to be then heard a shout of pain. A gun fired. I gasped, but I hadn't been shot. Then, I was shoved against a wall. My knee shot up, kneeing whoever was holding me in the gut or, more preferably, groin. I heard a groan, and I reached to take off the blindfold, but I was grabbed again, my hands pulled behind my back and I was pressed face-first against the wall. I bit the inside of my cheek, holding in a scream. Then I heard footsteps running our way, probably due to the gunshot.

"Oh Aaron, I'm glad you could make it," Edward stated, acting like this was some sort of event. I tried harder to push him off of me, but Samuel, at least I assumed it was him, held me against the wall. This isn't what I wanted. It was just another nightmare I was forced to endure. I needed help. I needed Aaron. I needed him to be my hero, now.

C H A P T E R   4 5

The Final Night

LISTENING TO THE WORLD AROUND ME was so much worse than actually seeing it. My mind conjured the images of pain, and I was left hoping they weren't true. I heard Aaron attack Edward, only to be shoved off all too quickly. I heard the click of a gun. *No, not again!*

"Back down, boy, or you will see your sweet little Carter bleeding out on the floor," Edward threatened. The gun wasn't pointed at Aaron, it was pointed at me. There was silence for a moment. No one even released a breath. Aaron must have nodded because Edward spoke again. "Good, now, back to the infirmary, unless you want more wounds for Owen to attempt to heal." There were footsteps, this time leaving. It was the right choice. While I wanted to escape now, it was impossible. Aaron and I needed to save our strength for the real battle. Samuel pushed me away from the wall into a different space. It wasn't until he closed the door when I realized we were in his room. I stood still like I had my first day on this ship. He slipped the blindfold off my eyes. The room was lit by candlelight. Samuel looked at me straight in my eyes. It was that pathetic begging look again. Anything and everything I thought I knew about Samuel, I quickly forgot. That man no longer existed. He was back to being his father's puppet.

"Was that all real?" I asked him desperately, but I already knew the answer.

"Carter, see beyond your own selfishness. See beyond

Jonathan. See me," he begged me.

"Love is selfish!" I exclaimed.

"No, that is lust! Love is selfless!" Samuel argued. I sighed in frustration. He wasn't wrong, but he wasn't right either. The way he defined selfless was stupid, ridiculous, and distorted. I threw my hands into the air and they slapped my legs when they came back down. I wasn't going to change his mind now. It was too late. I turned around and faced the wall; I couldn't even look at him. I tried to think about something different, but the fact remained that I was getting married in the morning. It was overwhelming. I turned around to face Samuel again. Before I could stop him, his lips pressed against mine, against my will. I grabbed his shoulders and pushed him away immediately. There was no longer a blindfold to hinder me. Or an Edward.

"Just stop Samuel. The more you kiss me, the more I loathe you," I snapped. Samuel huffed. "Samuel, I don't know what is going through your head, but I will tell you what's going through mine. I'm about to marry some strange man I met only a few days ago and the love of my life is nearly dead because of the same man's father. My only plan crumbled apart as I watched your heart change feelings, and your mind switch sides. I don't know what I am supposed to think, but it isn't good. Don't you think this whole situation is slightly off?" I questioned him.

"I'm not listening to your charm. This isn't one of your books, Carter. You're a ship girl," he snapped back, but with an edge of sophistication.

"I am NOT a ship girl!" I shouted back. Samuel didn't even seem stunned. "I am the first mate of the *Adventurer* and nothing you say or do can change that. You want to know why? Captain! Not Jonathan. And definitely not Edward. No, Captain James Rosten, my second father. I made him a promise to never leave my ship, I would stay with her until the end. I made him a promise, and I never break my promises!" I was on the verge of rage beyond control. My whole body shook as tears drenched my face in a way the ocean never could. Samuel stepped back, then composed himself.

"If you keep your promises, then I'll trust that you will keep the promise we will make to each other tomorrow," Samuel stated matter-of-factly. I was speechless. He caught my words, the same way his father would have, and distorted their meaning for his own gain. I turned around and walked into my room, slamming the door behind me.

I went straight to my bed and cried into the pillow. I cried for several minutes, tears of anger, and disappointment. At one point, I thought I might throw-up. *Get a hold of yourself!* I thought. I forced the tears to slow until eventually they stopped. I turned and laid on my back, staring at the ceiling. I imagined pieces of my recent past. Jonathan's kiss before the storm that killed Captain, and the other when I realized Edward was coming for me. These lovely thoughts served as a reminder of how trapped I had become. I so wanted to escape. Instead, I fell into a restless sleep.

"Jonathan!" I yelled. We were in a blank room. There were no objects, no furniture, no color. Just the two of us. We ran as fast as we could toward each other, prepared to hug each other tightly. The space between us slowly diminished until we were in finger's reach. As our hands nearly touched, an invisible wall formed between us. I slammed my fists against the invisible wall just trying to reach Jonathan. He was doing the same. My hands hit the wall again, and someone laid a hand on top of mine. I turned to face the owner of the hand. It was Samuel.

"Get away from me!" I screamed at him. But he didn't move.

"No, Carter. There is a wall here for a reason. Please stop fighting me, Carter," Samuel begged.

"I won't stop fighting," I replied, and started to smash my fists against the wall again. "I won't stop," I screamed one last time before the dream faded into darkness. I felt Samuel's lips gently touch my cheek, almost hovering over my cheek. My hand came around and slapped his face. Immediately his lips were gone. I opened my eyes, but I still couldn't see. I was blindfolded, again. It was my last morning as Carter Ellen Key, and I couldn't even look at the sun.

C H A P T E R   4 6

Wedding Day

"I won't stop fighting," I whispered behind clenched teeth. Those final words from my dream would be my final words of defiance. I didn't even know if I could make it through this wedding.

"You will one day," Samuel muttered. I could picture Samuel rubbing his cheek in pain and surprise. I wanted him to know I was angry. "Eva and Vivian will be in here soon to help you prepare for the wedding," Samuel explained. He said Vivian's name with such ease that it sickened me. I listened as he stood up and walked out the door. Once he was gone, I ripped off the blindfold. I didn't care if Samuel walked back in and slapped my face telling me to put it back on. I was going to see the sun on my last day as Carter Ellen Key.

But there was no sun to see. The sky was darkened by light gray clouds. The world outside seemed as miserable as I felt. Someone opened the door. I turned to see the saddened faces of Eva and Vivian. I couldn't imagine the grief Vivian was going through. She stood by the door, holding a simple white dress in her hands, the one she knew she should have been wearing. I was about to say something to her, but Eva ran to hug me.

"I'm so sorry things didn't work out Carter," she whispered in my ear. I nodded and slowly pulled myself out of her arms. I looked at Vivian. Our eyes met and she quickly looked to the ground.

"Vivian, I tried as hard as I could. I didn't want this wedding to happen just as much as you," I explained. Vivian nodded, still not looking at me. I couldn't blame her.

"I know, Carter. But maybe Edward was right. Maybe things really wouldn't have worked out between us. I mean, the way he looks at you is more powerful than he ever would have looked at me. And, if I'm honest with myself, I know I would return to the land to work. But Samuel would want to stay on the ocean. I know you would want to stay on the ocean. Maybe you two were made for each other. Edward was right; it was just a fantasy love," Vivian sighed. She was too young to go through this emotional road, both of us were.

"Don't listen to Edward's lies," I tried to convince her, grabbing her shoulders.

"Carter," she said, looking up at me, "Sometimes avoiding the truth is the only way to heal a broken heart." I didn't believe that for a second, but Vivian did. I had tried my hardest to convince her and Samuel that their love was true. Or at least truer than Samuel's feelings for me. Love was a delicate matter.

"Let's make you beautiful, okay?" Eva suggested, trying to break the tension between Vivian and me. I nodded and walked over towards her. I undressed and let the two girls help me with the corset and the white gown. It was the second time I had to wear a dress for Samuel. It was the second time I had to wear a dress, ever. I glanced at myself in the shattered mirror as Eva tied the last few strings in the back. I looked lovely in the dress. And it made me all the angrier. And yet, even with how miserable this entire situation was, I wondered about my mother, on her wedding day. It was nothing like this, that much I knew. This was like attending a funeral, but in white. Eva sat me down in the chair so that she could do my hair. Vivian, having no work left to do, exited the room.

Eva began to braid my hair and formed a bun on the back of my head. My blond hair seemed to glow with beauty, which annoyed me all the more. One little strand of hair didn't make the braid. I curled it around my ear. I thought of Jonathan and Aaron immediately. With all of their differences, they did one thing the same. They always curled a small strand of hair behind my ear with such care and affection, it made me feel important. But the longer I was here, on this horrifying ship, the less important I became. Here I was a token, a trophy, and an object. With Jonathan and Aaron, I was a woman, a human, a treasure. I wanted to see them so badly. I wanted to see Jopie so badly. I wanted to see David and the rest of the crew so badly. I wanted to see Sunset, Dawn, Aurora, and Luna so badly. I wanted to be home. My heart hurt.

"There, all done. And may I just say that you look dazzling," Eva exclaimed. I stood up and faced her.

"Please don't tell me that again," I told her. Eva nodded, understanding that I wasn't in the best of moods. I began to walk towards the door, but Jonathan came rushing in. He looked awful, covered in bandages and bruises and defeat. I got a weird feeling in my stomach again. I loved him so much. And wanted him here with me, by my side. This wedding was meant for him. At the same time, I wanted him to get away. He was only going to delay the inevitable. He could only make things worse. Hope and pain.

"Jonathan, what are you doing here?" I couldn't help but ask him.

"Aaron told me how to get here," he only briefly explained before wrapping his arms around me. I imagined it must have hurt him, but this hurt that we were experiencing together was so much worse.

"I love you, Jonathan. I can't imagine how hard this must be for you. But please understand that every time I glance your way, I am reminded that I wasn't strong enough. I am reminded that I didn't try hard enough. I am reminded that everything I did was worth nothing," I explained to him, my head resting against his chest. Jonathan nodded and released his hold on me. I began to turn to face Eva again, but Jonathan grabbed my shoulders.

"I told you that night that I loved you and you didn't have to love me back. That statement still stands. Everything that you do makes me love you even more. I don't want to hurt you any more than you already are. So, I will leave to prepare for the wedding," he breathed softly. And he kissed my lips lightly. As he walked out the door, I forced my sadness into confidence. It was the only way I could make it through this wedding. Or have a fighting chance to avoid it.

After a few minutes, Eva also left me alone, after informing me it wasn't quite time for me to make my entrance. I sat on the bed, alone with my thoughts. It was my last chance, a literal prayer. I whispered the words up to heaven, begging for a miracle. Something – anything – to stop this misery that had been eating me alive for the past few days. It forbid me to smile, walk, breathe, live. What felt like only seconds later, Eva returned, telling me an hour had passed and now it was time. The main deck had been prepared so that I could walk down the aisle. Reluctantly, I followed Eva out of the room and through the halls, headed straight towards the end of my life. The entire crew of the ship was up and awaiting my arrival. Samuel stood on the main deck and his father, above him, stood at the helm. The crew turned to face me as Eva walked me down to Samuel. Since I was seven, I always knew my father was not going to walk me down the aisle, but I never thought it would have been a stranger.

In a snap, I was standing across from the enemy – my husband-to-be. How had these days gone by so quickly and yet each was so painfully long? He looked at me with pleading eyes again and took my hand. I pulled away from him. We weren't married yet, no need to start pretending now. I was going to spend the rest of my life pretending. Edward began the marriage ceremony. I glanced at Aaron and Jonathan, who stood in the front row. I could tell that both were holding in their anger. Underneath their bandages and bruises were clenched jaws and tightened fists. It was torture for them to see me married off, and it was torture for me to watch them boil in their own furry. How I wanted to punch Edward in the teeth right then.

"I do," Samuel stated. I hadn't been listening, but now it was my turn to say, 'I do'. My stomach tightened. My throat constricted. This was truly happening. My nightmares were morphing into my reality, and this time, there would be no waking up. This couldn't be real. Edward finished asking all of the questions that he was required to ask me, all the promises I was being forced to make. It was my turn to speak. For a moment, I considered saying no. What would happen? Aaron, Jonathan, they would both be shot, I knew it. I would probably be killed too or tortured on this ship for the rest of my life. Then again, wasn't this torture? But if Jonathan and Aaron lived, it would be worth it. I looked out at my ocean one last time as Carter Ellen Key.

"I-" but I was cut off before I could finish my sentence.

"Captain, very sorry to interrupt, but a ship is heading this way!" yelled the man that was at the crow's nest. The man looked back out to sea. Jonathan, Aaron, and I all followed his gaze. I squinted my eyes to see what the crew member was seeing. On the horizon, I spotted the tiniest speck. Sure enough, there was a ship out there, heading our way. My heart fluttered with hope. *Did God answer my prayer?*

"Thank you for that Mr. Darrel," Edward stated. Then he glared at me. I was expected to finish this ceremony and do so quickly. I took a deep breath. Oh, how I hated him.

"I-"

"Sir!" the man at the crow's nest interrupted again. Praise this man and his neglect of proper wedding ceremony etiquette. "It's their ship! It's the *Adventurer!*" Jonathan, Aaron, and I all exchanged hopeful glances. Butterflies flew in my stomach. My prayers *had* been answered. I faced Edward with triumph painted on my face.

"I don't," I replied. He glared at me, but no guns appeared. Not yet at least. Jonathan, Aaron, and I ran to the side of the ship to look at our one last hope. Home was coming back for us. My whistle had been heard.

"Don't get your hopes up just yet, child," Edward whispered in my ear as he moved to stand beside me. Samuel was too shocked to move, but the rest of the crew was already bustling about. The thought hit me: Edward won't let us off this ship without a fight. *So, let's give him one!* And I ran from the main deck. Seeing my urgency, Jonathan and Aaron followed behind me. I saw Henry run from out of the crowd too. Surprisingly, Edward didn't stop us. *He thinks we'll lose.* We were all prepared to fight.

All of us reached Samuel's room and headed towards the corner, where the pile of weapons had been placed. Miraculously, they were all still there. This was our final fight. I grabbed a sword and picked up a dagger. But I found something better. I dropped the dagger and picked up Samuel's knife. Irony was the best form of revenge. Hopefully, it would be the last time I had to lay eyes on it. The third time's a charm. Jonathan picked up a pistol and shoved it in the back of his pants; Aaron did the same. They both grabbed swords. Henry held two guns in his hands, prepared to fight. I walked towards the door, but Eva, Vivian, and Owen came running in.

"We want to help," Eva exclaimed for the group. I nodded with a smile and gestured to the weapons in the corner. *The bigger the group the better,* I thought to myself. All three picked up a sword; Owen picked up a pistol as well. I knew that the girls weren't trained, but I wasn't either. I had to trust that, when the time came, we would step up to the plate. Our survival instincts would kick in. All of us were ready to fight.

"This is our final stand. We are going to have to fight our hardest for even a sliver of a chance of victory. Careful where you stab, or where you shoot. I want to have a clean conscience at the end of this," I stated. There wasn't enough time to take off my wedding dress, but a reassuring thought stuck in my mind. The dress would not stay white much longer.

CHAPTER 47
Final Rebellion

I WALKED OUT THE DOOR with confidence that no one in the world could break. I was ready to leave *The Cobra* and Edward and Samuel. This attack wasn't well-planned, well-coordinated, or well-manned. It was all thrown together because of a miracle. I prayed that miracle would extend with us into battle. We waited in the shadows of the hallway until spotting the *Adventurer*. With the crew also preparing for a fight, most of us blended in, all carrying weapons, per the orders of Edward. He was in a rage fit on the main deck.

"Why?" Edward was shouting. Samuel was yelling at his father to calm down, but Edward ignored his son. He was too angry with the entire situation to hear what Samuel had to say. Edward was barking orders, preparing his ship for battle. Someone took my hand and squeezed it. I looked up meeting Jonathan's shimmering blue eyes – tired from the sleepless nights, joyful with a new hope sailing our way.

"Looks like you're not getting married after all!" he whispered excitedly in my ear. I nodded happily, but, honestly, my mind was preoccupied. We listened as the *Adventurer* came closer and closer. And as the crew of *The Cobra* quieted down, I could hear David as he yelled across.

"Okay, Captain Jacobs! We have returned for our Captain, crewman, and first mate Carter, who chose to stay aboard! Send them across!" David yelled. It was so comforting to hear his voice again.

"I'm afraid I cannot. We have not finished our discussions," Edward replied calmly. It was shocking how quickly he could seemingly regain composure. I pictured David rolling his eyes.

"You have had enough time, sir," David argued. "We need our crew." For a moment, silence hung over the ocean. *Maybe he is going to call it off?*

"Fire!" Edward commanded his crew members. *Nope.* Only a few moments later, the sound of blasting cannons and splintering wood filled the air. I jumped at the loud sound that shook my core. I thought it would shake the ship, but it didn't, at least not as much as I thought.

"Good luck," I announced to our group, and we ran out of our hiding spot, weapons in hand. Suddenly, the battle wasn't just ship against ship but now had shifted into a civil war as well. I was battling two crew members with one sword in a dress. Not the best of situations. I held the knife tightly in my hand and aimed at one man's shoulder. I threw the knife. It sunk into his shoulder and the man screamed in pain. A twinge of guilt punctured my heart, but this was a battle for my future. Besides, I couldn't fight them both at the same time. I continued my fight with the other crew member. The swordplay continued until I found the spot of his body that he consistently kept open for stabbing - his legs. I swung my sword at his thighs. The blade cut open both of his legs. The man fell in pain. I jabbed the butt of my sword into his neck and the man passed out. I quickly pulled Samuel's knife out of the other man's shoulder. Knives and blood no longer scared me, not after Gargan and the pirates. I turned to face my next opponent. Samuel stood at the end of my sword's point, unarmed.

"Move, Samuel. Get away. Or pick up a weapon and fight with us. You might not love Vivian anymore, but you know what your father forced us into wasn't right," I yelled at him, trying to make my voice audible over the shouting, clanging, and cannon around us.

"I can't do that, Carter. You know I can't," Samuel argued. He was his father's boy. I sighed in frustration, but then shrugged my shoulders. I had given him one last chance. He was the one that refused.

"Fine." I swung my sword at him, and he slowly backed up. Until he launched forward. Suddenly, he was back in the fight, grabbing my arm, making my weapon useless against him. I lifted my leg and kicked his stomach. Samuel bent down in pain letting go of my arm. I stabbed his shoulder and he winced in pain, and, with him now distracted, I shoved him to the ground. My gaze fell on him with sympathy for a moment. He was the only man that was kind to me when I first arrived and now bore no weapon against me. I forced the thought away. This was a mutiny, but I wasn't going to kill him. I stabbed his knife through his shirt and onto the planks of wood on the main deck.

"Be thankful I didn't stab you instead," I muttered as I turned to look at the battle going on around me. Crew members from the Adventurer had come onto the ship to join the fight. At the helm, Adam was fighting Edward, which seemed unfair. Adam didn't need to be fighting Edward, I did. I ran up to the helm, barely avoiding tips of swords and bullets from guns that echoed in my ears alongside shouts of agony. I reached the helm and swung my sword down on Edward's, stopping the fight between him and Adam.

"Carter!" Adam exclaimed with a wide smile, though, he realized this was not a time of reunion. He turned and fought a different crew member. And I couldn't catch a breath before Edward's sword smashed against mine. I struggled to fight the pressure.

"Now I will kill you, Carter," Edward snapped behind clenched teeth. I slid my sword out from under his, dodging to the side, and I lunged for his shoulder. He blocked my stab. Our swords clanged against each other as we moved back and forth. I could feel my body resisting the intensity of this fight. I was weak and untrained; against a man whose job was war. He slammed his sword onto mine, and my grip gave way. The sword slid out from my grasp and flew down to the main deck amongst the fighting. There was no getting it back.

Edward dropped his sword. Was he trying to make it an even fight? *Surely not.* He shoved me backwards. I regained my balance, but he pushed me again, this time with enough force to bring me to the ground. He knew the injuries I had sustained on this ship. I had been here long enough for him to learn my fears. He knew how to exploit both.

"Edward, look at yourself! You're about to kill a fifteen-year-old girl just because you have a grudge against her mother! That's crazy!" I yelled at him, trying to get inside his head, despite knowing it was a lost cause. Edward ignored me and pulled out a gun instead. There was no swordplay stopping him any longer. He clicked the bullet into place. His finger hovered over the trigger.

This was how I was going to die. Despite my fear, a peace came over me. I would die for my family just as my mother had. I would die for my love and I would die to keep my promise to Captain. I would willingly die for all of those things no matter what the circumstance. Now was no different. I kept my eyes open the entire time, staring death in the face. I was going to show Edward that I was not afraid. As he was pulling the trigger, Aaron ran into him. The bullet missed my head but hit my shoulder instead, just grazing it enough to take out a large chunk of skin, but not sink into my muscle. I couldn't help but scream out in pain. Even with the pain, I had no choice but to stand and fight Edward. This was my fight. Aaron tossed me a sword and weakly smiled at me. He shoved Edward one more time and then left him to me. Aaron understood that this was my fight.

My shoulder throbbed in pain, but I ignored it. I had to. I swung my sword at Edward. The tip caught his face, cutting his cheek. I stabbed his shoulder, and he shouted in pain. I kicked his chest and he fell to the ground. I pointed my sword at him, and he looked up at me, defeated. He had no gun, no sword. I had the upper hand this time.

"Look at what you've done Edward. All of this for a silly little grudge," I said, nodding my head at the fighting happening all around us. At first, he moved to stand, but I pressed my foot on his shoulder. I wanted him to acknowledge the mess he had created. Edward slowly turned his head to look at the battle. He breathed heavily and closed his eyes. His head moved to face mine again. He opened his eyes and stared at me. The mixture of rage and fear in his eyes disappeared. The expression on his face, I couldn't identify.

"You won't kill me," he breathed. I shook my head.

"No, I don't kill people, Edward. I won't commit such an act," I told him sternly. Edward inhaled deeply, preparing to stand. I tightened my grip on the sword.

"If you won't, I will," he stated. He pulled a knife out from behind him. I braced myself, resituating my stance, preparing for a fight. Edward lifted the knife, but the point was facing him, not me. My eyes widened in shock.

"Edward no!" I screamed, but I was too late. The knife plunged into his chest. My jaw dropped in shock. His eyelids opened and closed slowly. As if everyone had one eye on Edward, all the fighting stopped. Samuel ran up and bent over his father.

"No, Father! Please don't leave me! I need your guidance! I need your help!" he begged his father. Edward smiled and put his hand on Samuel's shoulder. Then he nudged his son out of the way and looked at me.

"I might not be a good man, but I know right from wrong Carter. I know what I did to you was wrong. I know that the battle I created was wrong. I just didn't care. Until… until now. When I pictured myself dead," he paused, taking one of his final breaths, "It felt right," he breathed in deeply again. His eyelids began to close. I couldn't manage words. I couldn't believe the sight in front of me. An enemy, a father, a man bleeding out on his own ship, on his own deck, by his own hand.

"I'm sorry. I'm so very sorry," he said with his final breath. His hand slid off his son's shoulder as the last breath of life left his body. I stared in shock at what had just happened. I didn't cry, I didn't comfort Samuel, I didn't walk away from the scene and return to my ship. I just stood there in shock. I had seen dead men, but I had never seen a man die. I could have never imagined this. And I never wanted to see it again. Jonathan and Aaron ran up to me. Jonathan placed his hand on my shoulder. I did not need comforting. *Samuel does,* I thought to myself. I forced myself out of the trance and slowly placed my hand on Samuel's shoulder. He turned to me, tears rolling down his cheeks.

"Samuel I'm so sorry," I began. Samuel hugged me. I was shocked for a moment. But he wanted to turn to me for help, and I would let him. I lightly hugged him back. We sat there for a few minutes, with tears from his eyes dampening my hair. I didn't care. He had lost his only parent, and I knew exactly what it felt like to be suddenly left with no one. You want a shoulder to cry on, even if that person is someone you can't stand. It's better than no shoulder at all. As he cried, the crew started cleaning the deck, returning the weapons to their place on the ship. Other members helped each other to the infirmary. All the while, the silence of death weighed heavily on the ship.

Eventually, Samuel let go of me and nodded a thank you. I nodded back. He glanced at his father's body, bent down, and pulled the knife from his chest. It was dripping red with Edward's blood, and the hole in his body seemed unreal. I couldn't take my eyes off it even though it made me want to vomit. I had to hold it together for Samuel. Samuel held the handle and turned to face me once more. He placed the knife in my hands.

"Take this," he murmured. I did not want to take the knife. It disgusted and scared me.

"No, Samuel, I can't," I argued.

"If you ever wanted to forgive me, do so by taking this knife now," Samuel begged. And I did want to forgive him. I didn't want to be a burden on his shoulders. Not after this. So, I took the knife from his hands. He breathed a sigh of relief. I nodded a farewell and turned to Jonathan and Aaron.

"Let's go home," I told them. They both nodded. The three of us walked to the edge of the ship and grabbed a hold of the swinging ropes. We swung across the water and landed on the *Adventurer*. It only took a moment and suddenly I was home.

CHAPTER 48

Home Again

THE REST OF THE CREW MEMBERS FOLLOWED OUR LEAD. As they landed on the deck, I embraced each one of them. They all expressed to Jonathan, Aaron, and me how happy they were to have us back on the *Adventurer*. All of them wanted to know what happened, but there was a lot that had to be done before then. Jonathan needed to see Martin and I wanted to hug Jopie. I commanded David to help Jonathan to Martin's; he nodded and followed my orders. It was so nice to be treated with respect for the first time in a week. The rest of the crew prepared themselves to continue on route to the port. Still, an unsettling feeling lingered on board. I couldn't stand it any longer.

I ran through the halls until I reached the kitchen. Jopie was cleaning some dishes that they had probably used the night before. My mind went back to the last time I was in this kitchen. I had still never eaten anything she had made me. Now I could. She turned when she heard the door open. Her eyes widened and she ran towards me.

"Carter!" she exclaimed. I smiled wider than ever before. I picked her up and spun her around, pulling her tightly to my chest. It didn't matter how hurt I was, I wanted Jopie in my arms. "Oh, I'm so glad you're back!" she laughed. Then I set her back down on the floor.

"What are you wearing?" she questioned me. "A dress?" she asked. I had almost forgotten that I was still wearing the stupid wedding dress. It was so torn up and stained that it barely qualified as a dress anymore. We both laughed.

"Sadly yes, I had to wear this," I sighed in fake frustration. She laughed again, and I hugged her again. I was not going to leave her again. Her joy and happiness numbed the pain I had carried the past few days. She talked to me about the past week on the ship, what it had been like without the three of us. She repeated over and over how glad she was that the three of us were back. All the while, I helped her clean the plates. Then, the two of us walked back up to the main deck, my arm over her shoulder.

Everyone was celebrating our victory, telling stories of their battles against crew members of the other ship, and proudly revealing battle wounds Martin had cleaned up for them, insisting they had looked worse only moments ago. Fallier repeatedly mentioned how glad he was that he got those new cannons at our last port trip. Everyone agreed with him. Then, since everyone insisted on hearing my story, we all sat down, except for Aaron who was at the helm. And I began to explain everything. I would glance at Jonathan and Aaron during different parts. The whole crew was intrigued. At the end, everyone shouted in happiness, because they now knew what they were fighting for. The battle against Edward was finally over. My mother was right. Many tears had fallen from my eyelashes in these past few weeks. But I had won the war in the end.

"And the best part," David exclaimed, interrupting my thoughts, "is that you managed to stay alive to see your sixteenth birthday!" The entire crew shouted in happiness once more. David was right. I realized that my sixteenth birthday was exactly four months away. I was on track to turn sixteen as a Key -- hoping to avoid making any more enemies. It was a miracle. I looked at Jonathan. His smile was huge. He came over and hugged me. I kissed him quickly, hoping not too many people noticed. But I soon felt like the entire crew was looking at me. Jonathan and I both laughed. He kissed me again, with so much passion that the whole crew could feel the love we shared. I loved Jonathan. The crew cheered and teased, well, mostly David teased. Our lips parted and we both looked over at David and laughed.

I glanced at Aaron. Something was on his mind, his green

eyes lost in a trance, fixated on the sea. I left Jonathan's arms and walked up to the helm to meet him.

"Are you okay?" I asked him. He didn't look at me when he replied, but he smiled.

"You and Jonathan are so perfect together, I can't figure out why I was so blind to it before," he began. I swallowed. I thought we had already worked out all of this on *The Cobra*. Immediately I told myself that was unfair to assume. So, I listened. "I never want to get in the way of your love for him ever again. I would never forgive myself if I made the two of you unhappy," he continued. I rolled my eyes. Aaron glanced my way and chuckled softly. But then he looked down and bit his lip before he continued again. "Which is why I have decided to leave. The next time we go to the ports, I'm leaving. I want you to live a happy life." I was shocked.

"Aaron, no, *you* are part of my happy life. It wouldn't be better with you gone; it would be worse. We need you here. Jopie needs you here. I need you here!" I exclaimed. Aaron smiled weakly.

"You say that, but you don't mean it," he countered.

"Of course, I mean it. Every word I said to you while we were stuck with Edward was also true, so don't leave. You are so important to me, and I wouldn't have made it this far without you," I argued. Aaron sighed.

"Are you sure you want me to stay?" he asked me again, looking me dead in the eye. I nodded firmly and wrapped my arms around him.

"Don't ever leave me, Aaron. Don't ever leave me."

Madison Wade was born in Nashville, TN, where she discovered her passion for writing at a young age. She is a middle school librarian and helps foster the love of reading and writing in young minds. She published her debut novel, The Ocean's Daughter, in Feburary of 2020. When she is not writing, she spends her time with family, crafting, or roaming around Walt Disney World.

Find her on Instagram
@booksbymwade
and online
www.booksbymadisonwade.com